CRIME TRAVEL

Edited by Barb Goffman

TALES OF MYSTERY AND TIME TRAVEL

Melissa H. Blaine
Korina Moss
Anna Castle
Heidi Hunter
Adam Meyer
Eleanor Cawood Jones
Art Taylor
Michael Bracken
John M. Floyd
Brendan DuBois
James Blakey
Barbara Monajem
David Dean
Cathy Wiley
Barb Goffman

Introduction by Donna Andrews

ALSO BY BARB GOFFMAN

Don't Get Mad, Get Even

CRIME TRAVEL

Edited by Barb Goffman

WILDSIDE PRESS

CRIME TRAVEL

Published by Wildside Press LLC.
wildsidepress.com

TRAVELS

INTRODUCTION

Donna Andrews

Once upon a time I had a great idea. It started with what I thought was a brilliant title for a short story anthology: Crime Travel. Every story in it would have time travel...and a crime! Someone would travel in time—back to the past or forward to the future, author's choice—to do something related to crime. The characters could commit a crime...prevent a crime...solve a crime...or just watch one happen. I shared my idea with a few writer friends, and a reasonable number of them agreed that yes, it was a fabulous idea, and I should let them know when I sent out my call for stories.

Then life happened. As it does. I got busy with other writing stuff. With nonwriting stuff. My brilliant anthology idea remained just that—an idea.

Fast forward fifteen years. My writer friend Barb Goffman asked if she could pick my brain. She had a story that needed a home. Which doesn't happen all that often with her excellent stories, but this one was going to be a little tougher to place than most because a lot of the usual markets for mystery stories aren't that keen on paranormal elements. Like, in this case, time travel.

Time travel.

"Why don't you do your own anthology?" I asked. I knew Barb was an expert at every aspect of pulling an anthology together: she, Marcia Talley, and I have partnered on eight—soon to be nine—volumes of Chesapeake Crimes, an anthology benefitting our local Sisters in Crime chapter. Her excellent editing skills and her ability to focus on a project and get it done are two big reasons why we've made it to eight and a half instead of maybe two. "I've even got a title you can use: Crime Travel."

She loved the title. And we agreed—she could use my title if she gave me credit for it. And if I didn't manage to submit a story, I'd write the introduction.

So here it is: *Crime Travel*, with an introduction—but no short story—from me. Kicking myself now for not at least trying to pull together a story, because I'd love to be in this diverse and talented roster. Although I'd have been hard put to come up with a story to match some of these.

Why do we always assume the people using time machines will be either do-gooders intent on improving history or curious scholars seeking the truth about it? More likely they'll be like the teenage time tourists in Melissa Blaine's engaging "Living on Borrowed Time."

Korina Moss's "On the Boardwalk" features a rare example of time traveling for altruistic reasons, and if the ending leaves you dry-eyed, I don't want to hear about it.

"The Sneeze," by Anna Castle, introduces quite possibly the most ingenious method of time travel I've ever read—not to mention the most annoying for the traveler.

In "No Honor Among Thieves," Heidi Hunter successfully pulls off more unexpected twists than most writers even try.

Adam Meyer's "The Fourteenth Floor" shows there's no such thing as too late when you've got time travel on your side.

You can read "O Crime, in Thy Flight," by Eleanor Cawood Jones, as a crime story or as an inspiring tale of a woman breaking free from what was holding her back from discovering her real self. Sometimes it takes time travel to get there.

I'm still not sure exactly what happened at the end of Art Taylor's "Hard Return," but in a good way—it's the kind of story that grows the more you think about it.

If someone ever invents time travel, odds are it will be someone who wants it—needs it—as much as the protagonist of Michael Bracken's "Love, or Something Like It."

And John Floyd's "Ignition" is a cautionary tale—sometimes it's the seemingly unimportant things we overlook that come back to bite us.

Can you think of a reason why preventing one of history's worst crimes would be a bad thing? Brendan DuBois can—and does—in "The Dealey Paradox."

A hard-boiled 1940s private eye, a bottled-blond client, sinister Nazi thugs...and a time machine? James Blakey does a noir take on crime travel in "The Case of the Missing Physicist."

When you've double-crossed the Mob and can't think where to go... try thinking when, not where, like the heroine of Barbara Monajem's "The Last Page."

Even if you got a chance to go back in time and change that one moment where it all went wrong, could you figure out how? The title character of "Reyna," by David Dean, isn't going to give up without trying.

In Cathy Wiley's "And Then There Were Paradoxes" Dame Agatha Christie helps a modern police detective solve a classic locked-room mystery.

And the story that started it all. In "Alex's Choice," Barb Goffman breaks one of the biggest rules in crime fiction. But don't worry—time travel has a way of making things turn out okay.

Intrigued? Yeah. Glad this introduction's almost over, so you can start reading? Check. Go for it. You'll have fun. Not a stinker in the bunch, and I loved reading them. Well, except for that nagging feeling of being left out. My own fault, of course. It's not as if I haven't had months to write a story, not to mention those fifteen years of thinking "one of these days."

You know what I think I'll do? Write a really kick-ass story, then figure out the whole time travel thing so I can go back and submit my story to Barb for this anthology. If you're reading this introduction, I haven't figured it out yet.

But I'm working on it.

Donna Andrews is the best-selling author of twenty-six books in the award-winning Meg Langslow mystery series, including *Terns of Endearment* (August 2019) and *Owl Be Home for Christmas* (October 2019). Together with Barb Goffman and Marcia Talley she is one of the coordinating editors of the Chesapeake Crime series, whose ninth volume, *Invitation to Murder*, will come out in April 2020. She is currently the executive vice president of Mystery Writers of America and membership chair of the Chesapeake Chapter of Sisters in Crime. So far she has yet to write that long-anticipated crime travel story.

LIVING ON BORROWED TIME

Melissa H. Blaine

The moment I saw them I knew there was going to be trouble. I hadn't made it to twenty-six, teaching high school students and waitressing on the side, without developing powerful tradar (that's radar for trouble). The two teens huddled in the alley, peering around the edge of a big blue dumpster like children playing peekaboo. They would have stuck out like sore thumbs anyway since they were talking into their gloves like they were phones, but the Kansas City Outlaws NHL hockey jersey totally gave them away. Time tourists.

My roommate, Stell, and I had just watched a program on time tourists a few nights before. It was on one of those cable channels that shows all the weird conspiracy programs like aliens building the Great Wall of China and people trying to track down Bigfoot's buried treasure. Stell is a believer. Of everything. Give her the most outlandish explanation for something, and she'll buy into it with little more than a wink. Me? I'm more of an Occam's razor type of thinker. The simplest explanation is probably the right one. Even if it seems impossible.

There had been whispers and rumors about time tourists for years, but they were always pretty fringe. Most people rolled their eyes at the suggestion, laughing that if there were time travelers from the future coming back to the past, there would be no way they'd leave the environment in such a crappy state without trying to help it. They could end up living with our mistakes, after all. For the believers, though, time tourists were around every corner, making ripples in history. Stell and her crowd of tinfoil-hat wearers bought history books by the dozen, reading and rereading them, trying to spot the changing text that they knew had to be happening.

As I stood in the front window of the BookBQ Bookstore, I held up a coffee-table version of *Kansas City's Fountains and Park Art* to cover my appraisal of the alley. The teens, barely adults, were far enough back that they couldn't have seen much of what was happening on Nichols Road. The only visible shop window was the one I was standing in, straight in front of the alley. Three days ago, I would have thought they were casing the joint, although who robs a bookstore, especially on Country Club Plaza? Now, that not-right jersey was scratching at my brain.

Here's what kept running through my mind as I whipped open the door of the BookBQ and marched across the street: if they were time tourists watching me, I was in a hot mess and I wanted a way out. Think about it. If you're a time tourist from the future, where are you going to go? Kansas City? On Thanksgiving Day in 2019? Sure, the annual Plaza Lights spectacle would be great, with jewel-toned bulbs adorning fifteen blocks of buildings. And the stores and restaurants always did booming business as everyone trickled in to watch the lighting ceremony and fireworks. But still, it's Kansas City, not Paris, France. And it's not like I was a movie star or something. I'd worked the lunch crowd at Gibson's Diner on the Plaza and gone to the bookstore afterward while waiting for the festivities, still wearing my uniform, no less. Why would anyone pay money to watch me or the lighting ceremony...unless something big was about to happen?

"You're time tourists, aren't you?" I stuck my hands on my hips in my best superhero or angry mother pose. They were surprisingly similar.

"Wha...uh...no. I...uh...what?" The one closest to me stammered. A bead of sweat appeared at the line where his spiky-blue hair met his pimpled forehead. He slowly edged the book he was holding under the edge of his jersey toward his back pocket.

"Uh-uh. Hand it over." My fingers curled over my palm in the universal gesture for *give it.*

My five-foot-nothing dishwater-brown-haired wallflower look must be scary in the future because the guy flopped that book into my hand quicker than a bee sting. I turned it over slowly, wishing I hadn't once I saw the title, *The 50-State Stabber: History's Most Infamous Serial Killer* by Bhavin Jons.

"You're here to watch a serial killer?" My voice held a mixture of disbelief and judgment.

"I don't know what you're talking about, ma'am." This kid had dreads and kept his gaze pointed just beyond my right shoulder. He wouldn't meet my eyes.

"It's 2019. This book isn't published until..." I flipped to the copyright page and tried not to let my eyes bug out of their sockets. "Holy crap, not until 2073. You really are time tourists. Stell was right for once." I leaned up against the dumpster, feeling a bit lightheaded.

"Why'd you give her the book? You just broke about thirty-five different rules, Jeremy. We are so dead." Dreads glared at Jeremy, whose blue eyes immediately found a spot on the ground to stare at.

"She asked for it, dude. What was I supposed to do? Huh, Michael?" Jeremy tucked his head into his shoulders.

I held up a hand. "Look, I spotted both of you dingbats from the Book-BQ. You weren't doing an exemplary job of being inconspicuous over here. And you're wearing a jersey that doesn't exist. Kansas City doesn't have an NHL team, let alone the Kansas City Outlaws. It's 2019."

Jeremy's eyes widened before he smacked Michael across the arm. "I told you!"

"What's the deal with this serial killer?" I asked, paging through the book.

"The Fifty-State Stabber is only the most famous serial killer of all time." Michael's voice had a tinge of awe. "He killed fifty women, one from each state, over about fifteen years. Nobody even connected the dots on the guy until after the murders were over because they were so spread out. And then he just disappeared. After the last one, the murders stopped. No one ever knew who he was. Like Jack the Ripper, but like Jack the Ripper on steroids or something."

Jeremy nodded. "Yeah, the Stabber makes Jack the Ripper look like a kitten." He stood up a little straighter, puffing out his chest. "We're here to uncover his identity. Then we're going to write a book about it."

I cringed and lowered the book as I came to a picture of a woman splayed out across a parking lot, her organs arranged like a rainbow above her head. Whoever this 50-State Stabber was, he was evil. "Okay, so you're saying that the Fifty-State Stabber is going to get a victim here? At the lighting ceremony?"

"It's his last victim. Or at least the last known victim. Missouri was state fifty. After tonight, he disappears, and he's never caught."

How does someone get away with murdering fifty people and not get caught? And what did it say about 2019 that no one noticed a connection between fifty dead women? The thought made me want to cry. Maybe the book would give me some hint. After opening it again, with eyes squinted to shut out any more blood and gore, I swept through the pages until I got to a chapter called "Missouri." My next memory was waking up on the ground with Jeremy and Michael leaning over me.

"Are you all right? I think you fainted." Jeremy touched my shoulder.

"Wha? Why?" And then it all came flooding back. "The last victim is me. My name is the one in the Missouri chapter. Jennifer Elliot. Everything I did today is there, in the timeline. I'm going to die."

Michael gently took the book from me. "I'm sorry. You weren't supposed to know. We should have just waited at the parking garage instead of following you. The book was a little skimpy on who you were and what you were like. We thought maybe we could learn more for our book by watching you." He looked away before opening the book toward the back, scanning the page. "Oh, wow. Um. That's not good."

Jeremy looked over Michael's shoulder, his eyes growing wider by the second.

"What?" I sat up and tugged at Michael's sleeve.

"The book's changed. It looks like you tried to fight back."

"Do I survive?" I knew now. I could figure a way out of this.

"Uh, nooooo. It was probably better when you didn't know." Michael turned another page. Jeremy flinched, one hand at his mouth and the other reaching instinctively for his stomach as if protecting it.

I leaned against the brick wall and put my head between my knees. Great. I was going to die a horrible death at the hands of somebody known as the 50-State Stabber. What kind of name was that anyway? Stabber. Not very creative, that's for sure. It sounded like something a five-year-old would come up with.

"Wait! You said the book changed. That means that history changed, right?" Yes! A loophole.

"Yeah." Michael sounded a little unsure. "But we're not supposed to change history. Even this could cause all sorts of ripples that no one's expecting. Hell, it could create an alternate universe if the changes are too big."

"You should have thought of that before you started stalking me from the alley. History has already changed. I try to fight back, which by the reactions you two had, does not go well. What if we can save me and learn who the Stabber is? You'd still get your book, and I wouldn't have to die."

"Maybe." Michael raised an eyebrow in Jeremy's direction. "What did you have in mind?"

"You could help me! When the killer tries to attack me, you two can save me. Three against one."

Jeremy shook his head. "We can't. There are rules and consequences. We can't act to change history. We're already going to be in some serious hot water, but if we try to change history, we might screw it up forever. They might decide to just zap us out of existence as punishment. Sorry. No can do."

"Okay, what if I'm not in Missouri? I can't count as the Missouri victim, right? Look, the Kansas border is just a few minutes away. I'll drive over, and we'll see what the book says. That way you're not doing anything to change history. I am. You can stay here and try to figure out who Knifey McKnifeface is. If we can get a description or a photo, I can take that to the cops later. Maybe we can stop him at forty-nine. Maybe no one else has to die."

Michael and Jeremy exchanged glances, and then Jeremy shrugged. "Why not? We've already screwed up. We paid for this trip to try to identify the Stabber. If we can still do that and you can live, I guess that's okay." He looked at his shoes. "This was a lot easier when you were just a name, ya know?"

I still thought using time travel to watch a murder was gross, but I wasn't going to blow the sudden goodwill. If the two kids were giving me a shot, I was going to take it and think about it later. Hopefully, whatever I did wouldn't throw the whole of time and space into chaos.

Before Jeremy and Michael could change their minds, I ran to a nearby pharmacy and picked up a prepaid cell phone. It would put a dent on my credit card statement, but if I weren't alive, it wouldn't matter anyway. After giving the phone to Jeremy and Michael and explaining how to use it, I picked up my car and drove down Ward Parkway to Shawnee Mission Parkway and past the Kansas line. I stopped outside of the Border War Country Club and dialed the number for the prepaid phone.

"Did it work?" I asked when Jeremy answered.

"Hang on, we're checking." I could hear pages fluttering in the background. Michael made a noise that could have been anything from surprise to disgust.

"What?" My voice climbed about five octaves.

"Well, the good news is that you don't die," Jeremy said. "The bad news is that someone else does. Her name is Tiffany Kaler."

I frowned. "You mean the Stabber kills someone else?"

"Yeah," Jeremy said. "The details are pretty similar. She's abducted from the parking garage, the same one...ur, where you were supposed to be abducted from. Then he tortures and kills her. Her body is found three days later...or I guess, three days from now. So, you're good. You can go home or whatever. You're safe. We'll be able to identify him when he goes after Tiffany."

We hung up, but the horrible feeling in the pit of my stomach remained. Sure, I was okay now, but that just meant someone else was going to die a horrible death. I didn't want to die. But I didn't want someone else to die in my place either. That wasn't right. I laid my head on the steering wheel and made another call.

"Hey, Stell. I wanted you to know that you're right. I ran into these two guys this afternoon and guess what? They're time tourists. I didn't believe it at first, but they are, and I just wanted you to know that you were right. They do exist. The bad news is that they're here because they want to learn the identity of this famous serial killer. I'm supposed to be the last victim. They have a book that says he abducts me in the parking lot after the lighting ceremony and kills me. After I learned my history"—boy, time travel caused weird conversations—"I tried to get away and change what's going to happen, but then the book changed and someone else died. Dies. Will die." I shook my head. So confusing. "What it means is if I try to save myself, he'll kill someone else, and I can't live with that." Tears rolled down my cheek, and my voice caught. "I know that you won't get this until after your family Thanksgiving dinner ends because of your mom's no-cell-phone rule, but I just wanted you to know about the time travel and that you are the best friend ever. I love you. I'm sorry. This is the shittiest thing to do, but I need someone to know."

And I hung up. By the time she got the voice mail, it would be too late. She was with her family in Wichita. Even if she got the voice mail soon, she was hours away. I'd already be taken or dead, or whatever was going to happen to me. Not that she could have helped me anyway. But there was no one else for me to call. I started the car and turned it around.

Less than an hour later, I walked back into the alley. I'd stopped at the only open sporting-goods store I could find to buy the biggest knife they had. If I was going down, I planned to do it fighting. I would have bought a gun too, but a waiting period had just gone into effect earlier in the month. I didn't think walking up and down Forty-Seventh Street shouting that I needed a gun would be very helpful. Jeremy and Michael were hiding behind the blue dumpster again, watching a woman in the front window of the BookBQ. They jumped when I rounded the corner.

"What're you doing here?" Jeremy asked.

"You were safe!" Michael clutched my arm.

"I know. I know. But I can't let someone else die for me. That's not right." I sighed. "Am I back in the book?"

Michael turned a few pages. "You're back. Are you sure you want to do this?"

Shaking my head, I said, "No. But I do have a plan. Or at least part of a plan."

Jeremy and Michael listened to my idea. We knew from the book that I was abducted from the parking garage. I would call the cops before I went in or from close by. One of them might show up in time to save me. The plan was far from perfect. It would be a whole lot easier if Jeremy and Michael would just jump the guy, but it was the best I had. Call the cops. Fight like hell.

After shopping for a new outfit—I wasn't dying in my Gibson's uniform—and a last meal that started with dessert, I herded Jeremy and Michael toward a good spot to watch the lighting ceremony. We weren't sure when the killer spotted me, so we'd decided to do what I had been planning to do. We stood in the street with the rest of Kansas City, staring at the buildings in the Spanish-inspired shopping district.

Finally the bulbs flickered to life. I turned in a circle, trying to take it all in. Strands outlined each of the buildings with hundreds of thousands of bulbs. Each of the towers was outlined with single-color bulbs; my favorite was the red Time Tower. Elsewhere, multicolored strands outlined restaurants and shops. Green, yellow, and red lights shone into the darkness around us as a few snowflakes fluttered down from the sky. In the back of my mind, I remembered that over eighty miles of lights were used. That tidbit had won me fifty bucks at a trivia contest a couple of years ago. I tucked my coat around me, grateful that I could see this one more time. The lights were mixed with the memories of coming down here year after year with my family. My parents died in a car accident when I was in college, and if I had to pick a memory that encapsulated my childhood and my feeling of family, this was it.

I looked at my watch. Not long now.

"Have you seen anyone yet?" I glanced toward my two watchers, who hovered a few feet away from me.

Michael shook his head. "Nothing. Maybe he just grabs you. The book doesn't say that he stalks you or anything, just that he abducts you from the parking garage."

We wandered around a bit as the crowd thinned, leaving to go home to Thanksgiving leftovers and warm beds. Michael and Jeremy stayed behind me, keeping an eye out for whoever the 50-State Stabber might be, but trying not to spook him.

Finally, the time drew near. I nodded at the two time tourists and walked to the parking garage. Just before I went in, I called 911 and reported that I thought someone was following me. The operator promised to send someone as quickly as she could. I waited to see if Michael or Jeremy would yell that the book had changed with my call, but they didn't. My heart beat faster. If the call didn't change the book, did that mean that the police didn't make it in time to save me? I didn't know, but I had to follow this through. As much as I wanted to run as far away from here as I could get, I couldn't let someone else die for me.

Taking a deep breath, I stepped into the parking garage and walked toward the stairwell. I never took the elevator, but tonight I considered it, if only to get this over with. A few people were climbing into their cars as I opened the stairwell door. It creaked and groaned as if sharing my pain.

Forcing myself to keep going, I stepped onto the first step and then the next. Jeremy and Michael were going up the opposite stairwell, waiting at the fourth floor to catch a glimpse of the Stabber as he abducted me.

By the second floor, I realized tears were running down my face, and by the third floor, they dropped to each step as I climbed, marking the way to my death. When I reached the door to the fourth floor, I stood for a minute, gripping the handle. I could leave right now. I could save myself.

But I didn't.

I opened the door and walked toward my car. Closer and closer. One step and then two.

I took the knife out of my purse, clenching the handle.

The blow came from behind me, snapping my head forward. I fell into the back of my car. My knife skittered under the SUV next to me. I tried to roll, but he hit me again.

My last thought before I blacked out was that this was it, there was nothing to stop my death now.

I don't know how long I was out. It may have been minutes or just a few seconds, but through the haze in my head, I heard something thudding and someone crying in pain. Was it me?

My head hurt, but the rest of me seemed fine. Okay, not me. I cracked open an eye slowly, the light overhead too bright for my throbbing skull.

"Take that, you bastard."

"Get 'em, Rosie!"

"Oh, that had to hurt."

"Are you okay, Jen?" Stell leaned over me, slipping her hand beneath my head.

I tried to make sense of what was happening around me. If Stell was here, did that mean the Stabber didn't kill me? How did Stell get here? Where were Jeremy and Michael? Had the book changed? Did I just sentence someone else to death?

Stell helped me to a sitting position. In the middle of the parking garage floor, I could see her seven cousins, all looking like they'd stepped off a runway, surrounding a guy dressed in black. Ponytails swung and acrylic nails flew as they got in their punches. Jeremy and Michael were standing off to the side, reading the pages in the back of their book.

"How?" I started.

"There was a huge blowout during the soup course at dinner when my one auntie accused my other auntie's husband of cheating with the babysitter. It was not pretty. While they were fighting, we went outside to check the football score. I saw you called. As soon as we heard your voice mail, we piled in Mama's van and drove over here. You always park on the fourth floor as close to the nineteenth spot as you can, and your lucky number sure came in handy tonight. Your car was here. We've been waiting for about an hour. When that guy hit you from behind, we went for him."

The sound of sirens broke through the taunts of Stell's cousins. The guy was curled up in a fetal ball, his hands over his face. He didn't seem so scary anymore.

Jeremy and Michael ran over to me, wide smiles on their faces.

"You did it!" Jeremy yelled, making my head throb harder. "You got him!"

Michael knelt beside me. "The book changed. The last chapter is about you, but it's how you were almost abducted until some friends of yours saw it happening and stopped the guy. His name is Kyle Lars Fenton. The police are going to arrest him, and they'll link him to a similar abduction in Kentucky two years ago. Once they do that, he sings like a fat canary and confesses to forty-eight other murders."

"Are you mad that you didn't get to identify him?" I asked.

Michael laughed. "No, I'm happy that you're alive."

"You just can't tell the police about how you caught this guy," Jeremy said in a more normal tone, looking at Stell. "Say you were coming to meet Jen or something."

"Oh please, we had that figured out about two hours ago." Stell flipped her hand dismissively at Michael. "I see we need to do more work to dismantle the patriarchy if you still think women are that dumb in whatever year you're from."

As the sirens grew louder, Michael tugged on Jeremy's arm. "We have to go. We can't be here."

"Wait," I called, but they had already blended into the dark edges of the parking garage.

I don't know what happened to Jeremy and Michael after that. In the years afterward, Stell and I talked sometimes about what we thought they were doing. I wondered if they made it back to whatever time they were from safely, whether they had gotten into trouble for helping me. I hoped not.

I think I caught a glimpse of them once, at my and Stell's wedding. As we walked back down the aisle, I caught a flutter of something in the church balcony. Maybe it was my imagination. Maybe I just wanted to see them.

But it looked a lot like two Kansas City Outlaws jerseys ducking out the door.

Melissa H. Blaine is an author and executive coach for creative entrepreneurs and remote professionals. Although her time living in the Kansas City area did not involve time tourists from the future, she honed her time-travel knowledge with mentors like Bill, Ted, and The Doctor. Now living in Michigan with a rather judgmental old dog, Melissa is a member of Sisters in Crime, the Short Mystery Fiction Society, and the Grand Rapids Region Writer's Group. You can learn more about her work at www.melissahblaine.com.

ON THE BOARDWALK

Korina Moss

"You know I'm dying, right?"

Jacob's stomach clenched at Ruby's words. He'd just clicked the execute button on his MacBook, waiting to see those two glorious words—*TRANS-MISSION SUCCESSFUL*—that would indicate his latest de-bugging efforts worked. He popped out of the pod that overtook his dining area, still holding his slender laptop.

Ruby was resting on his couch, stroking the headscarf that trailed down one shoulder, the way she used to do with her hair when it was thick and came down to her elbows, and she'd complain she had more gray strands than black. He'd been watching his best friend die slowly since her remission abruptly ended and then the chemo stopped working. Her ochre-brown skin had dulled and turned sallow.

"Right now? You're going to die here on my couch?" He pushed his black rimmed glasses back up the bridge of his nose. They were old and loose but comfortable. Jacob didn't like change.

She chuckled. "No, not right now."

He exhaled his fear.

Ruby wasn't like anyone else he knew. They'd met when she welcomed him to the neighborhood with a half dozen homemade ube cheese rolls, a Filipino recipe passed down from her grandmother. She didn't seem to mind at all when he told her he didn't like the way the purple yam-and-cream-cheese filling felt mushy in his mouth, and that he preferred cookies. Afterward, he knew he should've just thanked her and accepted the pastries, but sometimes he couldn't keep the truth from spilling out before remembering to be polite. In this circumstance, it worked out. The next day, she brought over a dozen coconut cookies, and they were the best he'd ever tasted.

"You said the travel could be rough," Ruby continued. "I just want you to be prepared that if this works, I may be worse off when we return."

"Do you not want to go anymore?" He'd started working on coding his time machine during college but stepped up his efforts after meeting Ruby and hearing her story. It was nine years in the making, but this time it was going to work.

"No, I want to go," Ruby insisted, becoming more fervent as she spoke. "Your promise is the only reason I've held on. I don't know how my parents will survive losing both of their children. My brother has to be here after I die. I need to go back to the past and save him."

Jacob heard a ding from the computer in his hand.

TRANSMISSION SUCCESSFUL.

He smiled at Ruby.

* * * *

"Look out!"

Ruby and Jacob sidestepped just in time to save themselves from being run over by a four-wheeled surrey bike. Laughter followed the two teenage girls in bikinis who were pedaling it, their long hair waving in the breeze as they jostled erratically down the boardwalk.

Ruby glanced up and down the wooden promenade. *It really worked?* Giddiness bubbled inside her, causing goose bumps, despite the heat.

Jacob hopped up and down on the balls of his feet. "I knew it would work. I knew it."

"Where's the pod?" she asked him in a hushed voice.

"It didn't come with us. We just needed it to start the trip. It's all in here." He motioned to the computer in his hands, suddenly snapping it shut and wrapping his arms around it. He slipped his stars-and-stripes canvas daypack off his shoulders and stuck the computer inside, clearly not wanting to draw attention to himself. They didn't have laptops in 1975. That much he'd known even before he read everything about that year—decades before he was born—in preparation for this trip. Ruby appreciated how diligent Jacob was, as well as his nearly photographic memory, which might come in handy.

They stepped out of the shadow of a movie theater marquee. The bold black letters on it read JAWS and listed the two times it was playing.

"The pizza place is that way," he told her, pointing past the movie theater.

Ruby squinted her eyes against the intense sunshine. "I can't see anything. I forgot my sunglasses. Give me a sec." She blinked rapidly to help her pupils adjust. Jacob's lenses had automatically darkened in the sunlight within seconds.

As they stood among the throngs of beachgoers bustling past them, Ruby could feel the heat rising from beneath her sandals. She soaked in the smells of the Jersey shore that brought the summers of her childhood into focus—the salty air, the coconut lotion, the commingling of sweet taffy and chocolatey fudge with savory hot dogs and buttery popcorn. She tuned into the commotion of sounds: gleeful voices, the ocean waves, snippets of a crackly Captain & Tennille singing "Love Will Keep Us Together."

When she could finally once again see the stretch of boardwalk before her, her initial delight evaporated, as the memory that loomed larger than any other knocked the wind out of her like a bat to the gut. Her twin brother was going to die today.

Jacob broke into her thoughts, "From the photographs I studied, the Pizza Palace should be about ten shops down. Sorry, I couldn't get us closer."

"What time is it? Why didn't we just go to my house and keep Arvin from coming here in the first place?"

"I don't think your family would let us in, Ruby. We're strangers to them. Even you."

Of course, Ruby thought. Thirteen-year-old Ruby would be in her house right now and wouldn't recognize her fifty-seven-year-old self. Ruby swallowed the ache that she wouldn't get to see her childhood home again. But she had something more important to do.

"We only have an hour," Jacob continued. "Ninety minutes, tops. That's as long as I could get the time machine to work without error messages. It's four o'clock now. You said the pizza guy was the last person to see him?"

Panic lodged in Ruby's chest. "Yeah. Vic—that's the pizza guy. He was a friend of our dad's. We both liked to hang out at his pizza place, but Arvin especially."

"He estimated last seeing him sometime between four fifteen and four forty-five, according to the old newspaper article you gave me," Jacob said.

"Right. So we just need to meet Arvin there and keep an eye on him."

She propelled herself forward, desperate to see her brother again. Jacob followed. The rollercoaster in the distance looked like a squiggly line drawn from Harold's purple crayon, reminding her of a favorite childhood book. She and Jacob were a lot like Harold, in fact, creating the world they wanted with each step they took.

"What if we miss him, Jacob? What if the same thing happens and I can't stop it?"

"We got here in time," Jacob said evenly. "Seven more shops."

His monotone rarely broke, but over the years that they'd gotten to know each other as neighbors and then friends, she knew his lack of inflection didn't connote his feelings. It hadn't taken her long to understand his quirks. He was thirty years younger than she, but they would both readily agree they shared a special bond—two people who stood out, but didn't seem to fit in.

They passed a souvenir shop where display racks of postcards crowded the entrance. Ruby watched Jacob suck in and hold his breath as they hurried past a woman perusing the sidewalk-sale T-shirts with a lit cigarette between her fingers. She knew he was sensitive to odors, especially ones he hated.

"Five more," he said a few steps later, after they'd passed the worst of the cigarette smoke.

"What if he's not there?" Ruby couldn't tamp down her anxiety.

"We can go down to the beach where he was found."

"His body washed up the next day. Who knows how far off course the tide took him? He would've never gone in the water willingly. Not that year. We'd just seen *Jaws* the day before, and we vowed we would never go in the ocean again."

"We're close. I can smell it."

Ruby knew Jacob's heightened senses could be overwhelming to him, but she also knew this particular aroma he didn't mind—he loved pizza.

A *thwap, thwap, thwap* cut through the cacophony of noises.

"Oh my gosh." Ruby stopped abruptly, her head swiveling to follow the dark-headed boy whizzing by them, one hand on the handlebar of his red Schwinn bicycle, the other tucking a shoebox under his arm. A playing card smacked against the spokes. "That's him. That's Arvin." Ruby didn't wait for Jacob. She U-turned and ran after her brother.

Jacob followed, quickly catching up to her. "What's he holding? What's in the box?"

"I don't know."

It wasn't long before they lost sight of him. Ruby's chest heaved, and the sweat that had been forming beads on her skin dampened her headscarf and dripped down her back. She sucked in the humid July air, trying to fill her lungs.

She panted. "Find him. I'll catch up."

* * * *

Jacob continued on without her. He'd promised Ruby they would save her brother. He couldn't lose him now.

He slowed his pace so he could scan the packs of people. When he didn't see Arvin, he crossed to the painted benches lining the boardwalk, where beachgoers sat and stared at the ocean. Jacob's gaze followed a group of bare-chested guys his age with towels draped over their shoulders, wearing cut-off jean shorts and flip-flops, as they descended a column of stairs to the beach. The swath of white sand looked patched by the multitude of colorful towels, like the jeans Jacob saw in photos from the era. He had thought he would look the part when he chose his clothes for the trip, but he realized his shorts were still too long.

An insistent lifeguard's whistle cut through the hum and brought Jacob back to his mission. No bicycle near the stairs—Arvin hadn't gone down to the beach. Jacob crossed the flow of pedestrian traffic back toward the stalls and shops. He was drawn to a sign running the width of a corner building, which perfectly repeated above its doorways: ARCADE ARCADE ARCADE. He spotted a red bike propped against the side of the building, an ace of hearts playing card attached to a spoke of the back wheel.

Jacob stepped inside the wide entrance. The rapid-fire bells of a long row of pinball machines rattled in his ears. He tried to ignore them and looked around for Arvin. He had to find him for Ruby. Although he'd only gotten a glimpse of Arvin on the bike, Ruby had shown him family photos plenty of times in the six years they'd known each other. *Focus*, he ordered himself. But the *tick, tick, tick* of a roulette wheel competed with the bells and the endless *thwack* of pinball flippers. The racket magnified in his head. He saw two men hunched over a video game with their fingers on the triggers of toy rifles only seconds before the game started. A crack of a rifle shot sounded, and then came a ricochet of whirring bullets, followed by more shots. The noises assailed him, sending strobe lights flashing through his brain. He ran.

Ruby found him crouched on the opposite side of the boardwalk with his hands pressed against his ears.

"Jacob! Are you okay?" She knelt beside him, extending her arms, then pulled back. Jacob could tell she stopped herself from hugging him. She knew he couldn't handle it. She knew him better than any friend ever had, and this made him both happy and sad, for as strong as their friendship was, he'd never been able to hug her.

Her presence made him feel safe enough to cautiously lower his hands from his ears. The jumble of sounds that bounced around him no longer pierced his brain. "I'm sorry," he finally said. "It was too loud. I couldn't stay in there."

"In where?" she looked around. "The arcade?"

Jacob nodded and stood. "I saw his bike."

When Ruby tried to stand, she wobbled on weak legs. Jacob helped her up.

"We're going to need each other to do this, Jacob."

He nodded again. They walked toward the arcade and saw a boy emerge clutching the same shoebox as Arvin had.

"I think I know him," Ruby said.

The boy approached a bicycle, a yellow one. A ratty beach towel hung over the handlebars.

"That's Arvin's best friend, Stevie," she said.

"Do you think he killed Arvin for his shoebox?"

"No! He wouldn't have hurt Arvin. He was devastated when Arvin went missing and especially when he found out he died." She strode up to the boy as he swung a leg over his banana seat.

"Where's Arvin?" she shouted at him.

He reared back. "Over there." He pointed to the other side of the arcade where Arvin was pushing off on his own bike. In place of the shoebox, Arvin was now holding a small brown paper bag.

Ruby and Jacob went after Arvin, calling his name, but he cycled on, oblivious to their cries. They circled back to talk to Stevie, but he was long gone, as well.

Ruby's tears spilled onto her cheeks. "We keep missing him."

Jacob looked at his watch. "He went in the direction of the Pizza Palace. We can still catch him there."

* * * *

Ruby followed Jacob back to their original destination. Ruby's desire to keep her brother from his fate overpowered her weakening body. They'd said Arvin had drowned, that it was an accidental death. They said the gash to his head could've happened when his body was battered on the rocks. One of the detectives even mentioned a possible shark attack. He must've seen *Jaws*, too. Arvin's autopsy had shown that he did indeed drown. But Ruby knew there had to have been foul play. She felt it, as only a twin might.

Soon a heavy aroma of garlic welcomed them back to the open-air Pizza Palace. A clog of hungry customers blocked their way in, but Arvin wasn't one of them. Ruby and Jacob scanned the handful of clustered rectangular tables that crowded the interior, but her brother wasn't among the diners either.

Ruby cut into the line. An animated guy in his thirties with a five o'clock shadow was behind the counter taking cash and serving up hot slices on grease-sodden paper plates. Two more guys who resembled him were twirling dough in the air and making the pies. They all wore Phillies hats and white Pizza Palace T-shirts that clung to their broad shoulders and swollen biceps.

Ruby had to look at the men twice to recognize Vic. She remembered him as an older man, like her dad—older back then was twenty years younger than she was now. She realized Vic was the one at the cash register.

"Was Arvin just here?" she urgently asked him.

Vic broke his attention from his customer to look at Ruby. "How do you know Arvin?" He looked her up and down. "Are you related?" Considering her dark almond-shaped eyes and wide nose—it was a good guess. There weren't too many Filipinos in South Jersey.

"Yes, I'm his...great-aunt," Ruby lied. "Was he here?"

"Came and went just few minutes ago."

"Did he say he was coming back? Which way did he go?"

"Don't know. Sorry, I can't help ya." Then to the next customer, "How many slices?"

Ruby stepped away from the counter and rejoined Jacob.

"What if it was Vic who did something to your brother?" Jacob said. "He could've lied to the police about when he last saw him."

Ruby looked around. "I didn't see Arvin's bike. And I don't see how Vic could've gotten away from his customers long enough to do something like that in the few minutes Arvin was here." She gestured to the queue, which was constantly replenishing, to make her point. "What are we going to do?"

Her energy sapped, Ruby began to sway.

Jacob's eyes grew wide. "Let's sit down for a minute."

They grabbed two chairs at the end of one of the long tables that were recently vacated. A draft of air hit them at intervals from an oscillating fan. Jacob reached into his daypack—a Goodwill find—and opened a Thermos of chilled water for Ruby. She immediately put it to her lips.

"Maybe we should go home," he said. "We can come back after you've gotten some rest."

"No. You said yourself that you don't know if the pod will work again after we've laid new footprints on the past. You said the algorithm gets too screwy."

"I can try again to figure it out."

"I don't have the time for you to figure it out. We have to find my brother, and it has to be now."

Jacob hunched over the table and began rapping his knuckles against his forehead.

Ruby immediately regretted sharing her panic with Jacob. If frustration overtook his reasoning, she knew it would take some time for him to be able to think clearly again—time they didn't have.

She made an effort to calm her voice. "I'm all right, Jacob. I'm just a little tired, but I want to keep going. Okay?"

A moment later, he sat up and readjusted his glasses. "So let's use our heads instead of our legs."

Ruby was relieved that the logical Jacob was still in charge.

He continued, "Do you think the shoebox he gave his friend has anything to do with his disappearance? What was in it? Do you remember him taking it from home that day?"

Ruby thought back to that fateful day. She'd gone over it a thousand times in her head since she was thirteen. Arvin had asked her if she wanted to go to the boardwalk with him that afternoon. She'd said no, it was too hot to bike the eight blocks there, and they weren't about to cool off in the ocean. They were too afraid of that damn shark. If only she'd said yes.

"I was in my room when he left, so I didn't see him. My parents never mentioned afterward anything of Arvin's that went missing."

"Your brother had something in a little bag when he got back on his bike. Maybe he traded the shoebox for whatever it was?"

Ruby had no idea. She was starting to lose hope.

A customer shouted over their heads, "Hey, Vic, turn up the game, will ya?"

Vic turned the dial on his transistor radio on the counter behind him, and the booming voices of baseball announcers competed with the whirring of the corner fan.

Childhood memories swirled around Ruby like a tornado picking up strength. "That's it! Arvin kept his baseball cards in a shoebox. He kept some of his favorite players tacked up in his room, but the rest he kept in a shoebox. He traded with his friends sometimes. Never the whole box, though."

"You think his friend Stevie took it from him?"

"It didn't look like they left the arcade on bad terms." Her shoulders slumped again, and she took another swig of water. "Either way, I think Stevie has some answers. If we can't find Arvin, we need to find Stevie."

"Where would he have gone?"

Ruby thought for a moment. "If they weren't hanging out here, they were almost always at the bumper cars. Let's check the pier." But when she stood, she had to grab hold of the back of the chair to steady herself.

"I've got an idea," Jacob said. "I'll be right back."

In a matter of minutes, Jacob was at the front of the Pizza Palace in a covered, four-wheeled surrey. The boardwalk was dotted with surrey rental stands.

"Hop in," he said.

Ruby smiled gratefully and slid onto the bench seat beside him. "I don't think I'll be much help pedaling."

"Leave it to me."

Jacob steered around pedestrians, and Ruby tried to scan every face, searching for Arvin's or Stevie's. It wasn't long before Jacob stopped the surrey where the boardwalk met the pier. An AMUSEMENTS sign arched overhead. The melodious muddle of band organ music reached their ears and immediately brought Ruby's memory to the carousel. She had to beg Arvin to go on it with her that last summer. He made a show of not wanting to go—he was thirteen and too macho for a merry-go-round—but once they handed over their tickets, he scurried to the front of the line to make sure they got the biggest and best horses.

Ruby and Jacob disembarked from the surrey. They passed the ticket booth with its striped awning to reach the dozen or so rides that spun and whirled and lifted and dipped like mechanical octopuses. The constant din was routinely punctuated by gleeful screams. Ruby sensed Jacob tensing—she knew he felt loud noises like these vibrating within his body. She hated putting him through this.

"Do you want me to continue on my own?" she asked him.

He took and expelled a deep breath while rapidly clenching and releasing his fists. He still didn't look fully at ease when he said, "We have to do this together, remember?"

She smiled at him and gave him a determined nod.

They wound their way through the crowd, searching the faces. Ruby's breath hitched in her throat every time she saw a boy that resembled Arvin or Stevie, but it was never them. They expectantly approached the circular barrier that enclosed the bumper cars, but Stevie wasn't there either.

"Let's keep looking," Jacob said.

They reached the far end of the pier, where the roller coaster towered over the other rides. Shrieks of terror and delight rose and fell with its riders. Ruby recalled Arvin persuading her to ride it earlier that summer, and on one particular dip, feeling like their car was going to fall directly into the ocean. Arvin had held onto her then. She was not going to give up on him now.

They ventured beyond the coaster where the empty pier continued to the shoreline, and the crowds thinned. They were about to make another pass through the amusement park when Jacob stopped short. He stood staring at the pier for several seconds before walking toward the edge. Ruby was about to chastise him for wasting precious time, when he reached down and picked up a small rectangular object. He turned to her, holding it out in his hand. It was a creased playing card: the ace of hearts.

"That's from Arvin's bike," Ruby said.

They cast their gaze farther down the pier. The sun glinted off a misshapen heap near the stairs leading down to the beach. As they trotted closer to it, she saw the red and yellow colors, then spoked wheels and handlebars.

"Are those their bikes?" Ruby asked.

"I think so," Jacob said, and they began jogging toward them. Running would have been better, but jogging was the best Ruby could do.

The closer they got, the more certain Ruby was that they'd found the boys. Then Ruby spotted someone ascending the steps that led from the beach below. It was Stevie. Jacob took off past Ruby and ran toward him, as Stevie pulled his bike from the ground and mounted it. He used one hand to steer, while the other hand clutched the towel wrapped around his handlebars and held it to his face.

Jacob juked from side to side at the center of the pier, waving his arms for Stevie to stop. But the pier was too wide and Stevie ignored him, both hands on the handlebars now, pedaling in bare feet faster and closer.

"Stevie!" Ruby shouted, but her weak voice was lost in the sea breeze.

At the last minute, Jacob lunged at the bike, grabbing at the beach towel, but Stevie swerved. His shoulder caught Jacob's, delivering a glancing blow, and knocking Jacob to the ground. Stevie wobbled, then pedaled on.

Ruby rushed to Jacob. "Are you okay?"

He sat up and rotated his shoulder. "I think so."

As she helped him up, she noticed his white T-shirt was splattered with crimson dots where he'd been hit. "You're bleeding."

He looked down and pulled his shirt sleeve over his shoulder to look at his skin. "It's not *my* blood."

They stared at each other for a moment as the implication sunk in. They both raced down the steps to the beach, which was beginning to be submerged by the rising tide. They jumped into the wet sand.

"Arvin!" Ruby shouted. "Arvin!"

Jacob joined her in calling out for him. Ruby pushed through each sinking step with labored breaths. They let the sand take possession of their cumbersome sandals as they made their way under the pier. The tidewater grazed their ankles.

In the shadows, the silhouette of a boulder sharpened into Arvin's body slumped over it.

"Arvin!" Ruby cried.

They trudged over to him. His head was lying on the boulder just above the water, and his eyes were closed. Ruby fell to her knees and pulled him into a sitting position, his head flopping to the side. By the streaks of sunlight shining through the boards of the pier, she noticed a gloppy patch behind his ear—blood.

"Oh, Arvin." Ruby encased him in her arms and wept.

She suddenly felt him shift within her embrace. She pulled back and his eyes fluttered open.

"Can you hear me? Arvin?"

"Mom?" he said groggily.

She hugged him again. She only stopped when she felt Jacob's insistent fingers tapping her shoulder.

"The tide's coming in. We gotta get him out of here."

"Can you walk?" she asked her brother.

"I think so."

Jacob helped both of them to stand.

"Wait, my baseball cards." Arvin's gaze searched the ground. He appeared confused by the rising tide.

"Oh, Arvin, they're long gone. Let's go," Ruby said.

They clasped arms and helped each other make their way the ten yards to the steps. It felt like walking in quicksand as the water now lapped at their shins. They pushed Arvin onto the steps. He pulled Ruby up the best a scrawny boy could, and then Jacob pulled himself up behind them. The hardest part was over. They plodded up the steps.

"Where's my bike?" Arvin said as he reached the top.

"It was here before," Jacob said.

Looking down the pier toward the rollercoaster, they saw a teenager riding away on a red Schwinn.

"First my rookie baseball cards and now my bike? This day couldn't get any worse."

Ruby broke into laughter and Jacob joined in. Arvin looked at them like they were crazy.

"Who are you, anyway?" he asked them.

After a moment of bumbling, Ruby said, "We saw you stranded down there. It looked like you could use some help."

They glanced over the pier's edge where the ocean was now crashing against the pylons.

"Gee, thanks," Arvin said, but his obvious relief quickly vanished. He hung his head. "I never thought Stevie would cheat me like that."

"What did he do?" Ruby asked, as they wearily made their way back to the boardwalk.

"He said he had a signed Steve Carlton baseball card. You know, Lefty, the Phillies pitcher? Stevie just went to a game last week and said he got his card signed by him. He wanted my rookie set in trade, so I agreed. Besides, I felt kinda bad for him after he snuck his brother's rookie collection and ruined it when he brought it fishing with us. He stuck the cards in the cooler and forgot about them. The ice made 'em all soggy. No, duh!" Arvin shook his head. "We traded at the arcade, then I went to the Pizza Palace to show my friend, Vic." Arvin's face colored. "Vic knew right away the autograph was a fake."

"Wow. He cheated you?" Ruby would've never figured that. Arvin and Stevie were like brothers.

"I couldn't believe it," Arvin said. "He's been at his brother's mercy for weeks, but still…"

"How did you end up under the pier?" Jacob said.

"I went to look for Stevie to get my cards back. I finally found him watching the bumper cars, but as soon as he saw me, he rode away, so I went after him. There was no place left for him to go on the pier, so he ran down to the beach. I ditched my bike and followed him. We had a fight and I socked him in the nose. Drew blood. It made him drop the box of cards in the water, so he pushed me, and… I guess that's the last thing I remember."

"You must've hit your head on the rock when you fell, and lost consciousness," Jacob said. Ruby saw him avert his eyes from Arvin's gash.

"And Stevie must've panicked," Ruby filled in the rest. "He shouldn't have left you there, though."

She recalled how distraught Stevie was after Arvin's body was found. It never crossed her mind that it was because he was to blame for it. She remembered hearing a few years later that he'd dropped out of high school and was having trouble with drugs. Ruby was certain he never meant for Arvin to die when he left him under the pier, but he never told anyone what really happened either. All those years, she and her parents were left wondering about Arvin's final moments. Ruby could only hope now that Stevie would never get himself into a similar situation again.

"Now I don't have a birthday present for my dad." Arvin hung his head. "He woulda loved that signed Lefty card."

Ruby's heart melted. "Oh, Arvin." She briefly put her arm around her brother and squeezed his shoulder. She wished she could tell him who she was so they could hug properly.

"How do you know my name?" he asked.

"Uh… You told me when you were regaining consciousness. Don't you remember?"

He shook his head and put a hand to the back of it, wincing. "I've got a whopper of a headache."

"We'd better find a phone and call Mo—your parents. You might need some stitches."

"I hope I don't get grounded for losing my bike," he said.

"Don't worry so much, Arvin," Ruby said. "You're going to be just fine."

She looked at Jacob, tears brimming in her eyes.

* * * *

Jacob exited the pod in his dining area. He'd left the boardwalk with Ruby, but now he was alone—confirmation that they'd changed the past and things were now different.

Her whole life would've changed when they saved Arvin—so many new memories would've supplanted the old ones. It's possible she wouldn't even remember their time travel. He helped to change Ruby's life, but had he changed his own and lost a friend, too?

Fear tickled his belly. What if Ruby didn't live next door anymore? Or worse, what if she already died? He checked the tablet he held in his hands. Only eighty-four minutes had passed. She couldn't have died; could she?

With deliberate steps, he walked outside and through his front yard. He took a left around his picket fence, down the sidewalk in front of his own house, and cut in where stepping stones led to her front porch. He stopped, for a moment not wanting to know. Then he approached the porch steps.

The screen door squeaked as it opened.

"Jacob. Want to come in for some lemonade?"

Jacob exhaled in relief. He couldn't keep himself from staring. It was Ruby all right, but she had thick hair again that was swooped over the front of one shoulder, like she used to wear it. She'd gained some weight, but her cheekbones stood out. He'd almost gotten used to the puffy cheeks her chemo had caused. Her skin glowed.

"Ruby, you look great." He climbed the steps to make sure it was really his friend.

"Thank you." She smiled. "I think it's the relief of finally being cancer free. There's nothing like hitting the five-year mark since my bone-marrow transplant."

"I thought you couldn't find a donor."

Her brows made a V between her eyes. "Arvin was a match. You remember that. You brought us pudding in the hospital?"

Jacob's spotty memory started filling in the regenerated past. "Banana pudding."

"That's right. Dr. Wingate ended up eating most of it."

Jacob tried to capture the memories as they flooded in.

"I mean Doctor Steve," Ruby said. "I forget that he lets people call him that. I can't believe Stevie turned out to be a doctor. He was such a flake when he was a kid, always doing stupid stuff." She chuckled, shaking her head at the ground. Then she stared at Jacob's bare feet. "Hey, your feet are all sandy. Mine were, too, a few minutes ago." She stared into Jacob's eyes. "It wasn't a dream. You helped me, didn't you, Jacob?"

Before Ruby could even register her surprise, Jacob was hugging her.

Korina Moss writes cozy mysteries, and is represented by Jill Marsal of Marsal Lyon Literary Agency. When considering writing a time-travel mystery, Korina knew she wanted to revisit her childhood summers on the Jersey Shore. The story also had to include *Jaws*, a movie she distinctly remembers watching on her ninth birthday. Her next short story will be in Elm Book's anthology *Death by Cupcake*, due out in spring 2020. Korina lives in Connecticut with her son and their fat black cat. She is currently writing a mystery set in Maine, and she occasionally posts in her blog www.korinastake.blogspot.com.

THE SNEEZE

Anna Castle

I leaned against my kitchen counter, too weak to make it all the way to the sink. My head felt like it had been stuffed with damp, shredded paper from a hamster cage. I needed a pot of hot tea in the worst way.

I opened the cupboard and a puff of spice-laden air assaulted my aching nose. My nostrils started twitching—the first sign. My eyes filled with water as my mouth contorted into a grimace. Then a shuddering breath seized my whole body, releasing in an explosive sneeze so powerful it almost knocked me sideways. Before my wits fully cleared, another one blasted through me.

Eyes watering and hands braced against the cold countertop, I waited for another attack, but the third one failed to launch. I could feel it coiling back into my chest, waiting for a chance to catch me by surprise. I'd never had allergies this bad before. These sneezes were mind-blowing body-quakes. One of these times, they'd shake the brains right out of my head.

I snuffled and wiped my nose on the sleeve of the saggy nightshirt I'd been wearing all week. Enough of the herbal crap—I needed earl grey, hot, and plenty of it. Caffeine was my only hope. I was scheduled to discuss the most important section of my dissertation with my advisor in two days, and I still had no pithy insight with which to wow her.

The whole damn diss was largely speculation—no surprise for yet another rehashing of the literary scene in late Elizabethan London. The evidence about people's lives was scanty no matter how popular a writer was in his own time. My main subject was the lesser-known pamphleteer Henry Claybrook, who may or may not have coauthored one of the Bard's rumored lost plays. I said he did, but all I had was a note here and a handful of textual similarities there.

My advisor knew the period inside out and was famously intolerant of hand-waving, smoke-blowing, and other forms of academic bluster. She was also one of those tough old birds who thought allergies were the sad excuse of lazy feather-wits. So tree pollen or no tree pollen, I had to present a brilliant argument or suffer a curling of the lip and a withering dismissal.

It would help if I had more faith in my argument. But as the pollen invaded my head, my confidence withered. At this point, it all looked like bullshit. Two years of work tossed out like a wad of used tissues.

I hung two bags of earl grey in my tea Thermos and lifted the kettle from the stove, giving it a shake. Empty. I turned to the sink to fill it, moving into a patch of bright sunlight. Stupidly, I looked at the sky, getting a full blast of sunshine square in the face. My nose wrinkled, my head snapped back, and I convulsed in one almighty sneeze so intense, it felt like an out-of-body experience.

I gasped, pressing my hand to my chest. I reached blindly for the faucet handle to splash cold water on my face and caught air. Opening my eyes, I saw neither faucet nor sink.

How's this?

I cautiously shifted my gaze. No stainless-steel sink. No quartz-composite counter. No fake-cobblestone vinyl; instead, the floor beneath my scuffed leather slippers was covered in broken straw with dark wood underneath.

Okay. Okay. This was some allergy-induced hallucination. It would pass.

I took a quick personal inventory. My heart still beat, my nose still dripped. My hair was still long, brown, and unwashed. I was still wearing the old Renaissance faire linen shirt that hung baggily down to my knees.

But this was not my kitchen. No, sirree. I'd never seen this place before, except in movies, maybe.

I stood in a square room with stained white walls. Dark beams spanned a steeply sloping ceiling. Bigger than my bedroom, it held only a narrow cot, a wooden chest, and a three-legged stool. The stink of piss rose from a clay pot in the corner, joining the rank smells of stale beer and fusty straw. The bedsheets had been jumbled by a rogue tornado, and clothes straggled out of the chest onto the floor. I spotted a couple of cheaply bound books thrown into the chaos.

But underneath the mess lay top-quality materials. The floor looked like solid oak, not engineered planks with that sleek factory finish. The walls had the creamy sheen of real plaster. Who had plaster walls in Austin, Texas? Nobody in my late-sixties neighborhood, that much was certain. And no one who could afford this much oak and plaster would live in such squalor.

"Toto," I said to the empty room, "I don't think we're in Austin anymore."

A queasy feeling stirred in my gut. I frowned at the small window with its diamond-shaped panes of glass set in genuine lead lines, framed with genuine oak trim. I walked over and opened it with an iron latch that appeared to have been handcrafted. I looked out at a perfect replica of an Elizabethan townhouse. Gray oak beams crossed sand-colored plaster. A quaint thatched roof hung over deep eaves.

The room opposite looked just like this one but with less mess. There was no one in it, thank goodness. I had no way to explain my presence, and wasn't quite up to a wave and a "Hi, y'all!" Peering down and sideways, I judged my room to be on the fourth floor in a row of houses facing a cobbled alley with water trickling through a tiled ditch in the middle. Two men strolled by dressed in flawless Elizabethan garb.

My head swam. I sat on the bed and buried my face in my hands. I chanted, "Wake up, wake up, wake up," then squeezed my eyes shut and popped them open.

Nope. I was still in the garret of wherever the hell that sneeze had brought me.

It couldn't be real, yet it looked, felt, and smelled real. No doubt I was lying in a swoon on the floor in my kitchen in the grip of some feverish delusion. But if this were madness, yet there was method in it. I was an Elizabethanist who had somehow sneezed her way into the Elizabethan period.

Why fight it?

A wave of sound, like many voices laughing, surged under the door into my room. There were people out there somewhere. I should go look at them. And since it was just a hallucination, I didn't even need to comb my hair.

I opened the door and stepped onto a bare landing at the top of a steep flight of stairs. I tiptoed down, my slippers silent on treads too well built to creak. The landing on the next floor gave access to three doors, all closed. Moans and grunts of a particular nature emerged from one of them. I clucked my tongue at the injustice. Why should my own delusions mock my dissertation-induced celibacy?

The last run of stairs opened to one side, revealing a wide room full of tables occupied by men and women in full Elizabethan dress, drinking and talking. I crept down a few more steps and crouched to peer between the balusters. My sneeze had apparently brought me across the sea as well as through the centuries. This place looked like Ye Olde English Tavern, complete with straw on the floor and tobacco smoke hanging in the air. More smoke seeped from the big fireplace in the middle of the room. Stained plaster covered the inner wall; diamond-paned windows filled most of the outer one. All as authentic as an A-list movie. I was impressed at my brain for its retention of detail.

Three men sat at the table nearest me playing cards. One of them smoked a long-stemmed pipe. I clapped a hand over my mouth as I recognized him: Christopher Marlowe, looking almost exactly like his portrait. Young, handsome, with that knowing look in his brown eyes, he had the same collar-length brown hair and skimpy mustache, but wore a brown woolen doublet instead of the brass-trimmed velvet one in the portrait. I gazed at him in wonder, absorbing every nuance of his expression with a stalker's intensity. The greatest playwright of his day, right there, almost close enough to touch.

The towhead next to him with the jug ears and freckles must have been Thomas Nashe, the scurrilous pamphleteer. He also looked like the one sketch that had survived the ages. One of his front teeth poked out under his lip, and his clothes were looser and shabbier than Marlowe's. The two poets had become friends at Cambridge.

The third man wore a scarlet doublet with yellow lining, a cut above the other two. He had a tall hat, reddish hair, and a pointed beard. I didn't recognize him. He studied the cards in his hand as if reading their portents while the other two watched him with growing impatience.

"I don't have all day," Marlowe said. "And I want to win my money back before I leave."

"Just pick a card, Claybrook," Nashe said.

Claybrook? *Henry* Claybrook? *My* Claybrook?

"Henry!" I scooted down the stairs to get a closer look, and all three hallucinations turned to stare at me, their surprise turning to amusement.

"Looks like your doxy wants another tumble," Nashe said. "If you're too busy, I could lend a hand. Along with other parts of my anatomy."

I clutched the gaping neckline of my nightshirt. It had a high collar, but the much-washed linen was not precisely opaque. "You can see me?"

Marlowe nodded. Nashe giggled. Claybrook said, "She isn't mine, but if needs must..." He started to get up but was blocked by a waitress bearing a tray with a loaf of bread and a bowl covered with a folded cloth.

She cast a sharp look at me and said, "Up you go, dearie, right back to your room. You get your kirtle on and cover your hair before coming downstairs. The Goose and Gall is a decent house." She turned to the card players and clucked her tongue. "Fie, Mr. Claybrook. You know better than to leave your strumpet alone in your room."

"She's not mine." Henry's protest was interrupted by Nashe craning his nose toward the tray.

"What've you got there, Kate? Enough to share?"

Kate shook her head. "Fuel for the pair in number three. Lord knows they need it. But I can spare you a whiff." She lifted the cloth and flapped it, sending hot steam riddled with black pepper straight up my nose.

Achoo!

* * * *

I found myself on all fours in my bedroom, staring at the carpet through watering eyes. "Damnation!"

But wait: hadn't I passed out in the kitchen? And what was this? I sniffed at my sleeve, smelling tobacco and beef gravy, two things never found in my house. It was real. I had been there.

And I wanted to go back.

But this time I'd be ready.

I got out the plastic storage bin that held my garb for Renaissance faires and dumped it out on the bed: two skirts, a bodice, sleeves, and a polyester neck ruff that now looked way too fake. The ruffle on my shirt collar would have to do.

I argued with myself about allergy delusions while setting up the ironing board and ironing the skirt. What was the plan, exactly? To get into a costume and lie on the floor? Still scolding, I jumped into the shower and washed my hair. I wouldn't get any baths in Elizabethan London, and I couldn't predict how long I'd be there.

Kate had mentioned the Goose and Gall. I knew the place—a tavern just north of St. Paul's that had been the favorite haunt of printers and pamphleteers. Thomas Nashe had come down from Cambridge in 1588 and Christopher Marlowe died in 1593, so I'd landed somewhere in that span of years.

I'd bet a silver penny it was 1591, the year Henry Claybrook published the book that formed the basis of the lost play *Henry and Eleanor*, which might or might not have been at least partially written by William Shakespeare. Bits of it had been quoted by some lawyer in his diary, so we knew it had been produced. My dissertation triangulated between Claybrook's *True Historie of English Queens*, the lost play, and Shakespeare's *Antony and Cleopatra*, first performed in 1607.

As I laced up the bodice, my inner bitch demanded a rational explanation for how the sneeze transporter worked. But how should I know? I was a lit major. I'd squeaked through my B.A. requirements with Self-Paced Astronomy and Physics for Poets.

But I'd been a Trekkie all my life. As I braided my hair, I remembered something Mr. Spock once said. We could think of time as fluid, like a river, with currents and eddies. I'd been standing on the banks of Henry Claybrook's life for two long years. So when the time-travelling sneeze caught hold of me, it would naturally drop me at his feet.

Or in his bedroom. The thought of that tousled bed and those broad shoulders prompted me to tuck a couple of condoms in my pocket. I might be the first Elizabethanist in history to get lucky with her primary subject.

I sat on the bed to pull on my stockings. But I could only find one shoe. I flopped on my belly to look under the bed and there it was, nestled in a cloud of dust bunnies. I reached for it, stirring up a puff of ancient carpet dust. My nose started twitching. I barely had time to grab my shoe before it blew.

Achoo!

* * * *

I lay sprawled on the stairs at the tavern with the shoe in my hand. I stuffed my foot into it and got up, shaking out my skirts. I'd forgotten the damn coif to cover my hair. Oh, well. They already thought I was a whore, and I didn't plan to go outside.

The men had returned to their cards, seemingly unconcerned about the vanishing woman. Maybe the sneeze-porter had some kind of blurring effect.

I hovered at the foot of the stairs, trying to think of an opening line. There must be a dozen questions I wanted to ask Henry Claybrook, but my brain had gone blank. He was *vastly* better looking than I'd imagined; proof, of a sort, that this could not be the product of my limited faculties.

I wanted to know everything, but where to start? *"Hi! I'm Amy. Have you ever collaborated with William Shakespeare?"*

As I dithered behind the balusters, Nashe tossed a card on the table with a victorious "Ha!" The other men groaned and threw down their hands. Nashe scooped coins into his palm while Marlowe gathered the cards together, tucking the deck into a leather purse.

Claybrook crossed his arms and shook his head. He glanced toward the stairs and spotted me. A sexy smile curved on his lips. "Well, well! Look who's back."

Nashe grinned and showed me his handful of coins. "Look you, ladybird. I can pay with more than promises now."

"She's not here for you, my friend," Marlowe said. "She can't take her eyes off old Claybrook. Though what she sees in him is invisible to me."

A bell tolled the three-quarter hour, echoed by another at a different pitch, and a third one farther off. Marlowe set his hands on the table and pushed himself up. "That's it for me, lads. I'm off to Deptford. The tide waits for no man."

"You say that every year," Nashe said. "Try to think of something new while you're cooling your heels in the court of—whichever court you cool your heels in."

"Where are you going?" I asked. The chance to solve the mystery of Marlowe's annual absences untied my tongue.

He answered with a scornful grunt and a shake of the head. "Coming, Nashe?"

"We never ask, sweetling," Nashe told me as he rose. "Personally, I think he spends his summers at an auntie's house in Folkestone."

"Perish the thought," Marlowe said. "I just grow weary of you buffoons and require a respite to refresh my wits."

Claybrook shot me a wink. "Don't you gentlemen have a boat to catch?"

Nashe said, "Boats to catch or rent to pay, we'll meet your wench another day." He and Marlowe took their leave.

Claybrook hooked a stool with his foot, displaying a shapely leg as he drew it close. He gave it an inviting pat. "Come sit with me, sweet chuck, and beguile my solitary state."

Feeling like a cross between a groupie and a reporter, I sat, clasping my hands between my knees. "Tell me, Mr. Claybrook, were you born in London?"

He preened himself at the title. Like many writers of the time, he straddled the border between social classes. "I was, sweet chuck. But you're from the West Country, aren't you?"

"I am." Well to the west, as a matter of fact. He must have keyed into my throaty r's and broad vowels. Having listened to actors performing Shakespeare in the original pronunciation, I wasn't surprised at how easy it was to understand these people. His dialect wasn't much different from those reconstructions, especially for my Texan ears.

I set my elbow on the table and rested my cheek in my palm, gazing at my favorite subject with unfeigned adoration. He had deep blue eyes with laugh lines at the corners, and the style of a man who could show a lonely scholar a very good time.

"You're a writer, aren't you?" I asked.

He chuckled. "I've published a few books. And more than a few pamphlets."

"What sorts of books?" I didn't dare ask about the *True Historie of English Queen*, because I didn't know which month it had come out.

"Aren't you a curious wench, then? What do you care about writing and books?"

"I'm just interested in you."

Sensual sparkings warmed his answering smile, making me glad for the impulse that put condoms in my pocket. "If you want to know, sweetling, Wolfe just published my new book about notable queens in English history."

"That sounds fascinating." As he reached for my hand, I asked the most important question. "Have you ever written any plays?"

"Oh, it's plays, is it? I suppose you want to meet Ned Alleyn."

I blinked at him, derailed for a moment. Meet the most famous actor of the Elizabethan era? Why, yes. Yes, I would enjoy that, if we had time between sneezes. "Maybe later. What sorts of plays do you write?"

"I can't say I've written one yet, not a whole one. I wrote some scenes for a play about Henry the Second, but I doubt they'll appear in the final version—if there ever is a final version."

"Who wrote the rest of it? William Shakespeare?"

"You know your poets, I see. Will's a newcomer." He lifted my hand to his lips and kissed it, before pointing his chin across the room. "I sat right over there under that window and gave the ungrateful whoreson everything he needed for a superlative play. Political conflict rich in history, with a stirring romance to boot."

"How was he ungrateful?"

"Did he thank me? Did he offer to add my name to the billing and give me a share of the takings? He just stared out the window scratching his beard, like I'd suddenly vanished. Then he jumped up, clapped me on the shoulder, and walked away, leaving me to pay for the drinks."

"That varlet!" I stroked his hand, wondering how I could work that anecdote into my dissertation.

He frowned at my choice of words. "I wouldn't be that harsh. He is truly a prodigious poet. Mark my words, he'll do well for himself, once he learns how to get along." He opened my hand and planted a kiss in my palm.

It made me shiver with anticipation. Who knew my Henry would turn out to be so hot?

"I have a copy of my new book upstairs," he said, a husky thrum in his voice. "I could read a bit to you, if you like."

"I would like that more than anything in the world."

His eyes flashed. He helped me up and slid an arm around my waist, taking a gander into the filmy linen at the top of my bodice while he was at it. But before we reached the first landing, someone shouted, "Claybrook! Are you still here?"

Thomas Nashe sprinted up the stairs. "Thank God, I'm in time. Look you, Claybrook, you've got to scuddle, this minute. Go visit your lightskirt in Hackney for a week."

Henry looked down at me, his eyes dark with desire. "Not today, Nashe. Visit her yourself if you're in need of fresh air."

"This is no jest, man. You've been named in a killing. Some churl named Bishop, knifed in a ditch outside Aldersgate. They're saying you did it."

"No, that was Walter Radley," Henry said. "I saw it happen, but I had no part in it."

"Well, you're the one they're coming for. Best go out the back. Now. The constables are hot on my trail. You're lucky I heard them talking and beat them here."

The urgency in Nashe's voice alarmed me. My gut clenched. But Henry, still focused on the lusty option, said, "I suppose we could—"

"Clear the way!" The voice of authority boomed up the stairs, followed by two stout men wearing badges. "Claybrook?" They glared around the tavern like they'd take anyone who fit whatever description they had.

Nashe backed away, hands up. Some asshole pointed at Henry, who pushed me behind him.

"I'm not the one you want," he said, as one of the men grabbed his arms. "You've got the wrong man!" Henry struggled, pulling the officer back toward the fireplace, where a wench knelt, scooping ashes into a bucket.

I jumped into the fray, tugging at one of the constables. "Leave him alone!"

He threw me off with one flex of his beefy arm. I tripped on the wench's skirts and fell on my ass, knocking over the bucket of ashes and sending a cloud of dust straight into my nose.

"Not now!" I begged the universe, to no avail.

Achoo!

* * * *

"No, no, no!" I landed on my butt on my living room floor. I started to get up, then changed my mind, rolling over to stick my nose under the couch, snuffling for dust.

No joy.

I got to my feet and tried a few deep breaths. My whole respiratory system felt clear. Where was the damn prickle when I needed it?

I went to the fridge for a cold Diet Coke. No time for tea; I had to find a way to get back. I couldn't leave Henry in jeopardy—though he must've gotten out of it somehow because he published a sequel to the *True Historie* in 1593. I'd never read anything about Claybrook spending time in jail. That didn't mean it didn't happen, but he certainly didn't hang for murder and then come back to write another book.

I settled into my nest—the afghan-covered desk chair where I spent most of my waking hours. I logged in to my computer and sat there drinking caffeinated fizz while I opened my dissertation and scrolled to the table of contents. Then I sat forward so fast I splashed Coke on my keyboard. Section three was gone! That was the most important part—the part where I laid out my argument about Claybrook's influence on Shakespeare.

Section one, my long review of the literature, seemed to have lost a few paragraphs. Section two, where I discussed literacy and which sorts of people read what sorts of publications, looked okay, but it was followed immediately by the conclusion. What the blazing hell had happened?

I hadn't touched this file since yesterday, and section three had definitely been there then. I'd spent several fruitless hours tweaking words and moving commas around, my pollen-addled brain barely able to parse sentences, but feeling the need to work.

Horror squeezed my heart. Had I changed history by keeping Claybrook in that tavern? If I hadn't been there, he would've left with Nashe and Marlowe. He would've heard the constables talking, as Nashe had, and split for Hackney to hide out until the real killer was caught.

This kind of thing happened all the time on *Star Trek*. One crucial moment altered, and history changed. Only the time-traveler remembered the truth.

I'd broken the past, and I had to set it right. Henry's future—and mine, apparently—depended on it. But how?

I scrolled slowly through my diss, hoping something would ring a bell. Most of what I knew about Claybrook's life was in here. I scrolled to section 2.2.3, *Prison literature*, and an alarm starting clanging. Prison pamphlets! These were lurid confessions ostensibly written by men or women about to hang for a heinous crime. While they referenced real people and crimes, they were written, and liberally embellished, by professionals like Claybrook. Such works were madly popular back in the day and might pay as much as a pound to the writer—more than a country parson earned in a year.

My main resource for popular pamphlets was still around here somewhere, in one of the stacks of library books and journal articles that filled my house. I went on a rampage, throwing paper around like a junkie searching for a lost stash. At last I found the right book and brought it back to my nest. I started flipping through the sections marked with torn strips of sticky notes.

I caught the name "Walter Radley" on page 321. Score one for the queen of research! I reread the passage and found a fatal flip-flop had transpired between sneezes.

In the true timeline, the one before I stumbled into the past, Walter Radley had been arrested for killing Benjamin Bishop in April, 1592. The act had been witnessed by Henry Claybrook, resident of the Goose and Gall on Ivy Lane. Later, Claybrook had visited Radley in prison and obtained his full confession. Claybrook published it along with a couple of others, adding a nice, moralizing preface.

Both Radley and Bishop had been minor poets—very minor—which is why their names survived. The moral of the confession was that pride in one's own works led inevitably to strife and death. Nothing was said about the pride of the pamphleteer or the publisher.

So far, so good; that was the way I remembered it. But now the book said Claybrook had been arrested for the murder on Radley's testimony. Radley had been in prison for a week too, while the authorities sorted things out. He'd taken advantage of the time to solicit a confession from Claybrook, which Radley had published as a lesson to the prideful. The old time-traveling switcheroo in action!

The book didn't lay out the precise chronology of who was in jail at what time. Curse its slothful author. She did supply one useful detail: Radley wrote his piece in Newgate Prison. That wasn't far from the Goose and Gall. All I had to do was get back there.

I headed for the kitchen to stick my nose in a jar of pepper but had another thought and detoured into the bedroom to rifle through my jewelry box. Prison meant guards, and guards meant bribes. I'd need something negotiable.

One pair of genuine gold earrings, a graduation present from Mom, and a little gold cross Grandma gave me once upon a time—that ought to do it. I had no idea what they'd be worth in the sixteenth century, but gold was gold.

On to the kitchen. I opened the tea cupboard and inhaled deeply. Nothing, apart from the pleasure of the mingled aromas. Hmm. My head felt unusually clear. Where was the misery when I needed it?

I grabbed the jar of pepper and twisted off the cap, sticking my nose right into it. I breathed in so briskly, I got flecks of pepper on my face—but no sneeze. Was it over? Were those first sneezes only teases?

It couldn't be over. I'd changed history and destroyed my own dissertation. Worse, my interference had caused a good man to die too soon. I had to go back and fix things. I glanced out the window at the bright blue sky. Sunshine had taken me out the first time; maybe it would do the trick again.

I bustled out the front door, strode into the middle of the driveway, and looked straight up into the sun. Nothing.

I marched back inside and stuck my head in the freezer, flapping my collar to stoke up the gooseflesh. Then I raced back out and turned my nose toward the sun.

Nada. Zilch. Bubkes.

Standing on the concrete drive, I shook my fists at the implacable golden orb. "Sneeze me up, damn you!"

* * * *

I ended up going out to buy some jalapeños. The sneeze-porter took me out mid-chop. I found myself standing at the foot of the stairs on the ground floor of the tavern, nose-to-nose with one gobsmacked serving wench.

"Hi, Kate!" I said, not bothering to amend my speech. "Which way's Newgate?"

She pointed, eyes and mouth round with astonishment. I patted her on the shoulder as I sped past and out the door.

I had spent many happy hours poring over the *A-to-Z of Elizabethan London*, so I knew my way around. I held a vision of Henry Claybrook's seductive smile in my mind to stop me from rubbernecking. The sights. The sounds. The *smells*! How had Shakespeare never mentioned this olfactory extravaganza? Horse shit, dog shit, every kind of shit; but also spicy pies, baking bread, and old leather. Luckily, a fine English drizzle kept the dust down and soothed my twitchy nose. I couldn't risk a sneeze until this deed was done.

The prison in the gatehouse at Newgate stood only a few crowded blocks west of the tavern. The guard had no problem accepting a gold earring to let me visit Walter Radley.

I found him in a dank room as small as my cubicle at school, hunched at a tiny table, writing on coarse paper. He must've promised the guards a cut of whatever the publisher paid.

I waved off his startled questions. "No time for shilly-shallying! Is that your confession?"

He nodded dumbly.

"The truth? That you did it? Or are you throwing the blame on Henry Claybrook?"

He gaped at me, clearly aghast at my uncanny knowledge of his private writing.

"Is that lie truly worth your immortal soul?" I raised an arm and pointed straight at him. "Tell the truth, Walter Radley! God is watching you!"

He nodded, gulped, and picked up his quill.

"And write faster," I added. "Or your trick will put an innocent man's neck in the noose."

He dipped his quill and wrote a few lines, then stopped to stare at me again, his homely features twisted in bewilderment. "Who did you say you were?"

"I'm ah… I'm Henry Claybrook's fiancée. Er…his betrothed. I simply cannot bear to lose him, so hither I came to spur you on."

"But how did you—"

I cut him off with snapping fingers. "Write, write, write!"

He got it done. I snatched each page from him as he finished it, waving the ink dry. Then I rolled them together, clutching them in my fist. As I waited for the guard to let me out, I turned a sympathetic eye on the poor schlub in the corner. "Some of your poems survive with your name on them, if that's any comfort to you."

He frowned at me, mournful as a wet hound.

Downstairs at Intake or whatever they called it, I unrolled my document to show Henry Claybrook's name to the man at the counter. Should've guessed he couldn't read. "That's for the magistrate," he growled.

I held up the second gold earring. "Take me to him."

He beckoned at one of the lesser guards to guide me. Turned out the magistrate sat right around the corner in the same building. A waste of good gold! I clearly needed to broaden the scope of my research interests.

The magistrate understood the situation as soon as I got his eyes turned toward the confession and away from the drooping neckline of my disheveled wench-wear. He told the guard who brought me to release Henry Claybrook at once, with the city's apologies.

"Never good to get on the wrong side of a popular pamphleteer," he observed.

"You got that right." I fairly danced on the mud-streaked cobblestones, waiting for Henry to emerge from the gatehouse. He shook off the guard's hand and straightened his doublet, then grinned to see me waving at him from across the street.

In three long strides, he had me in his arms. "Ah, sweet chuck, I don't know how you did it." He smiled that smile of his and warmth spread through my drizzle-chilled body.

"You owe me a pair of earrings." I buried my nose in his woolen doublet, which still smelled more of tobacco than jail.

I tilted up my face to see a slight frown. Earrings were expensive. "But I'll settle for a button if it comes with a kiss." That brought a look hot enough to melt my quivering insides.

"You drive a hard bargain, sweetling." He twisted off a carved wooden button and dropped it into my cleavage. Then he kissed me, thoroughly, right there in the street.

Well, I'd already proven my wanton nature by running around ruffless with a bare head.

He tasted like dark ale and fennel seeds. His lips were soft and his arms were strong. It all felt better than awesome until he broke the kiss and started nuzzling under my ear. "Let's go back to my room." His mustache tickled my neck, and his dry linen ruff smelled of perfume, something musky….

Oh, God, not that! Musk always made me—

Achoo!

* * * *

I landed in the backyard. A squirrel chattered at me as I dashed into the house to look at my dissertation.

Phew! Section three was back. Bless you, Walter Radley!

I settled into my chair, still smelling of Newgate and tavern smoke, and scrolled through section three, zapping every weasel word and mealy-mouthed phrase. I knew what I knew. I just had to lay it out and connect the dots.

I even knew something no one else in this century did, not for certain. Shakespeare had definitely moved to London by 1591, not 1592, which was scholarship's best guess. Earlier, probably, to have time to meet Claybrook and collaborate on their play. Will's first play, hitherto unstudied. Research didn't get more original than that.

If only I had some solid proof, something that would hold up in a dissertation defense. What kind of evidence could that be? Pages in Shakespeare's handwriting? Claybrook could introduce me to him, though I'd want a more respectable costume....

I fished the button out of my shirt and studied the crop of pollen strands draping from the live oak outside my window. Plenty of sneezes left on that tree.

Award-winning author **Anna Castle** writes two historical fiction series: the Francis Bacon mysteries and the Professor & Mrs. Moriarty mysteries. She has earned a series of degrees—BA in Classics, MS in Computer Science, and a PhD in Linguistics—and has had a corresponding series of careers— waitress, software engineer, assistant professor, and archivist. Writing fiction combines her lifelong love of stories and learning. She physically resides in Austin, Texas, and mentally counts herself a queen of infinite space. Learn more at https://www.annacastle.com/.

NO HONOR AMONG THIEVES

Heidi Hunter

It was the sledgehammer in his left hand that told me it was not going to be our usual Saturday night.

"So, no movie tonight?" I asked when Anthony greeted me at his apartment door. I'd arrived for what I thought was going to be an evening of beer and Netflix, typical weekend entertainment for us twenty-somethings.

He grabbed the crowbar leaning next to the door and handed it to me.

"We have to do it now, Joanna. The house will be torn down on Friday, and if we don't find it, it may be lost forever."

I hefted the crowbar as I followed him down the sidewalk, glad none of his neighbors were out. Really, a treasure hunt? Had Tony lost his mind?

Everyone in town knew the legend of the stolen Florentine Diamond.

I had grown up on the story. Reginald Bertrand Sr., a well-known art collector—or art thief, depending on whom you talked to—came into possession of the Florentine Diamond, a 137-carat yellow diamond stolen from Austria after World War I. Senior, as he was known, held a dinner party in 1935 during which he was going to unveil the diamond, but he and all his party guests were gunned down. There were plenty of suspects—art thieves, the Mafia, crooked business associates—but the murders went unsolved and the diamond disappeared.

"Surely if it was here, someone would have found it already." I rushed to keep up with Tony. "The house has been empty for a year, since Reginald the third died. And he probably found it when he was living here."

"It's still there. It has to be," Tony insisted. "I've researched the diamond. There were a few possible sightings over the years, but they were all fakes."

"Then it was sold to a private collector, who has it stored in some climate-controlled room for his own viewing pleasure."

"It has to be hidden in the walls. It's the only place I haven't looked." Tony was sweating in desperation and not listening to me.

Tony needed the money from selling the diamond. Everybody did. After Reginald Jr. died, his family-owned manufacturing plant in town deteriorated until his son, Reginald III, shuttered it. It was the death knell for many people. Unable to find work, they created their own jobs, many illegal.

Only a couple of hours after sundown, the streets were deserted. Still, I felt exposed under the moonlight as we arrived at the Bertrand house, one of a row of vacant Victorian mansions that lined what used to be the rich street in town. Every once in a while, someone was caught in the house, but the treasure hunters had become more frequent since it was announced the house and several nearby would be torn down to build an assisted-living center.

"You can't be sure Senior ever had it." I tried one last time to make Tony see reason before we were arrested for breaking and entering. "Everyone who saw it was murdered. And Junior always said he didn't believe his father ever possessed the diamond."

"Yeah, but he was living with his grandparents at the time of his dad's death, so he wouldn't know for sure, would he?"

I followed Tony around to the back, where he jimmied the old lock on the solarium door—if the door was even locked anymore with all the people who had passed through looking for the diamond. Tony nudged the door open, and we slipped inside.

The house was dark, dusty, and empty. All items not nailed down had been sold at an estate sale months ago, including the light fixtures. Looters had pulled wiring from the walls and stripped it for its copper. As we passed through the solarium to the main hall, we dodged holes in the walls and floors, which I suspected were created by other treasure hunters also using sledgehammers. Even with our flashlights, it was treacherous to maneuver without breaking an ankle. The wood floors were original, oak. Too bad they were irreparably damaged.

A mahogany staircase with intricate carvings graced the main hall, some of the bannister posts missing, as if someone thought they were hollow and the diamond was hidden inside.

I heaved a sigh as I calculated how long it would take the two of us to break into all the walls in the house.

Tony pointed to one of the doors to the right of the staircase. "That's the parlor where the bodies were found. They were having pre-dinner drinks. Senior would have wanted the diamond close by."

The parlor was the most searched room in the house, judging by the damaged walls, pried-up floorboards, and the ornately carved mantel over the fireplace that had been ripped down and lay in pieces. Is this what the people of our town had become? I could see glimpses of the old wallpaper exposed through the holes, faded to an indeterminate color.

"Start on some of those floorboards over by the fireplace, Joanna. I'll work on the walls." He stared greedily at the pockmarked walls. "I think there could be a hidden room here somewhere."

"Tony, there is no point to this. Look at all the holes. If there was a diamond hidden anywhere in this room, it would have been found."

But Tony was a man on a mission. I turned off my flashlight and dropped it on the floor. Moonlight filtering in through the uncovered windows cast enough light for me to work by. I began to half-heartedly pry up the wooden floorboards, finding nothing but subflooring underneath. I listened to Tony's rhythmic *thud-thud* with his sledgehammer. That same hollow thump disguised the sound of approaching footsteps until I heard a snarl behind us:

"Anthony Truglio! What are you doing here?"

Ugh. Bobby Seeper, town thug. He strutted around town like a big man on campus, even though he was as unemployed and penniless as the rest of us. And he'd brought two friends. Were we going to rumble? Or break into dance like in *West Side Story*?

"Everyone knows only I have the right to search this room," Seeper said.

"I have as much right as you do," Tony shot back. "You don't own this house."

"We'll see about that, Truglio. Guys."

And with that, Bobby and his friends advanced on Tony. Tony waved the sledgehammer in front of him to keep them at a distance, but they'd come prepared with their own weapons, er, tools. Bobby swung his own sledgehammer at Tony, which he blocked.

They hadn't seen me in my dark corner. Tony could never fight off the three of them, so I reluctantly joined in. I sneaked up behind one thug and swung the crowbar into the back of his knees. He squealed and crumpled to the ground. The other thug turned on me with his shovel. I struck for his stomach at the same time he swung at my head. I ducked, and the shovel glanced off my shoulder and clipped the side of my head. I missed his stomach but got him in the groin. He buckled but remained standing and managed to grab the crowbar from my hand as I staggered from his blow.

By this time, Tony was down and Bobby was on top of him, pummeling his face. I needed to get help.

I stumbled through the foyer to the front door. I tugged on the door, but it didn't budge. Hearing Bobby yell, "Find her!" from the parlor, I looked for a hiding spot. I spied a door under the stairs. Perfect, a closet. I stepped inside and closed it just as someone ran out of the parlor.

I waited, holding my breath. I had no doubt Bobby and his gang would kill us. Millions of dollars were at stake.

But it was silent on the other side of the door. I waited a couple of minutes. Still quiet. Maybe Bobby and his gang had gone and I could see to Tony's injuries. I cracked open the door to take a peek, then threw it open in surprise.

Where was I?

I stepped out into the foyer of the Bertrand mansion, but not the Bertrand mansion I sneaked into half an hour ago. The foyer was lit by a massive chandelier. The mahogany staircase was intact and gleamed from a thorough polishing. The oak floor was unblemished and laid out in a tiled pattern.

I turned back to the closet, which was now filled with fur coats. I stepped back in, closed the door, then reopened it. Chandelier, polished staircase. Nope, still here. What had happened?

Then I noticed I was wearing a floor-length aquamarine evening gown. It was lovely—silky and clingy. A wide-cuff diamond bracelet adorned my left wrist. I sure wasn't dressed like this when I went to the mansion that evening! *Duh, I must be hallucinating.* Or maybe I was unconscious and dreaming.

I heard a murmur of voices from inside the parlor. As I walked toward it, its pocket door slid open. I ducked back into the closet and pulled its door almost closed, leaving a sliver of space to peek out.

A man in his forties stepped into the entryway, bringing with him the soft sounds of conversation and background music.

"George, make sure everyone has a full glass as we will toast the guest of honor when I return." Was this Reginald Senior? He was younger than I expected, and he looked like Fred Astaire in a tuxedo and white waistcoat. His shoes were as polished as the staircase.

He slid the parlor door shut and crossed through the foyer, striding down the hallway past my closet, turning into the last room on the left.

This was my chance to attend a glamorous party the likes of which I'd never seen. I had to go. I left the safety of my closet and tripped when higher heels than had ever graced my feet before got tangled in the hem of my skirt. Righting myself, I pushed open the door and glided into the parlor feeling like Cinderella at the ball, with no plan how I was going to blend in. But this was all a dream, wasn't it?

A quick glance told me there were eight people scattered around the room. A man and woman sat on a yellow velvet couch, a perfect match to the pale-yellow wallpaper covered in a design of off-white flowers and leaves. A second man stood behind the couch, looking ill at ease as he pulled on his starched collar. All three of them had cocktails in hand. The men were dressed similar to Senior. The woman wore an outfit even I would steal a diamond for, an emerald bias-cut evening dress, sleeveless, with a full, floor-length skirt. Diamond-studded combs peeked out of her wavy hair.

Soft orchestral music floated from a machine discreetly tucked into the corner. A lovely painting—a Van Gogh maybe—held the place of honor above the fireplace.

"Drink, miss?" A man in a white suitcoat appeared on my left, startling me.

"Uh, yes." I quickly surveyed the room to see what the rest of the guests were drinking. "A manhattan, please."

While the butler went to retrieve my drink, a man with a pencil mustache and a tang of cigar smoke replaced him. He was impeccably dressed in a black tuxedo with wide satin lapels and a matching satin stripe down the side of his pants.

"Hello, who are you?" He greeted me by seizing my right hand and kissing the back of it. Did men really do that?

"Jo."

"Jo," he rolled my name around on his tongue as if he liked the taste of it. "So nice to make your acquaintance."

He hadn't returned my hand, so I eased it from his grasp. Would it be rude to wipe the back of it on my dress?

"And how do you know Reggie?" he said.

"Edward, dear, it's obvious that she's Reginald's most current paramour," the woman in the emerald dress purred on my right. Up close, I noticed her diamond chandelier earrings and huge square-cut emerald ring, both of which I coveted. "She's exactly his type."

What was his type? Young? Concussed?

"Don't spoil my fun, Clarissa," Edward admonished with a smile.

Clarissa? Clarissa Hendley? If I recalled correctly, she was a former paramour of Senior's herself. She was wearing a cat-in-the-cream smile, which meant trouble. Edward must be Edward Bennington, an internationally known playboy and the man reputed to have stolen Cortez's cross right out of a museum in Switzerland.

The butler returned with my drink as the parlor door slid back open. I stepped behind Edward, looking for someplace I could stand unnoticed without appearing to be hiding. Dream or no dream, Senior was not going to know me. I backed into a dimly lit corner of the room by the door in case I needed to make a quick getaway.

Clarissa returned to the couch, but Edward stayed put, shielding me from view.

Senior stood in front of the roaring fire, drink in hand, shrewd eyes scanning the room, surveying his kingdom and minions.

"Ladies and gentlemen, as promised, our guest of honor, the Florentine Diamond." He flourished the yellow gem, which sparkled in the firelight.

A few guests "oohed." A couple applauded. I gasped at the sheer size of it.

"I came by this trinket more or less the honest way. I bought it." Everyone laughed, familiar with Senior's less legal methods. "From a man of questionable virtue who claimed he smuggled it in from South America for a less generous patron. He hoped to strike a better bargain with me, and I obliged." He admired the diamond, turning it back and forth. "I'd pass it around, but, well, you know." Senior smirked and there was more laughter. His friends at the party were light-fingered as well. "After tonight, I'll be sending this treasure to a much safer location. Not that I don't trust you all, of course, but there is no honor among thieves."

More knowing chuckles.

"Drink up! George, see to dinner. I'll return this trinket to its resting spot."

The legend of the dinner party was true. Which meant—oh crap—I was in the house the night of the massacre. I needed to find out where Senior stashed that diamond, then get out of there. It might be a dream, but if you die in a dream you die in real life, right? I didn't want to find out.

Edward turned, looking for me.

"I'm going to go freshen up before dinner." I hastened from the room.

I heard Senior's footsteps echo down the hall past the closet. I slipped off my heels so they wouldn't sound on the oak floorboards and padded down the hall after him.

He entered the last room on the left but didn't latch the door, probably because George was keeping his guests occupied. I nudged it open so I could see what Senior was up to.

The room was either an office or a library. A fireplace with an intricately carved oak surround faced me, and a leather wingback chair and side table flanked it on the right. Senior stood on the left side of the fireplace. He pressed the center of one of the many carved flowers that graced the mantel. I heard a small click before he pulled open a wooden panel in the surround, revealing a space into which he placed the diamond.

He spun around to leave. Afraid he'd spot me, I ducked into the room at the end of the hall.

A mouthwatering vision of oysters and smoked salmon greeted me, laid out on the counter waiting to be whisked away to the party guests. What a delectable first course! The aroma of roast beef filled the kitchen. I was sorry I couldn't stay to enjoy this feast, but I had a diamond to steal.

Movement at the oven drew my attention. Oops, I wasn't alone. The cook stood there with her back to me. I couldn't crouch behind the table in my tight gown, so I decided to get a move on to the office.

Unfortunately, the office door was locked. I should have expected that. Hoping I could find something to jimmy it open, I turned and smacked right into the servant in the white jacket. George? Where had he come from?

He grabbed my arm and squeezed, which hurt. Should I have felt it if I were dreaming? Everything seemed so real I was beginning to worry this wasn't a dream. And if not, I had to get out of here before the shooting started.

"Who are you? How did you get in here?" he demanded. He shook me, and as he did, his suitcoat fell open, revealing a gun in an underarm holster.

"I— I—" How could I explain I arrived through the closet?

"Sir! Intruder!" George sounded the alarm as he dragged me toward the foyer. Senior exited the parlor, gun already in hand. Several extravagantly attired guests, including the jealous Clarissa and the dapper Edward, gathered in the doorway to watch the spectacle.

"I found her trying to get into the library," George reported. "She won't tell me who she is or why she is here."

"Could she have seen…?" Reginald Senior began asking George, then turned on me. "Who do you work for? What did you see?"

"No one! Nothing! I saw nothing. I know nothing. I just want to go home." It was hard to be coherent with a pistol in your face.

"Lock her up," Reginald Senior ordered. "We'll deal with her after the party."

George manhandled me by the arm toward the closet.

Yes! The closet. I sighed in relief. Maybe I'd wake up before they returned to deal with me.

He had a powerful grip for an older man. I stumbled trying to keep up.

The front door burst open. Three men with machine guns entered. George dropped my arm and reached for his gun.

I stepped back toward the closet on trembling legs, once again hoping not to be noticed.

"Truglio! I never expected this of you." Senior, unruffled by the pressure of three guns pointed at him, greeted the man in the middle.

Truglio? I gasped in shock. Hey, wait a minute. Why had Tony never mentioned this? He had to know who killed Senior. Families feed off stories like this for generations. It explained why he was so hot to find the diamond.

"Drop your guns," Truglio ordered.

Senior carefully placed his gun on the floor, then motioned for George to do the same.

"You have something that was meant for me," Truglio said.

"Come, have a drink." Senior motioned toward the parlor. "We'll discuss this like businessmen."

"The time for talk is over." Truglio motioned to his buddies, who surrounded Reginald and George and herded them into the parlor, pushing the hovering guests into the room.

This would be a good time to leave, I decided. No diamond was worth death. I stepped into the closet and shut the door. Almost immediately, I heard the rat-a-tat-tat of automatic gunfire and screams.

I closed my eyes and put my hands over my ears, willing myself to wake up before they searched the house for the diamond, finding me cowering in the closet. It was horrible hearing people being gunned down in cold blood. A burnt gunpowder smell reached me, and I began to hyperventilate, thinking I was going to pass out.

Maybe I did. The next thing I knew, the gunfire was replaced by knocking on the closet door.

"Joanna? Are you in there? You can come out now, they're gone."

Tony! Crying with relief, I flung open the door and collapsed in his arms.

"Are you all right? I thought for sure Bobby killed you." I looked Tony over. His face was covered in bruises, his lip split. But he was alive.

"They're gone for now. Cops drove by. But they'll be back."

I looked at the closet, now a dusty space, empty of furs. I glanced down at my clothes, and I was clad again in jeans and a T-shirt. I mourned the loss of that beautiful gown and bracelet.

"I don't know what just happened. I was hallucinating…or dreaming… or I went back in time…."

"What?"

"I was at Senior's party…with the diamond…"

I stopped blathering when a feverish gleam popped into Tony's eyes. Uh oh. I should never have mentioned the diamond.

"Wait. Did you see the diamond? Where?"

Me and my babbling mouth. "What? No. I don't know what I'm saying. I was imagining things." I tried to laugh it off.

Tony's nostrils flared. "Show me where you think you saw it."

I looked into his cold eyes, so like his ancestor who led Reggie Senior off to his death, and my insides froze. Thinking fast, I hustled toward the office, Tony trailing behind.

The office was in as bad a shape as the rest of the house. Devoid of furniture, including that lovely leather armchair I had seen, with holes in the walls and oak floorboards pulled up. It looked like someone had tried to pry off the hand-carved fireplace surround as well.

I moved to the right side of the fireplace and felt around on the flowers, pushing a few flower centers. *Click.* I breathed a sigh of relief. "It worked." I groped around for the panel that should be ajar and slipped my fingertips in the crack, but it wouldn't budge. I took the crowbar from Tony and popped it open.

Tony thrust me aside to peer in with the flashlight. The space was maybe six inches high by a foot deep. Tony pulled out a whiskey bottle.

"Of course, he would have had hidey-holes." Tony seemingly spoke to himself. "They were popular during Prohibition, and Senior loved his whiskey."

He pulled a sheaf of papers out next, crumbling and yellow with age. Grunting, he tossed them carelessly on the floor. He groped around in the cubby again, then shined the flashlight in.

"It's not here." He took the crowbar and whacked at the fireplace mantel in frustration, causing some scrapes and dents, but no major damage, to the surround.

He turned on me. "Did you take it? Before I found you in the closet?" He scanned me with his flashlight from head to toe, then reached in a couple of pockets. I slapped his hand away, offended.

"No. Someone else must have found it," I said. "All I know is, this is where it was, right before the shooting. I watched Senior put it in here."

"The shooting. Maybe someone survived." Tony shone his flashlight in my face. "Did you see who was there?"

"Some, but none of them saw where he kept the diamond." I paused. "Except, I suppose George knew."

"Who's George?"

"I don't know. A valet? A bodyguard? We weren't properly introduced." I held back from checking my arm to see if he had left a bruise. That would be too weird.

"I don't recall reading there was a victim named George," Tony mused. "Maybe he survived, grabbed the diamond, and went into hiding." Tony warmed to his theory. "I'll need to do research on this George character."

"You do that. Let's get out of here before the cops or Bobby come back."

* * * *

It was nearing daylight and I had to hurry. I prayed neither Tony nor Bobby had returned to the house this early in the morning, and I was rewarded. The mansion was deserted.

Or appeared to be. As I entered the main hall, I thought I heard a creak overhead. I froze and strained to hear any additional movement, but there was only silence.

I raced to the office and stood on the left side of the fireplace. After a couple of false starts, I found the correct flower. *Click*. The panel opened under my fingertips.

I shone my flashlight into the cubby. Something sparkled back at me. The diamond! Untouched for over eighty years. I took it in my hand. It was heavier than I expected. Selling it to a private collector should net me enough to live luxuriously for the rest of my life, leaving this dead-end town in the dust.

I had taken a gamble with Tony, betting there was a matching cubby on the other side of the fireplace that I could open for him. I needed to convince him the diamond was gone and hope he would spread the word of a possible survivor of the massacre. That way, when the diamond resurfaced, it would be harder to trace it back to me.

Do I feel bad about not sharing the wealth with my best friend who so desperately needed the money and brought me on this treasure hunt? Why should I? As my great-great-great-Uncle Reginald Senior said, "There is no honor among thieves."

After a decade investigating financial crimes, **Heidi Hunter** is embarking on a career writing mysteries and short stories. Her stories have appeared in anthologies and e-zines such as *Flash Bang Mysteries*. She's a member of Sisters in Crime and their Guppies chapter. Heidi can be followed on her author blog, https://hollyhyattauthor.wordpress.com/ and her Wander Woman travel blog, https://wanderwoman376.wordpress.com/.

THE FOURTEENTH FLOOR

Adam Meyer

At just after nine p.m., Frank Russo—a night guard at the Hunter Building on West Sixty-Third Street on Manhattan's Upper West Side—dropped
his frozen dinner tray in the trash, glanced down at the walkie-talkie on the
table beside him, and began to make his rounds.

The nineteenth floor was clear...eighteen looked good...nothing to worry about on seventeen. No trouble tonight. Then again, there was no trouble
most nights—especially for Frank. He could make his rounds without ever
having to get up from the plush leather chair behind the security desk. All he
had to do was click the mouse and push a few keys. Every floor had a dozen
video cameras, and Frank could call each one up on the monitor before him.
It had taken him the better part of a month to learn how, twice as long as the
younger guys, but that was all right. At least he still had a job here, no small
feat after almost forty years.

He continued to check the building's cameras floor by floor. Sixteen was
quiet. Not a peep on fifteen. Fourteen was—

He blinked, looking at the bottom right corner of his screen. The grainy
image showed rows of empty desks, a tall filing cabinet, a photocopy machine. Standing in the middle of the desks was a young woman wearing a
flower-print dress that ended right below her knees. She spun slowly, her
eyes wide with surprise and a hint of fear, then hurried off.

Frank called up all the other cameras on the fourteenth floor, one by one,
but there was no sign of the young woman. Maybe she was hiding under a
desk. Maybe she'd tucked herself in a closet.

Or maybe she'd vanished into thin air.

Frank knew what he was supposed to do. Report the sighting to dispatch and go up to investigate. But that would set in motion a whole flurry of
events: an incident report, a phone call with his supervisor, and depending
what he found, maybe a visit from the NYPD.

So he had to ask himself: are you sure there was a girl up there?

Frank hadn't kept this job for four decades by being rash, but then he was
lucky to still have it at all. For years he'd been an employee of the same fam-

ily-run company that had owned and managed this midsized office building since the 1960s. Eight months ago they'd sold it to a giant developer, and now he was working for a security firm with thousands of employees worldwide. Frank had heard rumors of cutbacks the last few months. Most of the downsized guards were old-timers like him. Being almost sixty-five was enough of a liability. He didn't want to give them any other reason to let him go.

Like reporting a mysterious girl who'd never been there in the first place.

Frank checked the floor cameras a third time, lingering for several seconds on each one, and saw nothing. His finger hovered over the button on his handheld radio, and he hesitated a moment before deciding what to do.

"Colin, you see anything unusual tonight?"

Frank waited for a reply. His counterpart, Colin, was stationed at the building's side entrance on West End Avenue. Colin was about twenty-five, the same age Frank had been when he started here. Like Frank, he was supposed to watch the entrance and the cameras, though he usually spent most of his shift talking on his phone with various relatives, trying to sort out the latest family drama, and taking small nips from a flask of whiskey.

"Nah, Frank, quiet as St. Rita's on a Tuesday night." In the background, Frank could hear the faint burble of a TV show. "Matter of fact, I just got back from doing a circuit of the cafeteria. Not even the mice were out."

"Course not. Even they won't touch that grub."

Colin laughed, though Frank wasn't sure if it was at him or something he was watching on his iPad. "So why you asking me what I've seen? Did *you* see something?"

Did Frank want to own up to what he saw—*thought* he saw—or not?

"Nah, it's all quiet here. Just checking, that's all."

"You bored? 'Cause I can give you my Netflix password. You could watch some TV."

Frank touched the paperback he always kept in the inner pocket of his sports coat. Usually something by Lee Child or Michael Connelly, though his apartment in Rego Park—a rent-controlled one bedroom he'd lived in since shortly after being hired here—was jammed full of books. His parents were gone, he'd been an only child, and except for a few distant cousins up in Poughkeepsie, he was alone in the world—no wife, no kids, and generally no visitors either. At least he had his books for company.

"I've got something to read. I'm okay."

"You change your mind, you let me know."

"Thanks, Colin. Ten-four."

The radio went silent then. Frank scrolled through the images of the rest of the floors, then back to fourteen. Still nothing. Yeah, he'd probably imagined the whole thing.

He picked up the Reacher novel that he'd started on the subway ride over and read half a dozen pages before realizing he'd been paying no attention to it. He tucked in his makeshift bookmark—a receipt for the coffee he'd bought on his way into work—and slipped the novel into his inner pocket. A moment later he clipped his walkie-talkie to his belt, pushed out of his chair with a groan, and hit the elevator's up button. He'd just go take a quick walk upstairs. Not that there was anything to see. He wanted to stretch his legs. Nothing wrong with that, was there?

The doors swished open, and Frank got into the sleek silver cage, everything gleaming and bright, with buttons so sensitive his finger barely had to brush them. He swiped his card and hit the one marked 14.

Frank felt edgy as the elevator whisked him upward. Why hadn't he stayed at the front desk and found out how Reacher was going to dispatch that crew of redneck mobsters closing in on him? He could go back. Open the bag of popcorn he'd brought for a snack. Maybe even—

The elevator lurched.

Frank put a hand out to steady himself. He looked at the display above the buttons and saw that he was on the eighth floor when suddenly the numbers stopped changing. The elevator was still moving, however. Frank could feel it in his belly, that lurching feeling of being on an amusement park ride, something he hadn't done since he was a kid at Coney Island.

Then the lights went out.

Suddenly the elevator began to shake, the floor rattling beneath his feet, the sound of creaking metal ringing in his ears. Frank put a hand out to keep himself from falling, the floor swaying beneath him, the growing rumble of the elevator so loud it made his whole head hurt, and then without warning it all stopped.

The double doors slid open with a gentle *ping.*

Frank stumbled out of the elevator, no idea what floor he was on, not caring either. He wasn't getting back into that tiny cage, not tonight and maybe not ever. Wherever he was, he'd sooner take the stairs and risk a heart attack than try another ride in that death box.

Edging across the open floor, Frank found a rolling chair to sit in and rubbed at his forehead, the sound of clanking metal still ringing in his skull. He took a deep breath, leaned back, looked out. A bunch of metal desks were lined up in rows, each one outfitted with a Brother typewriter and a sturdy black phone with a rotary dial, the kind his father used to keep in the den.

What's this, he thought, looking around in disbelief. Which floor had he gotten out on?

Of course that was a moot point. None of the floors looked like this. Not since the renovation in the mideighties, and maybe even long before. Everyone had computers now, and though there were still landlines, the phones were small and sleek with lots of buttons.

He reached for his walkie-talkie and hesitated. What was he going to ask Colin now? If he saw anything on the video feed that suggested someone had completely rearranged one of the floors with desks and phones and typewriters that had been cleared out of here years ago? Frank thought a minute. They'd been emptying out the storage room in the basement lately, so maybe someone had dug up a bunch of this old stuff and put it out like kind of a stage set. Maybe they were deliberately trying to mess with the old man at the front desk and were all watching on the video feeds right now, having a good laugh.

The hell with it, Frank thought. If he made a fool of himself, then so be it.

He pressed the button on his walkie. "Colin, it's me."

All he heard was static.

"Colin, you there?"

Probably the kid had gone off to the bathroom and left his radio behind. Wouldn't be the first time. He gave it a minute, tried again.

More static.

He lowered the walkie and made his way across the floor, letting his fingers graze the metal surface of a desk, wanting to make sure it was real. Whoever had done this had gone to great lengths with the details. Near one of the desks he found an aluminum trash can. Inside were several sheets of crumpled typing paper, an empty package of Chiclets gum, and a folded-up newspaper. The *Times*. The headline said "KENNEDY FACES CARTER IN FINAL DEMOCRATIC DEBATE" and the date was September 18, 1980.

Exactly thirty-nine years ago today.

Frank felt like someone had pressed an ice cube to the base of his spine. For the first time he asked the question that had been niggling at him ever since he stepped off that elevator.

What if this was no setup?

What if everything was as it had been back in the summer of '80? Could he walk down to Fifty-Third and get a pastrami sandwich at Sammy's, his favorite deli, which had closed more than two decades ago? Could he ride the A train uptown to see his old friend Charlie Gruber, who had jumped from one of the Twin Towers on 9/11? Could he pick up one of those chunky black phone receivers and call his ma out on Staten Island, tell her to quit smoking those Virginia Slims before lung cancer took her in a couple of years?

"Hey! Hey you!"

Frank looked up, startled, at a thirty-something man in a pin-striped gray suit. The lapels were a little too wide, and his dark-blue tie seemed a bit conservative, but otherwise he would've fit in perfectly fine where Frank was from. *When* he was from.

"Do you get paid to sit around all night or what?"

"I uh…"

The man stared at him, his dark eyes brimming with suspicion. He had a narrow face and ears that stuck out too far, but his chiseled jaw and swept-back hair seemed to make up for it. Frank tried to remember if he'd seen this man before but couldn't.

"Look, there's no trouble here on fourteen. You might as well finish your rounds."

"Fourteen?" The number caught in Frank's throat as he remembered the girl on the video screen. "I…I've got a question. Who's the president right now?"

"Jimmy Carter, of course. At least for a little while." The man scowled, studying Frank. "You don't know who the president is?"

"Sure I do but—"

"Are you new here? Can't say I've seen you before."

"Just filling in." Frank took a last look around before turning to go. "Have a good night, sir."

He felt eyes on his back all the way to the elevator bank. Ornately carved maple doors faced him, not the burnished metal ones he was used to seeing every day. He pressed the old black down button set in a wooden panel and waited.

Off to the side, around the nearest corner, a shadow stirred. The elevator doors pinged even as Frank walked away. The shadow grew longer, and then he saw a swish of flowery skirt. Hurrying down the hall, his breath caught as he stopped outside the ladies' room. She was there wearing a shirtwaist dress with a flower print, her heart-shaped face slightly puffy from tears. She looked to be in her midtwenties, though at his age it was getting harder to judge. The woman he'd seen on the closed-circuit camera earlier. But of course that was impossible because now she was here, in what seemed to be 1980.

Then again, so was he.

"You all right?" he asked.

The woman hesitated, as if she wasn't sure. "I'm fine."

Faintly, he heard a voice call out, "Susan? Susan? Where've you gone?"

"Coming, Mr. Lerner. Be right there."

She wiped her face with the back of her hand and turned her lips into a smile. Even though it seemed forced, she looked suddenly radiant, and Frank had to make an effort not to stare.

He started to go after her. Maybe she knew something about what had happened to him. Maybe she could tell him how to get back to his own time, his own world. He hurried to the end of the corridor, catching a glimpse of the woman, Susan, walking with the man in the suit. Frank ducked behind the wall, out of sight. Lerner had made it clear he didn't want Frank around. He even seemed to have some sense that Frank didn't belong here, which of course he didn't, not really.

Frank waited a moment, hoping that whatever business Susan had with Lerner—her boss?—they would finish quickly and she'd be alone again. No such luck.

Frank leaned out and saw Lerner step into one of the offices along the far wall. Susan was already in there, her fingers twisted into knots against her skirt, her forced smile starting to slip. Lerner's office door closed with a *thlunk.*

For a moment Frank stood there, not sure what to do. Behind him the elevator doors pinged. Maybe he ought to stick with his original plan and head down into the streets of 1980 Manhattan. But he couldn't shake the feeling that somehow Susan had brought him here, or at least knew why he'd come.

"Sir?"

A young man stood outside the elevator bank. He wore a navy-blue uniform, neatly pressed, his unruly curls spilling out from beneath his cap. His thin lips made an expression just this side of a frown. Frank recognized the young man from countless photographs and of course from many years of staring at him in the mirror, though it had been a while.

"Evening," Frank said to the security guard, a younger version of himself, who would've started here about six months earlier.

"Evening." Young Frank moved in, eyes narrowing. "You work here?"

He repeated the lie he'd told Lerner a few minutes earlier. "I'm filling in."

"Who for?"

Frank tried to remember the names of some of the guys he'd started with here. There was Fat Lenny, who was skinny as a rail; Angelo, an old Korean War vet; and Sal, who was always calling in sick and ended up dying of cancer about a year after Frank started.

"Who's on the main desk, you and Fat Lenny?" Frank asked.

"Yeah, Sal was supposed to be here too but...you covering for him?"

"Only if you need me. Otherwise I'd be happy to go home and catch the Mets game."

Young Frank shrugged, looking uncertain. "That's not my call. Maybe you better check with dispatch."

"I'll do that. Soon as I finish checking things out up here."

Young Frank turned to go, then looked back. "Your uniform, where'd you get that?"

Frank touched the front of his shirt, which was pale blue instead of dark blue, and far more sleek than Young Frank's, with its square pockets and wide collar.

"They issued these about a month ago. You guys didn't get yours yet?"

Young Frank shook his head. "Nope."

"You will soon."

Frank took a step toward his other self, stunned by how young and innocent this guy was. He tried to think of all the things he ought to tell Young Frank. Bet big on the Mets in the '86 series. Be nicer to your ma; she really does love you. Find a pretty girl and ask her to marry you and start a family instead of just living alone, being alone, dying alone. He said none of those things.

"Hey kid…you know, you could do anything you want in life, right? Be anything."

"Sure, I guess. For now, I'm pretty happy right here."

Suddenly, Frank knew: he could've taken this kid out for a couple beers and told him all the things that would someday happen, all the ways in which his life would fall short if he didn't get off his ass right now, and he'd never do a damn thing. He didn't have it in him. Meaning I haven't got it in me, he thought, and felt his heart clench with sadness.

"See you around, sir."

He heard the whisper of young Frank's rubber-soled shoes on the carpet, then the ping of the elevator, and the whoosh of the doors opening. He fought the urge to look back.

Frank headed across the fourteenth floor, listening to the ticking of clocks on the wall, the faint sound of a soda machine humming. He looked out at the skyline, majestic and yet a little more stumpy than it would be almost forty years in the future, and, faintly, he heard a cry.

Frank stared at his own faint reflection in the window, cocked his head to hear better.

Again, that cry. A woman's voice.

Susan.

Frank turned around, heading for the row of office doors. He kept going past one after another, finally stopped when he came to one marked K. LERNER. The window beside the door was covered by blinds, and although Frank shifted position a couple of times, he couldn't see in.

"Hey, everything okay in there?"

He knocked on the door, waited.

A man's voice. "Everything's fine."

Frank reached for the doorknob. It rattled in his hand.

"Why don't you open the door a minute?"

No answer. Then: "I told you, there's no problem in here."

An obvious lie, but then this wasn't his problem. It wasn't even his *time*. All Frank had to do was walk away. In his younger days, he would've done exactly that, intimidated by a guy in a suit, prone to doing what he was told even when he knew it was the wrong thing. After all these years, had he changed? Not a bit. Seeing his younger self was all the proof he needed. He was the same as he'd always been, too scared and weak to do the hard thing.

Or was he? He turned from the door and started to walk off, but something inside just wouldn't let him.

He looked back and tried the knob again. Definitely locked. He touched the key ring on his belt, but of course these keys were useless, made for doors that wouldn't be installed for years to come.

"Mr. Lerner, let's not make a big thing here. Please open the door."

Silence, and then a faint yelp. Susan again.

"Right now, Mr. Lerner. I mean it."

"I told you, everything's fine. Now go away."

Frank wondered what to do next. He could go down to the lobby and find Young Frank, who probably did have a key to this door. But who knew what would happen in the meantime? Frank put his shoulder against the door and started to push, but felt no give. He could try to break it down, but he was too old for that. He rattled the knob again, noticed it was a bit loose, and looked back at the long rows of desks. He had an idea.

He unplugged one of those Brother typewriters and hefted it into his arms and swung it down against the doorknob as hard as he could. The machine was so heavy that with the added force of gravity he nearly dropped it. He smashed it again, then again, his muscles shrieking, his breath coming in quick bursts. The knob finally gave, hanging down lopsided, and the door swung open.

Frank put down the typewriter and peered in.

Lerner had Susan pushed against the wall, one arm against her throat. Her dress was rumpled, the skirt pushed up past her waist, and her face was flushed, her eyes unreadable. Lerner was looking at her with a mix of desire and fury, though when he turned to face Frank, only the anger remained.

Lerner stepped toward the door, smoothing out the cuffs of his white dress shirt. His jacket lay on the floor beside a pair of crumpled pantyhose.

"It's not what it looks like," he said.

Frank advanced into the office. "I think it's exactly what it looks like. But we'll let the cops decide."

"You're not calling the police." Lerner picked his jacket up, slid his arm into one sleeve. "We're consenting adults. Who cares what we do?"

Susan smoothed her skirt, a glimmer of fear showing in her face as she began edging away from Lerner.

"You all right?" Frank asked.

"I'm fine. Ken's right, you don't have to call the police. I just want to get home."

Susan made her way toward the door, stopping when she came close to where Frank stood.

"I'm going with her." Frank glared at Lerner. "And I'll be back for you."

He watched her flatten her hair as she walked past the long rows of desks toward the elevator bank. She pressed the button to go down.

"You sure you're okay?" he asked.

"I'm fine. Really. It's no big deal."

He felt flustered, knowing he ought to explain what was going on, but not sure how. Before he could think of an approach, the elevator pinged. He gestured for her to get in and after a slight hesitation she did. He went in after her, pressing the L button. Would his own younger self be down there, sitting at the front desk? If so, what would he say to him?

As the elevator doors shushed together, Susan studied him. "I don't think I've seen you here before. What were you doing on fourteen tonight?"

"The truth is, I'm not sure. I guess… I was following you."

She took a step back, bumping into the wall behind her. "Excuse me?"

He'd said the wrong thing. He decided to start over, try a new approach.

"I saw you, earlier tonight. Only not here, not exactly."

"I've been here all day. I work for Ken." She crossed her arms over herself, watching him with caution. "Mr. Lerner, I mean."

"Sure, I get it. And I know this is going to sound crazy, but I'm not from here. This time, this year. I'm from years and years into the future. How I got here, I have no idea. I know, this is totally nuts, and there's no way for me to prove it." He pulled out his wallet, fumbling through his cards and cash, looking for something, anything, to prove he wasn't crazy. "Here's my license, see, it expires in 2024. And look at these credit cards. I'm sure they're nothing like yours."

She glanced up at the brass arrow ticking down past the seven and then the six, looking like she wished it would move a whole lot faster. As soon as the doors opened, she would bolt. He knew he didn't have much time.

"Hold on, I got it." He pulled out the paperback from inside his coat and fished out the makeshift bookmark, his receipt from buying coffee earlier. "The date's right there, September eighteenth, 2019. You can see it plain as day."

He held the scrap of paper out to her and she took it, frowning.

"So now maybe you'll believe me when I say…"

He heard his voice trail off, and when he tried to start over, his tongue felt like mush. He looked around at the brass walls of the elevator, but everything had these black pixels and was starting to go fuzzy. He stumbled backward, trying to steady himself, and realized his hand went right through the wall. He looked back at Susan, but she was starting to go all hazy, even as he felt the floor beneath him shudder and he heard that clanking again, loud as a blocked pipe.

"Can you feel this too?" he asked, or thought he asked, as the shaking intensified, and then he felt something smash against his head, and he was out cold.

* * * *

When Frank opened his eyes, he was sitting in his chair in the lobby. The wide-screen monitor was there, full of little boxes showing the different floors, no sign of life in any of them. The back of his head throbbed, and his mouth felt dry as cotton, but he seemed okay otherwise.

"You're back," Colin said, handing him an ice pack. "I was about ready to call an ambulance."

Frank put the ice against the side of his head, wincing. "What happened?"

"Found you sitting in the elevator, mumbling. Got you to your feet and said we ought to call nine one one, but you made me promise not to. Figured I'd give you a couple of minutes and see." Colin studied him carefully. "You sure you're okay?"

"Positive." Frank sat up a little straighter, adjusted the ice pack. "Did you hear me on the walkie-talkie earlier?"

"Yeah, when you asked me if I'd seen anything weird tonight. That was like fifteen minutes ago."

Fifteen minutes. No, it had to have been more than that. Everything up on the fourteenth floor must've taken…

Frank shook his head, ignoring the pain radiating out from his skull. Of course nothing had really happened on the fourteenth floor. He'd seen some phantom image on the monitor, gone up to check it out, then fallen in the elevator and hit his head. He must've imagined everything else.

"You need some water or something?" Colin asked, frowning.

Frank almost laughed. "How about something stronger?"

"Sure, at my desk." Colin's face flushed. "You good for a few minutes?"

"Don't worry. I won't move."

Frank watched Colin disappear through a doorway that would lead him to the other side of the building. Putting the ice pack down, he glanced at the computer screen again. All the images were still. Frank felt like a fool and, more than that, he felt old. Any security guard who jumped at shadows and passed out in the middle of his watch deserved to be put out to pasture.

The sound of rattling glass startled him.

Frank turned to the front door of the building. A woman stood there, about to rap on the glass again. She had silver hair, elegantly cut, and wore a knee-length stylish coat. One of the execs catching up on a late-night project? If so, Frank didn't recognize her.

He hit the button under the desk that unlocked the door. The woman swept in, her high-heeled shoes clicking as she walked. She stared at him a moment as he stood up from behind the front desk, her eyes going wide.

"I can't believe it. It's you."

"I don't understand," he said, and then all of a sudden, in a rush, he did. And he realized that what he thought he knew about this night, well, he'd have to completely rethink it. Again.

"Susan."

She nodded. "I don't even know your name."

"I'm Frank. Frank Russo."

"It's nice to actually meet you, Frank." She looked at the ice pack with concern. "Are you hurt?"

"No, I..." He smiled at her. "I was going to say you probably wouldn't believe what happened to me. Although since you're standing here, I'm thinking maybe you might."

She shook her head, looking around in wonder, then turning back to him. "It's been years since I've been here. It looks so different. But the crazy thing is, you look exactly same as that night you burst in on me and Ken. Which is impossible. Because that was almost forty years ago."

"Thirty-nine to be exact. And I could try to explain. But I'm not sure I understand it myself."

She looked across the lobby, her gaze impossibly distant. "You know, a few minutes before I first saw you outside the bathroom, I'd gone to the sixth floor to return some files, and I was coming back up when the elevator lights cut out and the floor started shaking. Finally the doors opened and I got out and the place didn't look anything like it was supposed to. I remember it was really futuristic and strange. Although I suspect if you were to take me up to the fourteenth floor right now, I'd have a total sense of déjà vu, as if I had been there before."

Frank said nothing. But he felt pretty sure she was right.

"The elevator doors opened again a few seconds later, and I got back on. Then the same thing happened—the lights went out, there was all this shaking, and when I stepped out on fourteen, everything was normal again. I went into the bathroom to compose myself, and then a few minutes later, you were there too." She studied Frank, her eyes wide. "It was all so long ago, it seems like a dream."

"To you, maybe. For me, that was only a few minutes ago." He studied her closely: her heart-shaped face was lined with grooves, especially around the mouth and eyes, but the radiance he'd seen in the younger version of her was muted but still there. "I don't suppose it's any of my business, but what was going on with you and Lerner?"

"I was Ken's secretary, and we were having an affair. It was foolish, really. He was married, and I kept thinking he'd leave his wife for me. Then one night he asked me to stay late, and I knew what that meant, only I'd decided I was going to break things off. It didn't go over well. He didn't hurt me too badly, although I think I maybe owe that to you."

"Did you ever call the cops?"

She shook her head. "I didn't see the point. I quit without giving notice, and I never came back again. Until tonight."

"You didn't tell anyone?"

"Forty years ago, who would've listened? Besides, I wanted to put it all behind me, and I did, mostly. Then a couple of years later, I saw an obituary in the *Times* for Kenneth Lerner. Dead of a heart attack at thirty-six, and that was that. By then I'd already met the man who would become my husband. We had three beautiful children, a lovely house in Larchmont, a life. Everything that happened here, it was almost like it never happened at all. Maybe I even convinced myself that it hadn't. Still, whenever I come into the city, I always avoid this street. I never come anywhere near this building. The very thought of it makes me sick. But tonight, I felt like I had to."

"Why?"

She reached into one of the pockets of her coat and pulled out a yellowed scrap of paper. Frank couldn't read it without his glasses, and especially with the letters so faded. But he knew what it was. A receipt for a cup of coffee.

"You can't read the date anymore, but then I memorized it a long time ago." She tucked the slip of paper back in her pocket. "I always remembered what you said, about being from the future, and I figured on the off chance it was true…well, maybe you'd really be here today. And you are." Her eyes moved across his face, and there was something so kind and gentle in them. "So I wanted to come and say thank you. For everything."

"That's all right. I did what any decent person would do."

He studied her face, the lines grooved in around her mouth and across her forehead, all the years of life she'd lived in the time since he'd last seen her. They were strangers, but he felt like he knew her somehow, in some way that went beyond the brief encounter they'd had.

"Your husband…you ever tell him this story?"

She nodded. "About a year ago. It was near the end for him—he had pancreatic cancer—and I wanted someone to know. I'm not sure if he believed me or not. I don't suppose it matters."

Behind Susan, the heavy door swung open with a groan.

"Hey, sorry it took me so long, I got a call from my sister about…" Colin looked at Frank and then at Susan, hiding the small silver flask behind his leg. "Good evening, ma'am, I ah…"

"It's okay, Colin. She's an old friend."

Frank put his hand out, and Colin gave him the flask. He took a long sip, feeling the burn in his throat and noticing that the ache in his head was almost gone.

"You're working. I almost forgot." Susan smiled at Frank and started to back away. "I should go. But it's nice to see you again."

Her shoes clicked on the marble tile as she walked off. Frank could just let her go, same as he'd let other women walk out of his life, though truth be told there hadn't been very many. Besides, what was the point? Clearly her husband had given her a good life, while here he was, a security guard with a rent-controlled apartment full of books. And yet he felt something rise up inside him, the same thing he'd felt a few minutes ago—or thirty-nine years ago, depending on how you looked at it—when he picked up that typewriter and smashed his way into Ken Lerner's locked office.

"Hold on, Susan. Wait."

She stopped immediately, as if she'd been waiting for him to call out all along.

"Would you like to grab a cup of coffee or something?" he asked.

He handed the flask back to Colin, then looked at Susan to see her reaction. She turned, a huge smile breaking across her face, and for a moment thirty-nine years seemed to melt away, every single one of them.

Frank smiled back. "Thing is, I might switch to decaf. As you know, I already had some coffee a couple of hours ago." He nodded at the pocket where she'd tucked away the receipt. "If I have too much regular, I'll be up all night."

"Me too."

He unhooked his walkie-talkie and set it on the front desk, making his way toward Susan.

"You gonna be back?" Colin asked.

"Do me a favor. Tell dispatch I had to go home early. Just say I hit my head and needed a little time to recover."

He crossed the lobby to catch up to Susan. When he got to her side, she began moving with him, easily keeping pace. He held the front door open for her, and together they stepped out into the cool fall night.

A fiction writer and screenwriter, **Adam Meyer** has loved time travel ever since he first saw *Back to the Future*. Adam's short stories have appeared in the Mystery Writers of America anthology *Vengeance*, *Chesapeake Crimes: Storm Warning*, and *Landfall: Best New England Crime Stories 2018*, and he has upcoming stories in *Chesapeake Crimes: Invitation to Murder* and *The Beat of Black Wings*. He's written several TV movies and series for Lifetime, Discovery, and National Geographic. He's also the author of the YA novel *The Last Domino*. A native of New York City, he lives with his family in Northern Virginia. Visit his website at www.adammeyerwriter.com.

O CRIME, IN THY FLIGHT

Eleanor Cawood Jones

Backward, turn backward, O Time, in thy flight.
Make me a child again, just for tonight!
> —"Rock Me to Sleep," Elizabeth Akers Allen

Charlotte had always been told life got easier as you got older, but she wasn't buying it.

It was hard enough balancing day care and commuting to DC for her career as a data analyst, plus keeping herself and her family out of the press. And to top things off, that very morning Charlotte's husband had threatened to leave her because, in his words, she was "getting creepier."

"Seriously, Char, I can find my own shoes," Marco said. "You don't have to use your supposed magic powers to tell me where they are."

Yes she did, if he wanted to be on time for work.

And how did a grown man lose his shoes, anyway?

And why did he have to say "magic powers" in that sarcastic tone, as if he were Darrin and she were Samantha and he wanted her to stop being who she was? Of course, that *was* what was happening. Except she wasn't a TV witch—simply a woman who could find missing things by holding a piece of clothing the owner had been wearing before the item went astray. And he was a husband who wanted her to be normal.

"I wouldn't have to help you if you used this newfangled thing we call a closet. It's right upstairs if you're curious," she retorted, earning her an angry look from Marco.

Just as quickly, his expression turned from infuriated to dismayed. "You're pushing it," he said sadly. "You weren't like this when we got married."

He sat down at the kitchen table to tie his newly found black dress shoes. He had an important meeting this morning with the head of sales, and he was nervous and irritated to begin with. She should have ignored him and his missing shoes and kept frying the bacon. He would have found them eventually anyway.

Ah, hindsight.

"Well of course I wasn't like this ten years ago," she said, wondering if she sounded as unhappy as he did. "I can't help it if I developed special talents after Aranea was born."

He snorted. "Special talents, indeed." He stood and picked up his suit jacket off the back of the chair. "Skip breakfast for me. I'm out of here. And I have to tell you, the only special talent I can see right now is you showing off. You're going to drive me right out of this house if you're not careful. I wanted a normal life, and look what you've given me."

He stormed into the garage, slamming the door behind him.

And that woke three-year-old Aranea. "Mommy?" she called from upstairs.

Her daughter's voice wrenched Charlotte's heart. What would she and Arie do if Marco walked out? Or worse—what if he tried to take her daughter away from her?

Charlotte's breath caught in her throat, and she hurriedly turned off the bacon and rushed upstairs to hug her daughter tightly. She'd think about what Marco said after she dropped Aranea off at day care. She didn't have time right this second, so she shoved nursing her hurting heart to the bottom of her to-do list.

But she couldn't quite suppress the nagging sensation that what Marco said might be right. What if he deserved better? And maybe she was becoming a little…weird.

Her gift had emerged right after she and Marco brought their beloved daughter home from the hospital. When she held one of Arie's little baby booties and wondered where the odd one had gotten to, she felt a jolt and then could see it clearly lying in the back of the car, under the diaper bag. It was as if she was looking at a photograph in her mind. And sure enough, there it was.

Once was easy to write off. Even two or three times. But after fifteen or sixteen times of locating Arie's favorite stuffed bunny (under a table at the restaurant they'd eaten at the night before), her own car keys (under the newspaper), her grocery list (in the pocket of yesterday's pants), and her husband's rough draft of his speech (under the front seat of his car where he'd tucked it and forgotten)—simply by holding an item of clothing they'd each worn when they thought the items were misplaced—that same electric jolt would hit her in the chest, and the clear image would form in her mind.

She was always right.

She didn't tell Marco about her gift at first. She had a feeling he wouldn't like it. When she dared mention it to Arie's pediatrician, he'd taken little notice. "Lots of women become more intuitive after the birth of their first child," he told her. "You are more tired, and you see things you don't realize you're seeing, and your subconscious stores them. I'm sure that's all it is.

Just intuition and coincidence."

Dr. Warren, like Marco, liked logic and normalcy. So she didn't mention her new ability to anyone else and went about her business, secretly delighted by the amount of time and frustration she saved when she located misplaced items right away—until Dot Francis next door wandered away from home.

Dot was suffering from Alzheimer's, and her husband, Ben, was trying to care for her, but he'd fallen asleep, and all he could find of Dot was her knitted cap in their front yard. It was Dot's favorite hat, and she never took it off. Charlotte was holding it while she tried to comfort Ben, who was frantic, and the jolt came as she wondered where in the world Dot could be.

"She's in a blue car at the lake," she blurted out. "She's in the front seat, holding her coat and looking out at the water." Ben was crying and talking to himself and didn't notice what she said, but the young cop standing next to her sure did.

Dot was indeed at the lake. When they found her, she was standing beside the water in her coat and talking about going swimming. When she'd left her home, she'd walked across the street and into another neighbor's house, lifted his keys, and taken his car for a spin into the next county to the lake where she and Ben used to picnic.

Though relieved for Dot and Ben, Charlotte had been horrified that the cop, Officer Harris, might tell his colleagues or, worse, the newspapers, how she'd helped find her neighbor.

But he didn't. Instead, one morning two weeks later, before Charlotte left for the office, he showed up on her doorstep with a stuffed teddy bear and a tiny pink sweater. She'd known what he wanted when she opened the door. The family in the next town had been missing their little daughter for three days. She started to tell him she couldn't help. What if the child was not only missing but worse? What if she tried and failed, or was wrong, or people found out what she could do? She'd never have a moment's peace again.

"I'm here because I'm desperate," he said. "No one knows I'm here. Please try. I think you might have some special talents, if what I saw at your neighbor's house is any indication."

She let him in and poured them both a cup of coffee. At the end of the conversation, he was calling her Charlotte and she was calling him Officer Sam. She explained to him that her talent extended to missing objects, not missing people, with the single exception of Dot two weeks before.

He told her he wouldn't get his hopes up.

Doubtful and nervous, she held the sweater and bear and concentrated on where their owner might be. Then, to her surprise, she described the house—even its street number—where the missing toddler had been taken by a woman who, it turned out, desperately wanted a child but couldn't get pregnant. Charlotte even saw a stack of mail on the table where the toddler sat in a high chair, enjoying a tray of Cheerios.

And Officer Sam had been a regular visitor ever since. She didn't know what he told his supervisors, but he'd been promoted and, to her knowledge, still hadn't revealed her secret. Charlotte, too, had kept mum about her gift, and about how she helped Officer Sam, so she found herself on thin ice one day last year when Marco returned home early from work and found her sitting in their warm kitchen with a handsome police officer over half-drunk cups of coffee.

Officer Sam had left quickly to follow the clues she'd given him about the runaway teenager from the next town—he was camping in the deserted snack bar at the drive-in movie theater that was closed for the season—and she poured Marco a fresh cup of coffee, sat him down, and told him everything. From the baby booties to Dot and the half-dozen local missing-person cases she'd helped solve anonymously.

Marco listened carefully, finished the coffee, called her a freak and a liar, and slept on the couch, while Charlotte spent a sleepless night wondering why she was still trying to make their relationship work.

It had been a week before he'd come back to their bed, and a year since she'd told him about her talents, but he touched her infrequently now, and without passion. There was no doubt her marriage was in deep trouble. And her dream of a second child was becoming more and more unlikely.

Maybe, she thought now with a sudden flash of insight, he thinks if he touches me I'll see where he's been.

She dismissed the thought—rapidly—as she got her daughter into a jumper, tights, and coat, and fixed the bow in her little blond ponytail just right, before heading out the door to day care. When they arrived, another surprise awaited. "What are you dressing as tomorrow for Halloween?" Miss Tricia asked Arie as she gave the little girl a welcoming hug.

Arie loved Miss Tricia and day care, especially craft time. "Whatever Mommy says," her sweet little daughter said agreeably, and went off to play dolls and trucks with the other kids in the corner.

"Oh no," Charlotte groaned. "I completely forgot. I can't make her be Red Riding Hood again. I don't want her to look back at her childhood pictures and say, 'Mommy, why did I have the same costume every year? Didn't you care enough to shop for a new one?'"

Tricia laughed. "You'll think of something." She patted Charlotte's arm. "Look. It's DC at rush hour. Call in to work and tell them you're running late from traffic. The thrift store three door down opens at nine, and it's five of now. Pop in there, and check out the costumes for kids. They probably have a few left."

"What a great idea. You're the best, Tricia!" She hugged the young woman. "Maybe they have a Disney princess outfit."

"Or a fireman's uniform." Tricia grinned and pointed to the corner of the room, where Arie was running a fire truck up and down the carpet and ignoring the dolls.

Charlotte laughed. "Why not?"

She was waiting outside Thrifty to Boot when the doors opened, and asked right away for the kids' costumes. But her eye was caught by the costume rack for adults behind it. Pirate cloaks, two scanty French maid outfits, and a dozen assorted flowing witches' robes. And on one end of the rack was what looked to be an authentic flight attendant's dress, maybe from the sixties or seventies, complete with a darling hat and gloves, and even a little silver airplane pinned to the collar.

She grinned. It looked like her size. How cute would it be if she dressed up as a flight attendant to take Arie trick-or-treating, and Arie was dressed as a mini-flight attendant? Arie would only need a little suit, hat, and scarf to match her mom's. Her daughter would be adorable, and she knew her little girl would love the idea of dressing like Mommy. Arie even had her own plastic airplane pin for her lapel, a gift from a friendly Mesa airlines flight attendant during their trip to Tampa this past summer. It was a great idea for a costume.

Without thinking, she reached out to finger the dress, casually wondering where the owner might be. Spotting a mirror at the end of the aisle, she put on the hat and held the suit in front of her, touching the little silver pin. She laughed out loud with delight, and the jolt, when it came this time, almost knocked her off her feet. She tried to catch her breath and stumbled backward as lights flashed in her eyes.

In a few moments, she came back to herself and looked up to apologize to the thrift store employees in case they'd noticed her stumble and to tell them she was all right. Weirdly, in spite of the jolt, she still had no idea where the owner of the dress was, and wondered if it was because the woman was no longer living. But she did know what the woman looked like. An attractive brunette with her glossy hair pinned up under the hat and a dusting of face powder not quite hiding a sprinkle of freckles across her nose stared back at Charlotte in the mirror.

Wait—how was that possible?

Charlotte reached up and touched her hat, straightening it. She had a weird sensation that the movements weren't her own, as if someone else was controlling her arms. Whoever was moving her arms, and whoever was staring back at her in the mirror, all of it was someone else. She knew that on one level, but she still had the distinct sensation that she was *there*, in that brunette's body.

Not only that, but she looked good, and she knew it—both of them did, actually, Charlotte and the woman whose body she was in.

The brunette pulled on white gloves, then left the room and locked the door to 805 with a key labeled Airport Inn LAX before heading down the hall and around the corner. Her clunky heels didn't make any noise on the thick carpet. Without knowing how she knew it, Charlotte was sure this gorgeous flight attendant was on the way to somewhere Charlotte didn't want to go.

The brunette passed a few other flight attendants in the same type of outfit, but no one was around when the door to room 869 opened at her knock, and she stepped inside before the surprised-looking redhead who'd opened the door wearing a silky nightgown could shut it again. The brunette closed the door behind her, shoved the redhead back, and snarled at her.

Charlotte hadn't ever heard a noise like that come out of herself or any other woman. It frightened her. She would have liked to cry out, but she had no control over her vocal cords, her body, or the situation.

She was scared. It was like being at the movies and in the movie at the same time. She was powerless, both there and not there, and out of nowhere she remembered when Officer Sam had set her up on a phone call with someone he called "one of her ilk" after she'd confessed to him she was becoming frightened of her own abilities. That woman had told her that her talent was like a muscle. She could practice it and control it to a certain extent, but like any regularly used muscle, it would grow stronger with time and perhaps take unexpected directions.

She had no time to wonder if this was a new manifestation of her skills before the brunette snarled at the redhead again. No words. Just a feral growl that caused the redhead's eyebrows to stretch upward toward her side-swept bangs.

"You!" The redhead looked astonished as well as angry. "You're Ben's wife! Why aren't you back in DC with your kids? You're not a stewardess. You're not even qualified. Where did you get that suit?"

"This suit?" the brunette said, her voice low and menacing. "You're sleeping with my husband, the father of my children, and all you want to know is where I got this suit?" She laughed, but there was no mirth in her voice. "I'm just trying to blend in with the hotel clientele. And if you must know, my husband was foolish enough to pack your outfit in his suitcase. When I opened it to polish his shoes I naturally looked to see what else was in the bag. I suspected he'd been sleeping around with some tramp on the road—after all, a pilot has plenty of opportunities—but I had no idea he'd kept it so close to home, with someone from the same airline. I imagine you two have had some fun, planning your schedules and sleeping together in cities all over the country. What happened? Did you forget and leave your spare suit in his hotel room the last time you got together? Or did you leave it on purpose? So I'd find it?"

"You don't know what you're talking about."

"Don't try to deny it. I've used my family connections here in LA to have you followed, so I'm sure about what you've been doing. And with whom. But I had to see for myself the tramp my husband is sneaking around with. The one whose clothes fit me perfectly, by the way. Coming out here on the flight after yours was easy. As far as everyone else is concerned, I'm here seeing family." The brunette stepped toward the redhead. Close. Too close.

"Don't be ridiculous. It's not like that. You make it sound sneaky and sordid." The redhead backed away and sat on the bed, pushing her long, wavy hair away from her face. She actually had the nerve to look indignant.

"That's because it *is* sneaky and sordid. You *tramp*! What kind of woman sleeps with a pilot with two little children at home and another on the way?" The brunette wasn't showing yet, but somehow Charlotte knew that this woman was indeed pregnant.

"I said it's not like that. We fell in love. We couldn't fight it."

"You're what, twenty-two? Twenty-three? You don't know what love is. You don't know what living is until you've married the man you love, had his children, kept his house, and made it work, even when he's gone on the road. Ben and I are happy—or at least we were. And we're going to have this new baby and keep building our lives together. And you are not going to be in the picture."

"Too late." The redhead smirked, and Charlotte felt indignant on behalf of the woman she both was and wasn't. "Ben and I have a dream that has nothing to do with you. It involves a child of our own. The one *I'm* carrying. I just found out and told him last week. He's trying to think of how to tell you. You're out, I'm in. A newer model, I guess you'd say."

"You're lying." But Charlotte believed her. "And even if you aren't, my children come first, and there's no way I'm allowing their father to leave them."

"Very touching. The loving mother." She was smirking again. "Like I said, I'm in, you're out. And I'll take my clothes back, thank you." She eyed the brunette. "You're stretching the seams."

Charlotte could feel anger radiating throughout the brunette as she picked up the lamp on the bedside table—so heavy, so solid—and swung it at the redhead. Its base connected with a sickening smack on the side of her head. The woman fell over onto the covers, a dead weight.

As Charlotte shook inside, the brunette gave a little cry of astonishment and dropped the lamp, and Charlotte thought of nothing but flight. The brunette didn't even check to see if the redhead was okay, but turned to dash out the door. Not a soul was around as she ran in her clunky heels down the hall and back to room 805. With shaking hands, she unlocked the door, closed it behind her, leaned against it, burst into tears, and ran to the bathroom to throw up.

"I can't call the police!" she whispered, hanging on to the toilet. "They'll take me away, and I'll never see the children again!" She rocked back and forth on her knees, sobbing. Charlotte imagined being permanently separated from Arie and felt like crying herself.

The brunette stood up at last and examined herself in the bathroom mirror. She saw spots of blood on her face and began scrubbing it furiously. Then she tore off her clothes to wash them in the sink to remove more spatter. As the brunette draped the wet clothes across the sink to dry, Charlotte wondered why there was so little blood to wash out, deciding the bedspread and sheets in the redhead's room must have taken the brunt of it.

Finally, the brunette stretched out naked on the bed. Charlotte felt herself falling into an exhausted sleep along with her, powerless to stop it.

The next morning, Charlotte stretched and opened her eyes to bright sunlight. She closed them again and reached out for Marco but found nothing but pillows. The sheets felt rough, unfamiliar. She groaned out loud as the memory of the day before came flooding back. Surely it was a dream. But no, she was still with the brunette, still a part of her. And that's when Charlotte really began to worry. Was she going to be trapped inside this woman forever? She needed to go home. To Arie. But she had no control over this body. It was the brunette who was stretching and showering and wrapping the flight attendant suit in a plastic bag before hiding it in the bottom of her suitcase. Looking into the mirror while the brunette applied makeup, Charlotte ached for Arie, remembering the feel of those little arms wrapped around her neck.

Downstairs, the brunette was greeted at checkout as Mrs. Johnson. From the woman's increasing heart rate, Charlotte knew it wasn't her real name, that the lie made her nervous. Holding her small overnight bag, the brunette stepped into the street and hurried over to a nearby newsstand. She stared at the headlines on the local paper. "Stewardess found dead; pilot companion arrested." The brunette reached out and snatched the paper. "Dear God, where is he now?" she cried.

The jolt, when it came, was even more wrenching and blinding than the one before.

"Where did *you* come from?" The woman behind the counter was wide-eyed. "Oh, you must have stepped into the back to try on that darling vintage suit. Is it something a flight attendant used to wear? I swear, on you it looks perfectly natural."

Charlotte moved her arms and caught sight of herself in a nearby mirror. Thank goodness. She saw her own blond hair, her own trim figure, her own brown eyes, her own *self*.

"I don't exactly know," she said slowly. She looked at the newspaper in her hand. The *Los Angeles Times*. It was dated October 31, 2019. "Is this Halloween? And what store is this?"

The girl behind the counter raised her eyebrows. "Uh, yeah. I mean, yes, ma'am. Halloween. Right. And you're in Thrifty to Boot #4, right here in downtown LA. Best vintage clothes in town, that's for sure."

Charlotte looked around. She had no purse or luggage, only the newspaper in her hand. The LA newspaper. Her head spun. How had she wound up in the same clothes and the same chain store but in another city? Had it all been a dream? No, the newspaper she'd seen that morning had said there was a dead flight attendant, and it had all felt quite real. She hoped her powers weren't growing in some strange, new ways, but what else could it be? Well, at least she was back in her own time now, which meant she was in Arie's time. She had to get home.

"I, uh, seem to have forgotten my purse. Could I use your phone to call my, um, friend?"

"Where's your cell phone?"

"In my purse, I expect. Do you have a landline?"

"You're in luck. A vintage landline, just for you." The girl smiled at her and pushed the phone on the counter toward her. "I'm Sally, by the way. And tell your friend to bring enough money to buy that suit. It suits you to a T." She laughed at her own pun. "And hey, while you're here, I'm gonna run back to the restroom. Double coffee morning, you know?" She patted the phone. "Have at it."

Charlotte dialed the operator to place a collect call to Sam's cell phone. What did it say about her that she had the officer's number memorized? But when he answered, she almost sobbed in relief. "Sam, it's me, Charlotte."

"Charlotte, my God! Are you all right? Where are you? We've been looking everywhere! The woman at the day care said she'd sent you to the thrift store. And the woman at the thrift store was sure she'd seen you." He paused. "She thinks you stole some sort of old uniform for flight attendants. Then you never made it to work or to pick up Arie."

"I didn't steal the suit. And is Arie okay? Is she asking for me?"

"Of course she is. We told her you were visiting a sick friend. Your husband is beside himself. Where are you? I'll come get you myself."

"It's a long drive to LA. You'd best get started."

"You're in LA? How in the world—never mind. Just come home. You can tell me about it then. Is it talent related?"

"It is. At least I think it is." She was relieved not to have to explain herself. "Tell Marco—tell everybody I hit my head or something. I don't remember how I got here, and I can't find my purse."

"Charlotte, how can I explain that? And if it's true, you should be in a hospital. Where are you exactly?"

"I'm in a thrift store in LA. And I need you to do three things. First, find my passport and overnight it to me so I can fly home. Second, get me a room somewhere or have your cop friends here do it. I have to clean up and get out of this suit. It's—it's evidence. And third, look up a case where a flight attendant was killed in a hotel in this city. Somewhere near the airport, in the sixties I think, based on the hairstyles. A pilot was blamed. Find out if he went to prison, if he's still alive, what happened."

"Is that all?" Sam sounded sarcastic, then concerned. "Maybe you hit your head after all. Stay where you are. I'll send an ambulance. Let me talk to someone around you, and I'll find out what city you're in, where you are."

"You can talk to the store clerk in a minute. I'm fine, I'm in LA, and I'm thinking clearly." Her voice softened. "Trust me, Sam."

"I trust you, Charlotte. But this is crazy."

"We can talk about that later. Did you write down what I told you? About the dead woman and the pilot? Sam, it's important. He didn't do it. I know he didn't do it. And for all I know, I'm wearing the evidence."

"I said I believe you, crazy as it all sounds. Now let me talk to the store clerk."

"She'll be on the phone in a minute. She's in the bathroom. Now, Sam, most important, I need to talk to Arie. Wherever she is, wherever I am, there's nothing more important than hearing her voice, letting her know Mommy's coming home to her."

"I'll go to the day care, and we'll call you back. Now get that store clerk, and I'll have her look after you until I can send a car. And Charlotte, come home. Just come home." She heard the wistfulness in his voice. "We need you."

And I need you, she thought. Next to Arie, I need you the most. You believe in me.

She made up her mind then and there to surround herself with people who believed her. Her darling daughter. Sam. Others like her. Surely there was a way to get a handle on this growing gift before it went out of bounds again. One thing was for sure, Marco be damned, she was going to use this unexpected gift and let it take flight in whatever fashion it wanted, as long as it meant helping the police to find lost people and right wrongs. She realized how selfish she'd been, not wanting to look for Dot Francis or runaway teenagers out of fear, and she finally understood how utterly closed-minded Marco was.

She may be lost in a strange city, but she'd never felt more together. She closed her eyes and imagined Arie's arms around her again, focusing on where the child was. She had no clear image of her daughter as she had nothing of hers to hold, but she knew Arie would be at day care, maybe running her toy fire engine over one of the dolls in craft corner. She thought hard, willing herself there, but when she opened her eyes, all she saw was Sally, hurrying toward her.

Charlotte held out the phone to the smiling salesgirl and wished herself on the next flight home.

Eleanor Cawood Jones began writing in elementary school, using Number 2 pencils to craft crime stories starring her stuffed animals. She is author of twenty-one-and-counting short stories, including "Keep Calm and Love Moai" (*Malice Domestic 13: Mystery Most Geographical*) and "All Accounted For at the Hooray for Hollywood Motel" (2018 Bouchercon Anthology, *Florida Happens*). Coming soon: "The Great Bedbug Incident and the Invitation of Doom" (*Chesapeake Crimes: Invitation to Murder*). A former newspaper reporter and reformed marketing director, Eleanor is a Tennessee native who lives in Northern Virginia and travels often. You'll find her rearranging furniture or lurking at airports. Learn more at http://www.girls-gonechillin.com/.

HARD RETURN

Art Taylor

The man and the woman had reached that stage where the relationship would either turn more serious or slowly begin to dissolve. The seriousness wasn't about sex, a threshold they'd already crossed, but a step into some deeper, more emotional intimacy.

It was the woman who made the first move, but it was one the man had been asking for, hoping for, nudging toward.

Tell me something about yourself, he'd said, more than once. *Something special, something not many people know.*

Shared experiences brought people together. He believed this. Sharing them in the moment or a shared story, either one.

They'd been out to a nice dinner, had come back to her place. She kicked off her heels, lit a couple of candles, turned down the lights. They settled down in the living room—her plush couch, two glasses of red wine on a mahogany coffee table, the rim of hers already smudged with lipstick. A photograph on the end table caught a glint from the candle's flicker, caught his eye at the same time. A photo he'd been drawn toward before—her when she was younger, laughing, her head thrown back, her long blond hair falling.

A side of her he hadn't seen. With him, she'd always been more measured, more serious, melancholy even. Her hair was cropped close now.

"I had a boyfriend who…hurt me," she said.

"Broken hearts." The man made a motion with his hand, a throwaway kind of gesture. *Been there, done that.* A little laugh with it.

"Broken something else," she said. "Several things." She touched her arm in two places, touched her cheek, returned her hand to her chest—like she was trying to catch her breath, except she hadn't lost it right then. She wore a necklace, and she touched that instead, like an afterthought.

She began to tell him more about this ex: the bickering between them, the accusations and arguments, endless arguments after a while, the first time he knocked her around, the many times after.

"Then this one evening, the evening that *it* happened"—despite his curiosity, he felt a pang of distress, the way she inflected the *it*—"we were already broken up by then. Or I'd tried to break up with him at least. Actually, I had another guy at my place that night—nothing serious yet, but wondering where things might go, you know?"

"Like us," the man said.

The woman twirled a pendant at the end of her necklace, a small prism—catching the light from the candles as well.

"I was young and dumb," she said. "Living in a cheap rental house, not hardly the best part of town. Cheap furniture I'd picked up from Goodwill back in college, dragged along with me. Concrete steps on the front had a crack running down the center of them. Sometimes my life felt just as cracked."

"My grandparents had cinder block steps," the man said. "A stack of them piled up, not even connected together." But the woman didn't seem to hear him.

"So that's where I was, this house I'd rented, sitting here with the new guy I was beginning to see, trying not to think about the ex that everything had gone wrong with. Then he called. You can't put some things behind you."

"Nothing's easy. So you screened him out? Ignored the call?"

"It was a house phone, this was back in the nineties, before everyone had a phone in their pocket, before everyone had caller ID. I didn't know who was calling until I answered, and then he was…yelling at me, calling me names, ugly names. I know the new guy could hear. I should've just hung up. But I was trying to emphasize that it was over, trying to tell him not to call anymore—trying to reason with him, to be reasonable with someone who…wasn't." She took a deep breath. "And then he said something about how not only was he going to keep calling, and not only was I going to keep talking to him, but if I hung up, then he was going to come over there in person, and then…"

The man looked at the photo of her. She'd been happier once, and then this *it* had happened. It was coming together now—and who knew? Maybe talking with him about it would be a step toward healing.

"And then?" he said softly, urging without rushing.

She only shook her head.

"Did you hang up?"

"I did. And I regretted it almost instantly. I could feel it, in my bones suddenly, how it had been the wrong thing to do, how it was probably going to cost me. And cost the new boyfriend too, him thinking he was in for just a fun night. Don't they all?" She toyed with the necklace again, insistently now—*compulsively*, he thought. "But even if I hadn't hung up, would that have changed anything? In the long run, I mean? At the time, I felt like if

I was clear with my ex, if I stayed firm, if I just made the right decisions…
But looking back… Some things maybe you can't avoid. That's what I've
learned."

The candles flickered as she said it—startling him. Was there a window
open somewhere? It couldn't have been her talking that had done it, her
breath or his either. The candles were on the coffee table, too far away.

"So I guess this ex, he came over anyway?" The man shifted on the
couch, turned more fully toward her. Attentive. Concerned. "The way he'd
threatened?"

She nodded slowly, then shook her head. "We should've called the police," she said. "I see that now, saw that too late, or maybe that wouldn't
have made a difference either. But instead we left. The guy I was with, I
told him, let's just get out, go somewhere. So we left. Locked up the house,
even though my ex, he may have made a key. I knew that. We went down
the steps and started walking up the street. No hurry, it was a nice night,
cool air, crisp, so we were…strolling—until I turned and saw my ex about
a block behind us, coming around the corner of my house.

"Had he been watching us, me and this new guy? Had he been right
there the whole time? Calling from the pay phone on the corner? But he
would've seen us leave, I remember thinking that, because he was walking
up the steps, he was banging on the door, and then—suddenly—he turned.
Like he sensed me. Like he was an animal or something, smelling his prey,
even that far away. I saw him see me.

"It was a cool night, like I said—cold really. I'd felt chilly stepping out.
But suddenly I was raging hot. Anger and frustration and…fear most of
all, no other way to say it. The way he looked at me, that hatred, something
deep and dark and…*lunging* about his expression. And everything else on
the street, it was like it began to go out of focus, to spin and swirl, like the
ground underneath me was shifting somehow.

"I don't know if I said it or not. *Go. Let's go. Now!* But saying it, thinking it, I *went*. Up the street. Fast, but not running—no. I remember what I'd
been told about hiking. If you see a bear or a wolf or…don't run, because if
you run, they'll *know* you're prey. But going, *going* was necessary, getting
away, getting anywhere but there.…"

Listening to her, the man knew that this was the moment he should
reach out his hand, should take her hand in his, say something like *I know
what you mean* or *I feel like I'm there with you* or *I'm here with you now,
you're safe now.* Relatability builds connection, he believed that. Shared
experiences. Talking. Listening.

But when he did reach out, did take her hand…

The flickering candles, the glint of light off the picture and the prism,
the sound of her voice too, hypnotic in its flatness, and the story itself—

as he took her hand, so very cold it seemed, stunningly cold, everything changed.

He was there.

Not only *felt* like he was there—her storytelling drawing him in—but actually there. Some physical step back in time, into her time—seeing her running up the street ahead of him, seeing it as if through the eyes of that new man she'd been telling him about, feeling the crisp night air she'd described, and feeling too the *smack smack smack* of his feet against the sidewalk, his own feet rushing after her. Away from the house she'd described? Away from that ex?

"Wait," he called out. "Wait, stop."

She slowed, turned—surprised. "We can't stop. He'll get us sooner." Her face was the same, he recognized, but not the same—younger than herself but the same woman still, and the same solemnity about her. She wore low-slung pants, a top too thin for the weather, black with a silver sundial, a pair of Skechers. "We need to *go*." She started ahead again.

Could this be the same woman whose hand he'd taken on the couch? The same but transformed? Had he somehow traveled here with her? Or had he been transported here alone, to step into that other man's experience, to see firsthand this younger version of her? Someone who had no memory of—

Of what? Past? Future? Present? Where were they?

The street was two-lane, a small neighborhood—low-rent like she'd described it. Squat houses, small porches out front, folding chairs, clunky swing sets, some lawns tended, others overgrown. It was well past dusk, streetlights on overhead, TV screens shining from living room windows, the glow from each giving all of it the feel of a dreamscape.

Keeping up with her brisk walk, he touched his chest, his face. He was real.

A police car came barreling down the street, siren wailing. The man had the feeling the police might be coming because of them. But the car kept going—emergencies elsewhere, no knowledge of what the woman with him was facing, and him too.

"They didn't stop," he called out.

"They won't," she said. Her certainty confirmed it: she was a younger version on the outside, but haunted like the older one, the future one.

"You know what's ahead."

She nodded grimly.

He heard another siren, spotted more lights coming toward them. "But it could be different this time. We're here—*I'm* here."

He glanced at her. Her expression held something pitying in it, the way her lips turned down, that crinkling at the corner of her eyes, the sense of collapsing—that was the only way to describe it—inside the eyes themselves. "I don't think there's any way to avoid *it*," she said—that same emphasis again on the *it*.

But he felt sure that things could change, felt determined to prove it. The police car sped toward then. He stepped into the street, waved his hands wildly. The officer veered to avoid him, pulled to a stop.

"See. Have a little faith." But again her look, again that shaking of her head.

The officer got out, started toward them. But at that moment a door burst open at one of the houses on the street, two men spilled out onto the sidewalk between them. One of them had a knife.

The cop rushed toward the men, dancing around one another, the knife swinging. "Hey, hey, hey!" He pulled out his gun, pointed it at them.

"He thinks you signaled him to stop because of the fight." She pointed to the men, the knife making contact, the policeman leaping forward. "The cut isn't bad. You'll be a hero for saving his life."

Beyond the policeman and the fight, the man caught sight of the ex, walking at his same steady pace, coming at them relentlessly.

Like the Terminator, the man thought. Like Yul Brynner in *Westworld*—two of his favorite movies. He was surprised by the solace he felt thinking that—that whatever was happening here, he was still who he was in the middle of it. His favorites, his memories.

"Let's go," the woman said, tugging at his arm.

She quickened her pace. He struggled to match it—to keep up but not run ahead. To nudge her forward. To not look back.

"Where are we going?" he asked.

"There," she said—a corner convenience store, perched at the intersection of three roads, a corner slimmed to a point. Neon beer signs shone along a row of windows. Cigarette ads covered the door they pushed to get in. A peeling sticker carried the picture of a camera, announcing that the premises were under surveillance. The man took small comfort from it.

"Are we safe here?" he asked as the bell chimed over the door. The inside was only a few short aisles, with refrigerated cases lining the back wall of the store. A magazine rack equal parts comic books and pornography. A row of chips and candy. Stacks of canned vegetables and tinned meat. Were they going to hide behind the Spam? He looked for a restroom sign, some back room, someplace to hide.

"He's come back," the woman said—talking not to him but to the clerk behind the counter, the bulk of a wrestler, a thick beard on him. "Can you stall him a little?"

The clerk seemed to know her, knew the story, gave a firm nod—"I'll do what I can"—before he reached under the counter.

"This way," the woman said before the man could see what the clerk was after. Another entrance on the far side of the store, and another bell tinkling as they pushed through it. And was it an echo of that same sound from the first doors as theirs closed behind them? How far behind was that ex? How long could he be stalled?

"Now we run," the woman said. She took off ahead of him, sprinting along the new street back in the direction they'd come from. He hustled to keep up.

"Where are we going now?"

"Back to the house."

"To your house? Where you just left?" It had the logic—the *il*logic—of a dream, of a nightmare. No sense to it at all. What was her strategy? Was there a plan at all? "Why didn't you just stay there?" Frustration in his voice, disbelief—he heard it himself, couldn't keep it out.

"Because that wasn't what I did," she said.

"Whoa whoa whoa." He reached forward, grabbed her arm, pulled her to a stop. "You're just repeating the same thing that happened that night? What good is that going to do?"

She tugged her arm from his hand.

"What good is anything else?" She threw up her arms, dropped them to her side. "You saw what happened when you stopped the police car."

"Did that happen the first time too?"

She shrugged. "Nothing changes."

"And the clerk at the store back there," he said. "Look at me. The clerk— how long does he stall your ex?"

She wouldn't meet his eyes.

"He's not that lucky," she said. "Every time, he—" She cut herself off, defeated, ashamed. "I'm telling you. We need to run. Now."

From back at the convenience store, a gunshot.

The man's head flicked toward it. When he turned back, she was running again. He took off after her.

Another two-lane street, parallel to the first, an echo of it. More houses, more porches, a deeper darkness now, the streetlights struggled to cut through.

She turned abruptly down a small alleyway, then angled through a yard. Soon they were back at her house—the aluminum siding she'd described, the crack in the concrete steps, up to the front door. She didn't seem to fumble with her key but dropped it anyway—in her hand one second, then on the ground. "Every time," she said, half under her breath.

The living room was just as she'd described it too—cheap furniture, threadbare, dorm castoffs, and a smell like a dorm too, thick with memories of late nights drinking and smoking. A stack of paperback books beside a worn leather chair, a crocheted blanket draped across it. A fireplace with a pile of ashes, and above it a mantle lined with photos—groups of college students, the woman in a glamour shot wearing a seductive smile, an older couple who might have been her parents. Among them stood the same photo of her from back in the present, loose and laughing, that long blond hair, but in a different frame now, the edges dinged, the glass on this one cracked.

He heard the deadbolt click on the door, turned to see her hand raising to link a chain lock as well.

"He's coming this way," she said. "He knows we're here."

"We need to do something," he said. "Do you have a gun? Or a bat or—?" She was shaking her head, slowly. "The phone," he said. "The phone that he called you on. Where—?" He caught sight of it as he was asking—on the wall just inside a small kitchen. "We'll call the police. We'll—"

Still she shook her head.

"He cut the lines," she said—not with suspicion but certainty, even before he got the receiver to his ear, before he heard the emptiness there. She'd known. "The guy at the convenience store, he called the police already. They'll get here, but it'll be too late."

She was closing the blinds now, uneven venetians, a couple of slats broken, but she didn't hurry about it, easing them down slowly, swiveling them shut. *Going through the motions*, he thought. She began to push an end table in front of the door but without energy or urgency.

"You don't seem very distressed about all this," he said, and that did stop her short. She stood up from the table, still sitting short of the door. She seemed to puzzle over his comment.

"You can't change what's already happened," she said finally. "Happened over and over." She reached toward her neck, her fingers playing at nothing. He thought of the prism that had been hanging there—back in the present. "I feel like I'm reliving *it* constantly"—her same emphasis on the word *it*, rousing that same tremble of fear inside him. "Eventually you get numb."

He didn't feel numb. He felt everything—sharply. His body tensing for fight. The thrum of his blood. Pulses of adrenaline.

He watched her hands, the absence of that prism, the image of a sundial on her shirt. What was the switch to get them out of this? Take them back? Away from the broken blinds and the glaring streetlight and back to those warm candles she'd lit. Away from the worn sofa and back to that plush couch where they'd been having wine. Out of the past and into some future.

"Your hand," he said. "Give me your hand." Another puzzled look, but she stepped toward him, reached out, palm up. He took her hand in his, felt the warmth where there had been coldness before. He waited…but nothing happened.

He sighed, dropped her hand. As he leaned against the kitchen counter, he saw a knife block against the wall. He pulled out the biggest of the blades. Whatever was ahead, he needed to be ready.

"The guy," he said, remembering suddenly. "You told me there was a guy with you, a new guy you were seeing. What happened to him?"

She wouldn't meet his eyes at first—same as when he'd asked about the clerk. In her silence, he heard some dim echo of the gunshot from the convenience store.

Then another sound outside—a real one, something scraping the edge of the house. Feet on the steps and a pounding on the front door, pulsing with each blow.

The deadbolt struggled. The chain on the door swung and jangled. The ex's voice seethed and bellowed. "You let me in— You don't know what— You'll pay, you'll pay, both of you—"

"I'm sorry," the woman said finally, but the man could barely hear her over the raging outside. She turned toward him—the wilt of her lips, the vacancy in her eyes.

He thought about the night air, the way it whipped at him as he ran, the feel of his feet slapping against the pavement. *His* feet. He touched the frame of the doorway where he stood—solid, firm. The photo on the mantle—he could run his fingers across that too, he knew, feel the spiderweb of the cracked glass.

The pounding at the door grew louder. The Terminator, come back with a vengeance.

His favorites, his memories. All of him here.

The man lifted the knife in his hand, tested its heft, the actuality of it.

Without thinking, he ran his thumb down the edge of the blade.

He felt the sting, saw the blood begin to flow, brought his thumb to his lips—reflex.

He had just tasted it—that metallic tang—when the hinges gave and the front door burst inward.

* * * *

"I'm so, so sorry," she said. "But you...you wanted to know."

Art Taylor has won the Edgar, Agatha, Anthony, Macavity, and Derringer awards for his short fiction, and his work has appeared in the *Best American Mystery Stories*. He's also the author of *On the Road with Del & Louise: A Novel in Stories*, winner of the Agatha Award for Best First Novel. He edited *Murder Under the Oaks: Bouchercon Anthology 2015*, winner of the Anthony Award for Best Anthology or Collection. He is an associate professor of English at George Mason University. Find out more about his work at www.arttaylorwriter.com.

LOVE, OR SOMETHING LIKE IT

Michael Bracken

1975

While physics PhD candidate Kevin Thompson delivered a paper titled "Every Second Counts: An Exploration of Time Travel as a Fictive Device in the Works of David Gerrold, H. G. Wells, and Kurt Vonnegut Jr., and the Real-World Implications of Movement Through Time" to a group of bored scientists in Cleveland, Ohio, the love of his life was stabbed to death with a kitchen knife in her Waco, Texas, apartment, an act so violent the apartment's entire living room became a Jackson Pollock-like canvas of blood spatters.

The apartment door and all of the windows were locked from the inside, the murder weapon could not be located, and Kevin's were the only fingerprints in the apartment other than the victim's. Yet, he had an air-tight alibi and no discernible motive for killing Baylor University senior Michelle Radcliffe. They were college sweethearts who met during her freshman year, and they were nearly inseparable from that moment forward. An English major, she had helped him with the literary allusions in the paper he presented the day she died, but the math had been all his, and it caught the attention of a recruiter in the audience.

2018

Kevin kept a framed photograph of Michelle on his desk at the Department of Temporal Services, a government agency that recruited him following the receipt of his PhD in physics, and coworkers had long known not to ask about it.

Darryl Johnson, a recent hire out of Stanford, had not received the message. He leaned his hip against Kevin's desk and asked, "Who's the hottie?"

"My fiancée," Kevin said, the truth a story too long to tell the cocky young man interrupting his train of thought.

Darryl picked up the photograph to examine it. "She's a little young for you."

Kevin snatched the frame from Darryl's hand, wiped off the younger man's fingerprints, and replaced it on his desk in the exact spot from which it had been taken. "We met in college."

Darryl examined the overweight, balding scientist. "That must have been a long time ago. What's she look like now?"

Kevin's pasty, hound-dog face flushed red, but before he could respond, one of the other men in the office grabbed Darryl's elbow and led him away. Kevin stared at their backs until they disappeared into the break room.

"It's okay," Charlene Johnson said. An engineer, she sat in the cubicle across from Kevin's and was tasked with the practical application of Kevin's theories. "He didn't mean anything by it."

Ten years earlier, only a few months before she was transferred to Kevin's work team, Charlene lost her husband to a drunk driver who'd ignored a stoplight and T-boned his Prius. Each of the three other team members had lost loved ones in a similar manner. Grover lost his mother to an accidental overdose of prescription medicine. Angela lost her twin sister in a mountain-climbing accident involving a faulty carabiner. Matthew's daughter drowned in a neighbor's swimming pool. For each member of the team, unlocking the secret of time travel had become more than an interesting intellectual pursuit, but one that would, perhaps, allow them to alter that moment in each of their lives that came to define them.

The flush slowly drained from Kevin's face as he stared at Charlene. "That doesn't give him the right—"

"I know," she said, interrupting what could have become the kind of indignant rant in which each member of the team had too often engaged.

Kevin had been the first scientist recruited as much for his skill as for his loss, and he had grieved the longest and the hardest of them all. Michelle's death was not a preventable accident, but a cold-blooded murder, and he attacked it from two directions. At work, he and his teammates strove daily to discover ways to move through time other than the inexorable second-by-second slog into the future. During his off hours, he collected, read, and reread everything he could about Michelle's murder, thinking he could identify the one clue investigators had overlooked that would lead to the arrest and conviction of her killer. The long-cold case returned to public attention when *20/20* devoted an episode to it, but the producers uncovered no new information, and the crazies who came out of the woodwork only briefly resurrected the long-dormant police investigation.

Charlene understood Kevin's obsession but not the extent of it. Neither she nor any of their coworkers had ever seen the inside of Kevin's apartment, and they were unaware that it had become a shrine to the dead woman. He had covered the walls with photographs of his deceased lover, mounted in glass displays the change of clothes Michelle had kept at his Waco apartment, and displayed on a shelf he dusted daily her makeup, toothbrush, and hair dryer from that apartment.

Hers was the last face he saw before sleep and the first face he saw upon awakening. He swore he would never love again, and he didn't. And every day he made some infinitesimal progress toward solving the conundrum that was time travel.

* * * *

Every six months Kevin met with his handler, the man who had recruited him into the Department of Temporal Services after hearing his presentation in Cleveland and subsequently learning of his girlfriend's murder.

His handler asked, "How much longer are you going to carry her weight?"

"You wouldn't understand." He had never understood.

"Try me."

Kevin stared at the man sitting on the far side of the table, unable to remember how many times they'd had variations of this conversation. "Have you ever lost someone you loved?"

"Of course," the man said. "You don't reach my age without losing someone."

"How did they—?"

"Cancer, heart disease, the usual panoply of diseases."

"All expected. Anticipated. Planned for, even."

"In a sense, I suppose."

"My girlfriend was murdered for no apparent reason," Kevin said. He lifted his left hand and yet again showed the other man the diamond solitaire he wore on his pinky finger. "I was planning to give this to her."

"I know. You were going to propose."

Kevin nodded. "Michelle pointed it out to me when we were Christmas shopping, said it was the most beautiful ring she'd ever seen. She never even knew I bought it."

"Because she was murdered. Brutally murdered."

"As long as I love her, she's still alive."

"She doesn't exist without you, is that what you're saying?"

Kevin crossed his arms and said nothing.

"And your apartment?"

The conversation had taken a new direction, one Kevin had not anticipated. He leaned forward. "What about my apartment?"

"We know all about it. You think you've kept it hidden from everyone, but you haven't."

"I keep her alive."

"But you've done nothing to save her."

Kevin stared at his handler.

"You know why we recruited you, don't you?"

"My paper," Kevin said. "That's what you told me."

"Because we thought you had an incentive to turn your theories into reality," his handler said, "and you've been a bit of a disappointment. We're not sure you've made any progress in the entire time you've been with the department. That's why we've given you help, assigned other members to your team who have similar incentives."

He was wrong. Kevin had made progress. Though he could not focus on much of anything outside of work—he did no socializing, participated in no form of recreation—Kevin was able to concentrate so completely upon his work because he believed it would allow him to protect Michelle from the tragedy of that night and allow them to live happily ever after. His obsession to see her again, to hold her in his arms, to tell her how much he loved her, drove him in ways the Department of Temporal Services used to their advantage. To the other scientists outside of his immediate team, time travel was an intellectual challenge, but Kevin was determined to make it a reality.

"You're running out of time," his handler said, amused at his own little joke. "Soon you'll be too old to—"

"I'm close," Kevin insisted.

"If something doesn't happen soon," the handler threatened, "we're going to close down the entire project, give you all civil-service jobs in some Podunk town in Montana."

Kevin had told no one, but earlier that day, while contemplating lunch, a second orange had appeared on his desk, and that afternoon he stood with Charlene in the laboratory and sent his original orange back several hours in time.

* * * *

Three more months passed before Kevin discovered how to retrieve something sent back in time. Soon the department prepared to test the process by sending Darryl Johnson, their first human test subject, through time, using a device Charlene had designed and first tested on a pair of lab rats.

After dinner the night before the scheduled test, Kevin returned to the laboratory and found Charlene there adjusting the wristband Darryl would wear the following day. She looked up when he entered the lab.

"I'm surprised to find you here," Kevin said.

"Just making sure everything is ready for tomorrow."

"Is it?"

"Of course, it is, but Darryl's life is riding on this."

"His isn't the only one."

A wan smile crept across her face. "My husband's, Matthew's daughter's—"

Kevin stopped her with a glare. "You needn't make an exhaustive list."

She shrugged.

"You should go home now," Kevin told her. "Get some rest."

"Come with me," she said. "We'll stop for a drink to celebrate all we've accomplished."

"You'd best just go."

"But—"

The senior scientist glared at her again, so Charlene gathered her things and made to leave. She stopped at the door. "I'll see you in the morning."

"Yes, yes. Just go."

When he felt certain Charlene had gone, Kevin clothed himself in a specially designed suit, strapped on the wristband that controlled time travel, and programmed it to place him in Michelle's apartment shortly before her demise. Then he activated it.

1975

Years rolled off the chronometer, and Kevin found himself standing in Michelle's kitchen, listening as the apartment door opened. Michelle had grown in his memory from the love of his life to a mythical being of near angelic stature, so he was not prepared for what he witnessed.

"No," she said. "Not again. Not here. You can't come in."

"But—"

"Kevin will find out about us."

"How?" a man's voice asked. "He doesn't suspect a thing, and he's presenting a paper at that conference in Cleveland. He won't know anything happened as long as you don't tell him."

The kitchen door stood open about an inch. Through the gap Kevin saw a man kiss Michelle, and it was clear she welcomed it, enjoyed it, and had difficulty resisting the man's insistence that he enter the apartment.

But resist she did. She put her hands on his chest and pushed him backward, into the hall. She closed the door, snapped the deadbolt, and walked toward the kitchen, the look of bliss betraying her emotions more than any words she might express.

When she pushed the door open and saw Kevin standing there—sixty-nine-year-old Kevin, overweight, balding, his face a hound-dog duplicate of his younger face, fury radiating from every pore—her eyes opened wide in surprise. When she saw the engagement ring on his pinky finger, she clearly recognized it from her Christmas shopping trip and realized Kevin had turned his far-fetched time-travel theories into reality. She opened her mouth to scream, but his hand quickly covered it, and only a muffled sound escaped.

"I loved you!" he raged as he grabbed a kitchen knife from the counter with his free hand. "I loved you, and this is what you did behind my back?"

She pulled away, stumbled into the living room, and fell across the coffee table. Kevin was on her, the knife plunging into her again and again and again until he no longer had the strength to lift it.

Then someone pounded on the apartment door.

Kevin stared down at the body, looked around wildly, and realized he had to get away. He triggered the switch on his wristband—

2018

—and materialized in the Department of Temporal Services laboratory covered in blood, gripping a bloody kitchen knife, and facing Charlene, his handler, and several police officers with weapons drawn.

"I was afraid this would happen," his handler said, "and it's a good thing Dr. Johnson thought to call."

Kevin dropped the knife and collapsed on the floor beside it, having realized what he'd done.

"Kevin Michael Thompson, you are hereby under arrest for the murder of Michelle Anita Radcliffe," one of the officers said. "You have the right to remain silent. Anything you say can and will be used against you in a court of law. You have the right to have an attorney. If you cannot afford an attorney, one will be provided for you. Do you understand the rights I have just read to you?"

Kevin nodded.

Charlene watched the entire process before asking his handler, "If you knew he killed her, why did you wait so long to arrest him?"

"He hadn't committed any crime until now."

2026

Several years later a young doctoral candidate delivered a paper titled "The Government's Use of Obsession as a Motivating Force in the Development of Travel Through Time," asking, but never quite answering, the ethical question of whether Michelle's murder could have or should have been prevented, and if the murder *had* been prevented, would the younger Kevin have been sufficiently motivated to unlock the secrets of time travel.

Although Edward D. Hoch Memorial Golden Derringer Award recipient **Michael Bracken** has written several books, including the private eye novel *All White Girls*, he is better known as the author of more than 1,300 short stories published in *Alfred Hitchcock's Mystery Magazine*, *Ellery Queen's Mystery Magazine*, *Espionage Magazine*, *Mike Shayne Mystery Magazine*, *The Best American Mystery Stories*, and in many other anthologies and periodicals. Additionally, Michael has edited or coedited several anthologies, including *The Eyes of Texas* and *Guns + Tacos*. He lives, writes, and edits in Texas. Learn more at www.CrimeFictionWriter.com.

IGNITION

John M. Floyd

11:30 p.m., October 25

Eddie Hollister sat alone at the small table at the end of the room. Facing him were two seated rows of older men in business suits and lab coats. Some of them Eddie had met, but most were familiar to him only because of their positions here at the institute. All of them were frowning.

Dr. Lawrence Walcott, one of the senior managers, said, "Mr. Hollister, let me make something clear: this is not a trial or even a hearing. All of us in this room work for the Adlerton Institute, and the purpose of this meeting is to find out exactly what happened between you and Professor Thomas Milano here in the laboratory earlier tonight. Do you understand?"

Eddie nodded. He also understood that this group wanted to ensure that what happened would not jeopardize the upcoming announcement of the most stunning scientific breakthrough in recent memory. That ceremony was scheduled for the following morning, and it was now—Eddie checked his watch—almost midnight.

"These proceedings are being recorded," Dr. Walcott said. "Please state that you understand what I've just told you."

"I understand," Eddie said.

"Then please describe to this group, in your own words, what took place here approximately three hours ago."

Eddie cleared his throat. "To do that, I'll need to start at the beginning."

"Very well. We're listening."

He took a long breath and looked at each of the faces in the room. "Earlier today, as I was about to break for lunch, Professor Milano phoned me in my office and asked me to meet him at the south door. I recognized his voice right away, from the accent."

"The south door of our facility, here?"

"Yes. I was both surprised and curious because the professor and I hardly knew each other. But we met as he'd requested, and walked together to the little clearing behind our building. There are a couple of picnic tables there, and—"

"This is the grassy area near the perimeter road?"

"That's right. The professor brought a sandwich for me from the food court, although he brought nothing for himself. It was—"

"Did you have any idea, at that point, what was going on?"

Eddie sighed. "Do you want me to tell you what happened," he asked, "or not?"

Dr. Walcott paused, then nodded. "Proceed," he said.

11:18 a.m., October 25

"Thank you for meeting me," Professor Milano said.

Eddie Hollister smiled as he unwrapped the foot-long Subway. "Thanks for the sandwich. I'm surprised security even let us leave the building, as close as we are to the big day."

"Oh yes. The announcement. That is one of the things I want to talk to you about."

Eddie couldn't help turning to look. Twenty yards from the picnic area where they sat, preparations in and around the main laboratory of the institute had reached a fever pitch. Employees of all grades and specialties were scurrying about, the news media was circling like buzzards awaiting a feast, and armed guards were posted everywhere. The long-awaited "reveal" of the Ellipsiar TimeLiner—referred to by those at the institute as the Machine—was less than twenty-four hours away.

"I heard there'll be a press conference," Eddie said. "Will you be a part of that?"

The professor smiled. "You overestimate me, my boy. Like you, I am but a minor player in all this. Support personnel, I think we are called."

"But you helped design the system's energy converter. You've worked on almost every part of—"

"So did the team of which you are a member," Milano said. "But the TimeLiner project itself is not mine. Others came up with the idea and the funding. They will receive the glory." He shook his head. "I am a midlevel physicist, and that is all I will ever be. Since this operation is complete, I fear my future is dim here at the institute."

Eddie took a bite of his turkey-and-cheese sub and thought that over, chewing. Fallen leaves, yellow and red and orange, littered the ground around their table. "Is this," he said, "what you brought me here to tell me?"

"One of two things, yes."

"What's the other?"

Professor Milano looked out over the landscaped industrial park and pointed. "I want to talk to you about this place," he said. "Our surroundings."

"What about it?"

The professor paused as if deep in thought. "Many years ago, almost everything you see here was empty countryside. The institute had not yet been built, and our neighbor, the Irondale Corporation, stood alone across the way, in those fields over there."

"The plant, you mean?" Irondale Enterprises—half a dozen long white buildings—covered fifty acres or more and employed almost a thousand workers.

"No. It was just a single three-story house back then. And over there, beside the present-day plant, was a city park."

"How do you know all this?" Eddie asked.

"Old pictures. Hundreds of them, from different sources: the library, public records, historical websites, even files at the Irondale facility— among them are panoramic photos of this entire area at all stages of development." Professor Milano pointed again. "Most of it has changed, but a few things are still around. That open field just across the road there, with the odd-looking mound in the middle? It looks exactly the same as it did back then, except it is grass now, instead of dirt. And that fenced cemetery, there. One old photo shows that same graveyard, except with smaller trees and whiter headstones."

Eddie was no longer looking. He was watching the older man's face, studying it in the noonday sun. "All this is interesting, Professor—but what does it have to do with me? Or with tomorrow's announcement?"

"I am getting to that," Professor Milano said. "You see, I have done quite a bit of research lately into something that happened here just over fifty years ago. At exactly nine-fifteen on the night of July twelfth, 1968, an armored vehicle drove down this road right here, carrying a delivery of cash for the vault at the headquarters building of the Irondale Corporation. For some reason—possibly not an entirely legal reason—the money was transferred here from the banks downtown, and was apparently intended to finance the upcoming construction of their new research-and-development center. Are you with me so far?"

"Go on."

"Well, this particular night was stormy, or had been, just before the arrival of the armored transport. As a matter of fact, one of the big trees that lined this road back then had just been struck by lightning and had fallen across the roadway. The driver of the truck didn't see the downed tree until it was too late—he braked hard but swerved and crashed into it sideways, just east of here and around that curve. Neither of the passengers—the driver and a second guard—was injured, but the truck was badly damaged and leaking gas onto the road. The two men climbed out, and while one of them checked the cargo the other began the long walk around the bend to the Irondale house, to report the accident and place a call for help. According to the report I saw, the wind had eased up by then, and the storm had brought very little rain."

The professor paused again at this point, and Eddie, who'd put down his sandwich and sat waiting, said, "I ask you again—why does all this matter?"

Milano broke out a slow smile. "Because, my young friend, tonight I am going to take the TimeLiner back to 1968. I am going to show up right here, at this spot, at nine o'clock on the night of July twelfth of that year. I am going to stand here and watch that armored truck drive past and hit the fallen tree, and then..."

"Then what?"

"I am going to steal the cash."

Eddie sat there a moment, staring. "You're what?"

Milano smiled. "And I want you to come with me."

* * * *

"Wait a minute," Eddie said, raising both hands. "Hold on. First things first. What makes you think you could do anything with the TimeLiner tonight? It's being guarded as if it were the Hope Diamond."

The professor shook his head. "It is being guarded from outside. We have a small army watching the entrances and exits—but nobody is guarding it on the inside. The Machine is safe in there, or supposedly so. You and I work there, going in and out all the time. All we have to do is stroll in, enter the device, and set the controls. It will disappear for the duration of our journey, yes, along with us, but—as you must know—it will reappear when we return. And if the controls are set such that we reappear several seconds *before we left*...no one will notice anything amiss. Not even the security cameras. No fuel will be expended, and I will erase all evidence of the trip. The cameras, if examined at all, will show you and me approaching the device and walking right past it, with maybe a tiny hiccup in between, like a blip of interference."

Eddie's mind was whirling. "But...even if that works, how do you propose to—"

"Steal the loot? That is the simplest part of all. I will merely wait until the remaining guard comes out of the back of the truck, and when he does I will incapacitate him with an anesthetic. He will sleep like a baby for the next hour and wake up with no ill effects, except that the money he was guarding will be gone."

"Gone where? Where would you put it?"

"I would move it the fifty yards or so to the base of the small hill I told you about, the one I saw in the photos." Milano pointed again. "That one there, on the other side of the road. It would require a couple of trips, but there would be plenty of time before the other guard could get in touch with someone to come help with the accident. I would merely dig a hole in the near side of the hill, seal the money inside a wrapping to protect it from the ravages of time, drop it into the hole, cover it over, and return to the Time-Liner and come home."

"And once you're back home…"

"I would dig up the still-buried cash."

Both of them were quiet a moment. This was the craziest thing Eddie had ever heard. Finally he said, "Why me? Why not do it all yourself?"

"Because I have had, as you might know, some heart problems. I have an implanted pacemaker and defibrillator."

"Which is why you need me along. For the digging and such."

"Correct."

Eddie shook his head in wonder. "This is too weird, Professor. Even if I agreed—and I don't—there are all kinds of complications. The butterfly effect, for one."

"That theory is overrated, Edward. The idea that someone could harm something during time travel, and thus alter future events—that is mostly fiction. One would have to cause or prevent a crucial occurrence of some kind, or kill somebody's ancestor, or destroy a place that would later be vital to someone's survival."

"Are you saying those things couldn't happen?"

"Certainly not. But I am saying that such situations would be extremely rare. Let me give you an example of something that *could* happen. Let us say you travel back in time with an iPhone in your pocket, and you kidnap Steve Jobs as a young man. Suppose you tie him up and throw him down a well and leave him there to die. I maintain that your iPhone will remain operational throughout all this because there is always the chance that Mr. Jobs will survive, and will go on to invent whatever it is that he will invent. Who knows, you might have a change of heart, and go back and set him free. But if you don't, and if you return to your time machine and fire it up to leave, then fate, or the cosmos—or whatever maintains balance in the universe—will then take over, and your iPhone will vanish." Milano studied my face. "Do you understand?"

"I think so."

"But remember, we will not be doing anything like that. Nothing will die. Nothing will be destroyed. Nothing of any consequence will change as a result of our actions. All I plan to do is drug an armored-car guard and steal a sum of money."

"A lot of money," Eddie said. "Money that might be used for life-changing purposes, if it weren't stolen."

"No. This is money that would disappear anyway."

"What do you mean, disappear?"

"According to my research, the guard who stayed with the wrecked vehicle grew tired and careless while waiting for help to arrive, and around nine forty-five he tossed a cigarette to the ground near the vehicle. It accidentally ignited a pool of spilled gasoline, and everything went up in a fireball. The guard lived, but his truck and its cargo were incinerated." Professor Milano leaned forward, making sure he had Eddie's full attention. "The cash I plan to take burned to a crisp that night in 1968, right down to the last bill."

That made Eddie stop and think. But even so...

"Even so—this is breaking the law. Grand theft. Why would you think I'd agree?"

"Three reasons. First, as I have explained, it is not theft. The money will be gone afterward, whether we are there or not. The second reason is that we would then be rich, you and I. After our return we would simply pick a dark night—tomorrow, maybe, or the next—and dig up our buried treasure. Eleven million dollars, tax free."

"Eleven million?"

"How is that for a nest egg?"

Eddie fell silent a moment.

"Let me ask you something, Edward. Is there not something you would like to have, someplace you would like to go, that you cannot afford?"

He swallowed. Hawaii, he thought. He'd always wanted to see Hawaii...

Ignoring the question, Eddie replied, "You said three reasons."

"The third only applies if you are reluctant." Milano paused. "Are you reluctant?"

To commit a felony? Of course he was reluctant. "What's the reason?"

"Your criminal record," the professor said. "The one you never bothered to mention to your employers here at the institute."

"What?!"

"I told you I did my research. I know about the shoplifting incident in college."

Eddie's stomach muscles clenched. In a small voice he said, "I was a freshman, seventeen years old. A minor. As such, those records were sealed."

"But not inaccessible. What do you think Dr. Walcott would say if he knew you were hired on under false pretenses?"

Eddie felt his face heating up. "It was just a prank. A stupid stunt. He would understand."

"I do not think so," Milano said. "Do you ever wonder, Edward, why everyone calls me Professor? I have a Ph.D., like most of us who have been here awhile, but no one calls me Doctor. Just Professor." He propped both elbows on the table and rested his chin in his hands. "It is because I taught college physics for fifteen years. If I bring your unsavory collegiate history up to your bosses, I assure you they will listen to me. And you will be out on the street."

Eddie tried to swallow but failed. His mouth had gone dry. "You would do that?"

"I do not want to, no. All you have to do is go with me on this journey tonight. This adventure. No crime would be committed—as I said, you cannot steal money that does not exist. And you would return to the present a wealthy man."

A long silence passed. Eddie's mind was racing. After a minute or more he said, "Are you even sure it'll do what it's supposed to do?"

"The Machine? Of course it will. It is a time-travel device. You think they would be inviting the news media in to see it tomorrow if it will not do what it is supposed to do?"

Eddie wiped a trembling hand across his face. The lunch that had seemed delicious ten minutes ago was now a cold lump in his stomach.

"What if I tell them?" he said. "I could go to them right now and tell them what you're planning."

Milano shook his head. "They would never believe you."

"They'd believe enough to make sure nobody comes near the Machine tonight."

He shrugged. "In that case, my plan would fail. The difference is, I would still have a job."

True enough. Eddie squeezed his eyes shut. Another minute dragged by.

"Decision time, Edward. What will it be—the poorhouse or the penthouse?"

Eddie opened his eyes and heaved a sigh. "How exactly will all this work?"

* * * *

As things turned out, it worked very well. At 8:10 that night Eddie Hollister entered the office of Professor Milano, and together the two of them took the elevator to the first floor, where the much-anticipated Ellipsiar TimeLiner sat waiting and encircled by velvet ropes as if it were an exhibit at a convention or a museum. Up close, it looked nothing like the gaudy time machine Rod Taylor had used in the movies to visit the Morlocks. This was a giant clear-walled cube with a vertical console installed in one of the sides and three recliners that looked like barber chairs with seatbelts. As the professor had said, there were, incredibly, no guards nearby—they were all stationed outside the doors of the building.

His heart pounding, Eddie watched Milano step over the ropes—a little clumsily, he thought; Milano was wearing a baggy jacket and walking stiff legged, like that skinny deputy in the *Gunsmoke* reruns. Clumsy or not, he entered the device, Eddie followed, and they buckled themselves into two of the seats. Behind them, the wide door of the TimeLiner eased shut. Milano punched dates and times into the console, pushed three power buttons, and said into a black microphone, "Ignition." It was, Eddie thought, a strange thing to say because there was no resulting sound—no rev of engines, no buzz of electricity, no rumble of rocket boosters.

They just left.

Not only was their departure quiet, it was visually unremarkable. Eddie saw only a single blink of bright light, and then—

Then the Machine and its two occupants were sitting on a grassy patch of land two dozen yards north of where Eddie and the professor had talked during lunch earlier that day. Or actually, Eddie thought, *not* that day. A day fifty years in the future.

It was now 1968.

The two of them were sitting in the spot that would eventually be the lobby of the central laboratory of the Adlerton Institute.

Eddie was vaguely aware that his mouth was hanging open, his eyes wide as billiard balls. All around them was dark countryside and a starless, moonless night. Which made sense: the sky was overcast. A storm was coming.

He also realized, for the first time, how fortunate it was for Professor Milano that the Machine had been recently relocated to the ground floor of their building. When it made its journey backward in time, it—unlike all other forms of transportation—stayed in the same place; it was the surroundings that changed, as time spun backward. If the device had been located on an upper floor, it would've been positioned too high when it reached its destination—and would've come crashing down to ground level.

Even as these thoughts dawned, a gust of wind buffeted the Machine, and a few raindrops spattered its top. In the chair beside him, Professor Milano unbuckled his seatbelt, pressed the button to open the door—for something so advanced, Eddie thought, the door took a really long time to open and close—and stepped outside. Eddie followed. The air was surprisingly warm, much warmer than in 2018. Again, that was logical: when they'd left, it was October. This was July.

Standing there, Eddie was also surprised to see Professor Milano unzip his coat and raise his shirttail to reveal the blade of a shovel sticking out of his belt. He then pulled the rest of the shovel out of his trouser leg—that's why he'd been walking stiff legged—and held it beside him.

"I came prepared," the professor said. "I also have some large plastic bags"—he patted a pocket of his jacket—"inside which we can seal the money before we bury it. The way they are made, and without exposure to sunlight or oxygen, they should last far longer than the fifty years we require."

Having said that, the professor took a moment to get his bearings and then strode away into the humid darkness. Eddie followed, and after a moment heard and felt the crunch of gravel underneath his shoes. Overhead, lightning forked the sky, and just for a moment Eddie could see a road underneath his feet, a tree-lined road that wound its way east, into the gloomy distance. Thunder boomed and rolled.

A moment later they left the roadway and waded through an expanse of grass on the other side. The wind was howling now, the flashes of lightning almost constant. In their illumination Eddie saw several things that he recognized from the future: an iron footbridge over a fast-flowing stream, the edge of a cemetery (one of the graves bore a new headstone and was piled high with fresh dirt), and—most important for them—the small isolated hill that Milano had pointed out to him earlier. When they reached the base of that hill, the professor paused and stabbed his shovel into the dirt as if to mark the spot. Then he checked his watch—Eddie assumed he had reset it to match their current time period—and turned to face the road. Lightning continued to crisscross the sky, and suddenly Eddie heard the splintering crack of a nearby tree, followed by a deep THUD as its trunk hit the ground.

Then, only seconds afterward, Eddie heard the sound of a motor vehicle, approaching from the west, and watched it rumble into view. A tall boxy truck, moving fast. Too fast, Eddie knew, to avoid the tree that would now be blocking the roadway a short distance from where he and the professor were standing.

They didn't have long to wait. Tires skidded in the gravel, the armored truck swerved and slammed into the tree with a muted crash, and both Milano and Eddie crept forward, moving past the footbridge and the cemetery fence. As they drew closer they saw the two guards standing outside the disabled truck, collars turned up against the wind. Eventually one crawled over the downed tree trunk and headed west on foot while the other unlocked the back door and stepped into the bent and twisted truck. No one else was in sight, in any direction.

Professor Milano took something from his jacket pocket, motioned to Eddie to keep out of sight, and waited for the guard to emerge from the truck. When he did, Milano shot him in the back with a taser gun. The guard spasmed, fell heavily to the ground, and lay motionless. Moving fast, Milano put away the taser, took a small case from his pocket, opened it, and removed a syringe. As Eddie stood gawking, the professor knelt and injected the syringe into the guard's upper arm. "That should do it," Milano said, rising to his feet. "He will be out for at least an hour." Then he looked at Eddie and smiled. "Let us begin."

They did. Transferring the shipment of cash took only fifteen minutes, and burying it at the base of the hill took only ten. When a sweating Eddie Hollister had patted the final shovelful of dirt into place, Milano took the shovel from him, threw it into a weed-choked ditch, and looked around. The coast was clear.

They trudged back to the scene of the accident under a clearing sky. As expected, the short-lived storm had brought only a sprinkle of rain. After a final check of their surroundings, Eddie dragged the unconscious guard well away from the truck and Milano tossed a lit match into a pool of gasoline. They didn't stay to watch the fire. The professor had left about a tenth of the money inside the truck in an effort to convince the cops that the entire shipment had been burned, which Eddie thought was a smart move. He wasn't sure how thorough investigators had been back in the late sixties, but one thing was certain: if they thought nothing had been stolen, they wouldn't bother searching for it.

Silently the two thieves made their way back to the Machine. It sat waiting and—because of its transparent sides—almost invisible in the dark grassy area. Eddie, who was still breathing hard, half from the work he'd done and half from fear and tension, waited while Professor Milano stepped into the open door of the device. Eddie was about to follow when Milano turned to face him. The older man had a weapon in his hand—but not the taser. This was a big shiny revolver.

"Stay where you are, Edward," he said. "I want no blood on the floor of the Machine."

Eddie froze. Something in the back of his mind told him he shouldn't be surprised, but that made him no less scared. The words he managed to get out—"Don't do it, Professor"—sounded lame even to him.

"I am sorry," Milano said. "This is the only way." Still aiming the gun through the doorway, he pushed the button to start the closing of the door, and as it eased slowly along its track, Milano smiled, cocked the revolver, aimed it...

11:56 p.m., October 25

"And?" Dr. Walcott said.

Eddie, lost in his thoughts, blinked and focused on him. "Excuse me?"

"Professor Milano 'cocked the revolver and aimed it,' you said. What happened then?"

"Then he fell dead."

The large crowded room went quiet. The officials gathered here knew about the professor's demise, of course—his lifeless body had been sprawled on the floor of the TimeLiner when Eddie returned it to its spot at the institute at 8:15 tonight. But hearing the words spoken aloud were still enough to make those listening fall silent.

"Do you know why?" Walcott asked.

"Why he died? I have a theory, yes. I imagine those who have examined his body know for sure, by now."

"We'll come back to that," Walcott said. "For now, tell us what happened next, after the professor collapsed."

"What happened was, I jumped into the Machine, and quick. The door was closing."

"And then?"

"Then I strapped myself into one of the seats and did what I'd seen the professor do, earlier: I pushed the three power buttons and said, 'Ignition.' A moment later, I was back."

"Back here. In 2018."

"Yes." This had already been verified, Eddie knew, from the security cameras. Professor Milano had pre-programmed the Machine to return several seconds earlier than the time they had first approached the device, so that the footage would show the two of them nearing the Machine's door and then continuing past it. In reality, it instead showed Eddie and Milano approaching the Machine and then showed Milano dead on its floor, his hand clutching the gun, and Eddie sitting in one of the passenger seats. Not exactly the planned outcome.

Walcott studied Eddie's face. "What *do* you think caused the professor's death?"

Eddie stayed quiet a moment, choosing his words. "I've had time tonight, since all this happened, to do some thinking. And I believe Professor Milano lied to me about the fire that was started from a stray cigarette that night in '68. I don't think there was a fire. I think the money in that armored truck, the millions of dollars intended to finance the future of Irondale Enterprises, survived the accident that night and was indeed used to build a multinational manufacturing corporation. Why do I believe that? Because *before* our trip tonight, Irondale had a huge R and D facility located here, just south of the institute. I couldn't help noticing, since my return, that it's no longer there. In fact, do any of you even remember a company called Irondale Enterprises?"

Those in the group looked at each other. Some said no; most just shook their heads.

"We changed that," Eddie said. "What the professor and I did three hours ago—what he forced me to help him do—changed history. I'm not proud of it. In fact I'm deeply sorry it happened—and I hope that'll factor into any decision that gets made regarding regulations on time travel, after tomorrow's announcement. But I'll tell you something else, too: I'm not nearly as sorry as Professor Milano would've been."

"Why?" Dr. Walcott said.

"Because most of the products Irondale Enterprises developed and manufactured were electronic devices. Primarily medical equipment—ventilators, prosthetics, dialysis units, monitors…"

"Monitors?"

"Pacemakers," Eddie said.

Another silence. Many of the attendees had known Thomas Milano well and were aware of his heart trouble.

Walcott was frowning. "Are you saying—"

"I'm saying that there are many things we don't yet know about time travel. But Professor Milano felt that whatever governs it doesn't change things right away—he said it might wait until there's no chance that certain actions cannot be reversed. As long as he and I were there, in 1968, there was a possibility that we would do something to right our wrongs, to restore everything to its proper balance. Dig up and return the money we'd hidden, maybe, or tell someone else where it was. But we didn't. And when the point arrived that we could not reverse the things that we'd done—in other words, when the professor pressed that button to close the door and prepare to leave—it happened."

"*What* happened?" Walcott said.

"His pacemaker and defibrillator disappeared. I suspect that they were among the very first produced by Irondale Enterprises, which was itself a pioneer in that field. In that instant, all their wires, electrodes, and pulse generators vanished, leaving only the incisions made to install them. Death wasn't instantaneous, but—considering the stress of the moment—it didn't take long."

This was followed by a deep silence. After several minutes and a dozen muted conversations among the attendees of the meeting, Dr. Walcott cleared his throat and said, "It is my belief that the presence of the weapon in Professor Milano's hand confirms Mr. Hollister's claim that he was an unwilling participant in this…endeavor. If nothing is found in the professor's autopsy to contradict the other things we've heard here, I suggest as chairman of this body that we label this an accidental death and pursue the matter no further. I also put forward the official motion that we proceed as planned with the announcement of the TimeLiner, but that we restrict any official operations of the device until further study. Do I hear a second?"

12:20 a.m., October 26

The parking lot was almost empty when Eddie left the building through the side entrance and trudged to his car. Even though he was bone-tired, he paused a moment at the driver's-side door and looked out at the mostly flat fields south of the institute grounds. As he'd mentioned in the meeting, there were no buildings there now, nothing to indicate the vast Irondale complex that had filled that area in the version of 2018 he'd lived in a few hours ago. It was a little overwhelming to think that he and Professor Milano were the reason all that was gone.

He couldn't help wondering how many lives they had affected. Other patients in this current 2018 had cardiac pacemakers, of course—technology had not come to a halt as a result of tonight's actions—but theirs would've been manufactured by places other than Irondale. The professor had been unlucky in that regard. Or maybe, Eddie thought, that was a form of justice.

Which made him think again about the upcoming announcement of the Machine. When would its use be authorized, he wondered, in light of his and Milano's (mis)adventure? Journeys into the future were of course possible—but he suspected that trips to the past would be rare, and tightly regulated.

He sighed, clicked his remote, and opened the car door. One last time he looked south, at the picnic area where all this had started, at the perimeter road beside it, and then, beyond those, at the small hill the professor said had remained unchanged for all these years.

It was still unchanged, in this latest version of the present. Grassed over, yes, but still there, like the iron bridge and the stream and the cemetery. Before adjourning the meeting a few minutes ago, Dr. Walcott had stated his plan to assign a team of excavators to dig up the entire north side of that little hill, to find whatever remained—if anything—of the fortune the two time travelers had hidden there. Some ten million dollars, after subtracting the million or so that had been left to burn. Walcott had suggested that the proceeds, when and if found, should be presented to the institute.

Eddie couldn't help smiling. What Walcott didn't know was that Eddie hadn't told them the whole story. For one thing, he had omitted the blackmail issue—why advertise his long-ago shoplifting fiasco? So much easier to say the professor had threatened to kill him and his family—and the second thing was that the excavation team would find nothing at the base of that hill. That part of Eddie's story had been an outright lie.

The money, safely sealed in those plastic bags, was buried in that last grave on the edge of the cemetery, the one that had been freshly covered that night in 1968. Where better to hide something that needed to remain hidden for the next fifty years?

Eddie climbed into his car, started the engine, and headed for home, and some much-needed sleep. And after that? Well, he didn't plan to attend the big event later this morning—in fact, he didn't plan to come in to work at all today. But he did plan to visit Home Depot. He needed to buy a shovel.

Eddie had already decided not to keep all the money. Most would go to charity. He hoped to find one that was connected somehow to the once-promising Irondale Corporation.

But he would keep some of it. The professor had been right about that. Everyone needs a nest egg. And besides…

He'd still like to see Hawaii.

John M. Floyd's work has appeared in more than 250 different publications, including *Alfred Hitchcock's Mystery Magazine, Ellery Queen's Mystery Magazine, The Strand Magazine, The Saturday Evening Post, Mississippi Noir*, and two editions of *The Best American Mystery Stories*. A former Air Force captain and IBM systems engineer, John is also an Edgar Award nominee, a three-time Derringer Award winner, and a recipient of the Edward D. Hoch Memorial Golden Derringer Award for lifetime achievement. His seventh book, *The Barrens*, was released in late 2018. Visit John at www.johnmfloyd.com.

THE DEALEY PARADOX

Brendan DuBois

The weather is perfectly gorgeous this morning near Dealey Plaza in downtown Dallas, on November 22, 1963. Monroe is checking his antique Timex wristwatch as he gently pushes through the crowds gathered on Elm Street, seeing it's 12:05 p.m. and he has plenty of time.

Among the many things he finds amazing—besides actually living and surviving in this trip back, knowing he's the first human to actually try the damn thing—is the smell of the city. It seems like every other person is puffing on a cigarette or a cigar, and the stench from the exhaust from nearby vehicles is enough to nearly make him stop and have fits of coughing. His poor long-deceased mom, a historian and environmentalist, would probably freeze in place if she were here, horrified at what she was smelling and seeing.

But he presses on.

The crowds are impatient, laughing, talking, some clapping, as they expectantly wait for the presidential motorcade to slowly come this way on its trip to the nearby Trade Mart, but Monroe has a mission in mind, to get to the Texas School Book Depository and up to the sixth floor before the deadly time of 12:30 p.m. finally slips into reality.

Time, he thinks.

It's all about time, to prevent one of the world's most famous crimes.

* * * *

If Monroe were to ever confide in another about what his life meant—which would never happen, and will never happen—he would blame his mother. And not in the "I became a serial killer because Mom made me ate my peas" kind of blame.

No, poor old Mom had been obsessed by JFK and his promise, and legacy, and how he had been killed...for nothing.

As his retired historian mom had said once, in hospice and with a biography of JFK that she had earlier written clasped in her wrinkled shaking hands, "It all fell apart then. The incompetence of the Secret Service, the

FBI, the Dallas police. The Warren Commission never really learning about the Mafia and CIA connections. President Johnson getting us into Vietnam and his lying, which led to the riots, the demonstrations, Nixon…more and more lies, more and more cover-ups, more and more wars, from the Persian Gulf to Spratly Islands…"

He had checked her vitals and stroked her hot forehead and said, "Mom, it was decades ago. And he was just a man. A man with vision, strength, and lots of faults. But still…just a man."

Mom had smiled and coughed and coughed. Her room had large windows overlooking a fully blooming garden, with lots of flowers, bushes, and shrubbery, and the distant peaks of the White Mountains. Once she had whispered to him, "Don't tell the staff, but early morning, before anyone gets up, deer come in and nibble on the plants. Oh, there's such beauty out there…"

And she had said, "Ah, but when he was killed, the innocence and dreams were killed. Maybe the innocence and dreams would have died at some point…but they shouldn't have died then, not because of a loser with a rifle."

Then, maybe loopy because of her mind slipping some, or the painkillers doing their business a bit too efficiently, she had looked to him and whispered, "Fix it, Son. Fix it."

And damn if he hadn't said, "Mom, I will."

* * * *

The noise of the crowds is getting louder, and Monroe is finding it harder and harder to move through the packed sidewalks to the Texas School Book Depository up ahead. His clothes feel funny and are itching him something awful, and he wonders who the dead man was who once wore these clothes. It had taken some effort and time, scouring through thrift shops and flea markets, before he was able to find a suit that would make him blend in with the average male in this time and place so many decades in the past. Monroe had been tempted to go online, of course, but he didn't want to get the attention of any of the very curious and paranoid security staff who worked at Lawrence Livermore Labs, where Monroe is currently employed.

So he had purchased the suit, the white shirt, the skinny black necktie and very uncomfortable shoes at thrift stores and yard sales, but in the hour he's spent in November 1963, Monroe realizes his mistake: no hat.

Most of the men here are wearing some kind of hat, from straw hats to regular dark felt hats with narrow brims, and he's mentally kicking himself, wondering what else he might have forgotten.

He slips a hand into the right pocket of his smelly suit jacket, reassuring himself that his metal folding combat knife, used in the field by Special

Forces, was still in its place.

It is.

It's 12:10 p.m.

He's less than twenty feet away from the door of the plain brick building that later today would become one of the most famous buildings in the world.

He squeezes the knife.

Not today.

* * * *

And the funny thing is, Monroe is not a scientist. He's a numbers man, has always been a numbers man. Except for a brief stint in the US Army—the draft had returned with no college exemptions—he has spent his life in numbers, beginning with graduating near the top of his class at Wharton, and then entering government service.

Based on his military experience and some summer internships at the Department of Defense, Monroe had begun working his skills on the black part of the government's annual budget—the secret part. There were many military and defense-related programs that operated in the dark and without congressional oversight, and Monroe became skilled at keeping his mouth shut and floating money around so that favored highly classified programs received necessary funding without some senator or congressperson getting wind of it.

And all the while, seeing up close the various black-budget programs—particle-beam weapons systems; unauthorized, manned military space transportation; drones the size of houseflies; and even genetic-modification experiments on various primates—he had kept his eyes wide open as to what he saw, looking for opportunities.

Looking for evidence of time travel, even though the thought of it was so outrageous he couldn't dare say it aloud, even to himself.

During one of the very few times he'd brought a woman home to his condo in Arlington, Virginia, his guest had spotted a framed black-and-white photo of a man from the 1940s, wearing rimless glasses, an ugly wide necktie, and a suit jacket with wide lapels, his thick dark hair cut high and tight.

His guest had looked up at the photo on a bookshelf and said, "Who's that? Your grandfather?"

"No, that's Perry Spencer, a scientist from the 1940s. You should know him."

"Why?" she had asked.

"Because you use his invention nearly every day."

"Really? What's that?"

"The microwave."

She had laughed and he had said, "And you know what? He invented it by mistake. He was working at MIT in 1945, building magnetrons to be used in radar equipment. One day he walked by a magnetron with a chocolate bar in his pocket, and it melted from the equipment. More research later, the microwave was developed. By accident."

She had laughed again and had a wonderful night—and no more—and he'd never told her that what he was looking for in his black-budget work (all to prevent the biggest crime of the last century) were accidents, things that didn't fit in.

And more than a year ago, he had found one, in a budget line item that didn't make sense:

Guinea pigs.

* * * *

Now he is so very close to the building entrance, his hand in his coat pocket, still holding on to the combat knife. No pistol, no firearm, nothing that could prevent him from getting to his target if he encountered a police officer. Nope, just carrying a simple knife to slit the throat of a twenty-four-year-old loser who had in his hands and twisted mind the ability to change the world and its future.

In his years of research following Mom's death, he had talked to a JFK assassination expert, and Monroe had posed the question: Who had killed JFK?

"Oswald, by himself," the old man had said.

"But...the cover-up, the old secrets that have come out..."

The old man had shaken his head. "It was Oswald. But there was a cover-up, and it does go back to the CIA."

Confused, Monroe had said, "I don't understand."

The old man explained, "There's no hard evidence the CIA was behind the killing...but there is evidence that the CIA knew of Oswald's visit to Mexico City several weeks before the assassination. There it's believed he met up with a Cuban intelligence operative, who told Oswald—a fan of Castro—that JFK and his brother were working to assassinate Castro. Classic blowback."

"What?"

"Blowback. When an operation turns around and strikes you instead of the target. JFK was trying to assassinate Castro via the CIA and the Mob. The Cubans knew. They told Oswald...out of spite, a drunken comment, a slip of the tongue...and Oswald went back to Dallas, and killed JFK to save Castro. That's the cover-up. Governments don't do cover-ups to keep secrets from being revealed. They do cover-ups to prevent embarrassments from being known."

"So if Oswald wasn't there that day?"

The old man had shrugged. "JFK would have lived."

Will have lived, Monroe now thinks. Almost there.

And as he walks he's remembering one government secret and embarrassment that had been revealed to him.

Guinea pigs.

* * * *

The program administrator at Lawrence Livermore had been embarrassed when Monroe pressed her about an unexpected budget line item.

"Explain to me again how this facility, working with various concept devices involving particle weapons, needs to have dozens of guinea pigs delivered on a weekly basis," Monroe said.

She shrugged and pretended to shuffle some papers around her neat desk in a part of Lawrence Livermore that took two keycards and a retina scan in order to gain admittance.

"It's part of the development process," she said.

"No, it's not. I've checked your purchase orders, your order requests for the past year. For the past nine months, your section had four guinea pigs delivered every week. Then, last month, your request went from four to twenty."

The program administrator didn't say a word, so Monroe pressed on. "Why does your section need so many lab animals?"

"I'm not in a position to answer."

"Then put yourself in the position."

"I don't think you have the correct clearance."

"You'd be wrong. So give me an answer—one that's real and verifiable—or I'll leave here, and in a month, your budget will be zeroed out. Don't screw with me."

Monroe couldn't explain it, but he knew he was close. That this government scientist in front of him had the answers…and he was going to do everything and anything to make her talk.

She finally sighed. "It was something that we didn't expect. We were having an in-house demonstration of a possible particle-beam weapon. A guinea pig was eventually used as a test subject. It was…it disappeared, as projected."

The program administrator paused and sighed once more. "Then…it was back in the facility. At first, we thought the creature had slipped off the test platform before the weapon was fired. We tried again. The guinea pig disappeared."

"And it returned again?"

She nodded. "Yes. We've been…repeating the experiment on a continuous basis since then. We need a number of guinea pigs because…they don't last long with the instrumentation we install in them as part of the experiments."

"What are the results?"

"This will show you our best result so far." The woman swiveled the screen on her desk computer and tapped a few keys. A video appeared, showing a room jammed with different types of electronic equipment, computers, cables, and display screens.

The screen went black.

The video returned. It was jumpy, moving, and it seemed to be filmed from ground level.

"Where is this coming from?" Monroe asked.

"Surgically implanted video-recording system, on top of the subject's skull."

The view was of grass. Trees. The blue sky.

"What am I seeing?" Monroe asked.

"Watch," she said.

A few seconds passed.

Shadows appeared.

Then humans.

Carrying spears. Wearing clothing made from hides. The people were dark skinned.

Monroe took in a deep breath.

"Looks like Native Americans," he said.

"That's correct," the woman said. "Based on their weapons, clothing, and stature, it seems that these Native Americans are part of the Ohlone people. They resided here in the Livermore area."

Monroe stared and stared at the screen. "What year is this?"

The woman softly said, "Not sure. But…pre-Columbian for sure."

"You don't know?"

"Not at the moment. We're barely understanding how this process works, why it works, and when it works. Just the physics and computation involved in trying to determine how the animal traveled back and landed in the same geographical spot is challenging."

"What do you need to make improvements?"

"Another ten million. At least."

Monroe nodded. "I'll get you fifty."

I knew it, he thought. I knew it. If he looked hard enough, he'd find scientists conducting the research he needed.

I'm going to do it, Mom. I'm going to save him.

* * * *

Now.

So close.

Monroe checks his Timex one more time.

It's 12:16 p.m.

Exactly 12:30 p.m. is when the first shot was fired from the sniper's nest up on the sixth floor. That's what all of the history books, films, and commentaries agree on.

But Monroe is about to change history, to stop this horrible crime.

When 12:30 p.m. comes around this time, Oswald will be lying on the wooden floor, blood gushing out of his severed throat.

Monroe knows he can do it, know he can easily overpower the slight twenty-four-year-old man, and he steps forward, going up the steps to the Texas School Book Depository—

And his foot travels down.

Down.

He's missed the step.

He's falling!

* * * *

Now he's sitting.

He doesn't know where he is.

Or how he got here.

He tries to stand up.

He can't move.

He can breathe, he can blink his eyes, lick his lips, but he's frozen in place.

The room…it's dimly lit, and he appears to be sitting in some sort of soft chair, but one that can't be seen.

Around him is darkness, and it looks like the light source is right in front of him.

A pleasant woman's voice speaks to him.

"Sorry for the shock," she says. "I trust you weren't injured."

Monroe tries to say something. He can't do it. His heart is pounding so hard it's like a continual thrumming sensation underneath his breastbone.

The soft voice says, "You won't be harmed. You won't be injured. You'll be returning soon to the time and place from whence you came."

He chews his tongue, trying to work up some saliva to moisten his mouth, and he says, "Who are you?"

"I'm afraid we don't have enough time to discuss that matter. And you don't have the necessary background to understand."

He tries to move again. No joy.

"But where am I?"

"A place."

"I know that," he shouts out. "What kind of place?"

And the voice says again, "I'm afraid we don't have enough time to discuss that matter. And you don't have the necessary background to understand."

He tries to move again. It's like being stuck in place with soft, unyielding taffy.

"How did you know I was from away?" he asks. "Were my clothes wrong? My haircut? My shoes?"

"No," she says. "We have...detecting means. You are different from anyone else here at this time and place."

Monroe's mind calms down. "Okay...I see what you mean. My body... the normal radiation level it contains must be widely different from the population of 1963. Among other things."

"Very good." The woman sounds pleased. "Not many grasp that so quickly."

"Many? You mean others? Others have been here?"

"Yes."

"But...damn you...I'm trying to prevent a crime! The worst crime of the last century! I'm trying to save the goddamn world! What gives you the right to prevent me or anyone else to do it?"

"The world does." The tone of the woman's voice changes, almost reproachful. "This is the Dallas of your world at this time."

And before his eyes, a three-dimensional overhead view of Dallas appears, slowly rotating to show buildings, moving vehicles, and even tiny dots of people walking on the sidewalks.

"And a century after Kennedy lived and was not slain, this is Dallas."

He suddenly feels sick.

The view drastically changes. The office buildings, the highways, the bridge spans...are gone. All that's there are broken piles of debris: smashed buildings, collapsed highway spans, broken roads. And in the distance, a flattened area that looks like a sheet of dirty gray glass.

"And another hundred years after that."

Grass and brush is growing among the debris. There are two faint smoke plumes, where huddled groups of what looks to be people are gathered around the small fires.

"What...what happened?" Monroe finally stammers out.

"The politician named Kennedy lived. Other politicians followed. War came. The few survivors who were able to live and thrive elsewhere, they were able to go back and change what happened on November twenty-second, nineteen hundred and sixty-three, common era. His survival...that is the crime *we* are preventing."

"But…how?"

"Does it matter?" the voice says. "Your time here is almost over. You will be shunted back to your original time."

"I'll come back!"

"And you will return here. Others have tried. Others have failed."

"I…I'll tell someone else. They'll come back at another time…kill Oswald as a child, or when he was in the Marine Corps."

The woman's voice—some form of artificial intelligence, Monroe is sure—says, "When you depart, nothing from this trip returns with you. Nothing. Including memories."

Monroe is about to say something else, when he's in a familiar room.

The one at Livermore, from where he had secretly and illegally departed for 1963.

A group of men are there, watching him. Some are federal law-enforcement officers, stationed as security at Lawrence Livermore.

The supervisor he first dealt with steps forward.

"Before you're arrested," she says, "what did you see? What did you do?"

Monroe struggles to say something. He feels like he's woken up from an extraordinarily detailed and vibrant dream, and the memory of it is quickly slipping away, like an ice cube being held in his hand during a hot August day.

"I can't remember," Monroe says, feeling deep sorrow strike him, sorrow made even worse because he can't figure out why he's so sad.

The administrator gestures to the closest officer. "Well, I'm certain you'll have plenty of time to think about it. Years and years."

Wait, he thinks, just wait for a moment.

"Tell me, please, one thing," he says. "When did Lyndon Johnson become president?"

The administrator smiles, shakes his head. "What is this, *Jeopardy*? November 1963. Come along now."

Now he knows the source of his sorrow.

He has failed, though he doesn't know how.

* * * *

But the administrator was wrong about years and years, for those in charge of that section of Lawrence Livermore Laboratories decide they don't want to prosecute Monroe for everything that happened because they don't want to be embarrassed.

Monroe finds that extremely ironic.

So he is sent away for some months on an unpaid sabbatical as a punishment for his "misuse of government resources," and the first place he goes is his mother's grave, in a rural part of New Hampshire.

He lays a single rose upon her headstone, and then sits down on the grass.

"Sorry, Mom. I failed.... Kennedy was still murdered back them. Somehow, I didn't succeed."

He sits there for long minutes and then gets up.

Monroe takes in the gentle landscape of the cemetery, the unpolluted bright blue sky, and the lush green of the near woods and grassland, and even the hard beauty of the near mountain peaks.

He can't explain it, but for some reason, he now doesn't feel like he failed.

Brendan DuBois is the *New York Times* bestselling author of twenty-two novels, including *The First Lady* and *The Cornwalls Are Gone* (March 2019), coauthored with James Patterson. Brendan's short fiction has appeared in *Playboy*, *The Saturday Evening Post*, *Ellery Queen's Mystery Magazine*, *Alfred Hitchcock's Mystery Magazine*, and numerous anthologies, including *The Best American Mystery Stories of the Century*, and *The Best American Noir of the Century*. His stories have thrice won him the Shamus Award from the Private Eye Writers of America, two Barry awards, a Derringer Award, the Ellery Queen Readers Award, and three Edgar Award nominations from Mystery Writers of America. He is also a *Jeopardy!* game show champion. Learn more at www.BrendanDuBois.com.

THE CASE OF THE MISSING PHYSICIST

James Blakey

Captain Nemo.

I circled her name in the paper. They'd been sandbagging that mare all season. Billy Bruck, a groomsman who owed me a favor, had tipped me off that her owner was ready to cash in. I slipped into the phone booth, dropped a nickel, and asked the operator for Klondike 5-2368.

"Yeah?" Joey answered, nasal as ever.

"What are the odds on Captain Nemo in the fourth at Keystone?" I asked.

"Who's this?"

"Sturgis. Mike Sturgis."

Joey roared. "Mikey, Mikey. You still owe me money."

"C'mon, Joey. Give a guy a chance to get even. I haven't stiffed you yet."

"Okay. I'll take the bet. That gluebag's going off at eight-to-one."

"Put me down for a double sawbuck. To win."

"Got it. And Mikey, win or lose, we settle up by Saturday."

I hung up without replying.

I exited the phone booth and walked the ten steps to my current office: the corner booth of Bob's Diner, Roxborough's finest eating establishment. Clients were scarce, forcing me to cut expenses. Sure, the Formica was chipped, but it came with a window seat, the best cup of joe in Philly, and now a dame, decked out in red, sitting across from my grilled cheese.

"Mr. Sturgis?" Her blue eyes were the color of the summer sky before a thunderstorm, but the blond hair came straight from a peroxide factory. "I hope you do not mind. The waitress pointed me to your booth." She flashed a smile that could light up Shibe Park, but her speech was stilted and the inflections all wrong.

"Not at all, Miss?"

"Nancy Hainsworth."

"So, Miss Hainsworth, what can I do for you?"

"Call me, Nancy, please." Again, with the smile. "I want you to locate my father. He is missing."

"It's not often I'm asked to find people who aren't missing, Nancy." I pulled a notepad from my jacket pocket. "And your father's name?"

"Dr. R. C.—Robert Charles—Hainsworth. He is professor of physics at the University of Pennsylvania. Very highly regarded. You may have heard of him."

I shook my head. "I'm more of a chemistry man."

"He is not at his home. I asked about the university. No one reports seeing or hearing from him in weeks."

"When's the last time you saw you father?"

"Four years: 1946."

I raised an eyebrow.

"My father and I are not close. I live in Washington and recently became engaged. I thought this would be a good time to reconcile."

"What about your mother?"

"She died when I was nine."

"I'm sorry."

"Thank you."

"Any siblings?"

"None."

"What about the folks at Penn? Aren't they concerned that your father's missing his classes?"

She shook her head. "He does not teach. He is research professor."

"Do you have a photo of him?"

She pushed a snap across the table. Fancy black-and-red half-moon manicure. Slim fingers. No ring.

I picked up the photo. With his crazy shock of white hair and thick glasses, the professor could have come straight from Central Casting.

"Will you take the case?"

"I charge fifty a day." Let's see how desperately she wanted to reconcile with her *father*.

She didn't blink. "That is acceptable."

"Plus expenses."

"Also acceptable."

The real test. "In advance."

She fiddled around in her purse and pulled out three crisp fifties.

I squinted at General Grant and rubbed the corners of the bill. No smudging. "Looks like we're in business."

She handed me a slip of paper. "That is his address."

"Did you live there?"

"Excuse me?"

"Is this the house you grew up in?"

She paused for a moment. "Yes."

"How can I reach you?"

"I'm staying downtown at the Bellevue-Stratford."

"I'll get right on the case." I jammed the bills into my wallet.

"Thank you." She rose from the table, her skirt swishing as she walked out the door. Whatever her game, my client had amazing legs.

* * * *

The drive to the Hainsworth house took me through rural Chester County with its rolling green hills and pastures filled with horses and cows.

At the thought of horses, I snapped on the radio.

"And now the results of the fourth at Keystone," the announcer blared. "The winner, Youngstown Kid, paid seventeen-forty, five-eighty, and three-twenty. In second, Magnetic Pole, six-even and three-fifty. And third, My Fair Dixie, four-ten."

My nag didn't even show.

I found the house: a two-story white colonial set back a furlong's length from the road. No neighbors for at least a mile. I stopped at the mailbox and grabbed a handful of letters and bills. My first felony of the day, and it was a federal beef. I pulled in the driveway and parked my Ford in front of the attached garage.

I knocked on the door. No answer. Turned the knob and pushed. Locked. Peering inside, I saw a formal dining room. Circling the house counterclockwise, I stopped at the garage, wiped grime from the window, and spied a powder-blue late-thirties Buick Century. Around back another locked door and a vegetable garden with some tempting tomatoes. I glimpsed through more windows, didn't see anything interesting, and returned to the front.

Figuring the owner was an absentminded professor-type, I lifted the welcome mat. Aha! A brass key.

Unlocked the door and pushed it open. "Hello?" I stepped into the foyer and slipped my trilby on the hat rack, next to a black porkpie. From the foyer I moved to the sitting room. Bookshelves lined the wall, filled with science texts, half in German. Even the English titles I couldn't make sense of. A thin layer of dust coated the floor. No footprints. I found the professor's study (and more dust) and rifled his desk. The last entry for his calendar was on the twenty-fifth, almost a month ago. I opened the mail that I grabbed outside, sorting through bills, bank statements, and letters from colleagues. Nothing to indicate where he might be. No photo of "Nancy" on the desk.

In the kitchen, no plates in the sink, and the garbage was empty. In the fridge I found a bottle of milk, popped the top, and sniffed. Sour.

Upstairs. One bedroom. All made up. The other rooms might have once been bedrooms, but like the rest of the house, they contained nothing but more books and dust. No one had been here in weeks.

I descended the stairs and turned into the hallway. Footsteps behind me. Before I could whirl, a blow struck the back of my head. The world spun, and icy darkness swallowed me up.

* * * *

Woke sprawled on the floor with my head throbbing as if I'd gone the full fifteen with the Rock from Brockton. I rubbed the back of my skull. The lump was the size of Mount Pocono. My wallet lay on the floor next to me. The three fifties were still there. Robbery wasn't the motive. Whoever clubbed me wanted to know who I was.

A set of footprints in the dust led to and from a door I figured for the basement. Judging from their size, my attacker and I were equally matched, and I wanted an advantage. With my piece residing in the front display case of Gleason's Pawn Shop, I searched for a weapon and retrieved a fireplace poker from the den.

I descended creaking steps to a finished basement. Blackboards, covering three walls, were filled with chalk scribbling: numbers, letters (some Greek), and a bunch of unrecognizable symbols. Shelves lined the fourth wall with relays, spools of wire, vacuum tubes, and more. No attacker and no place to hide.

A worktable covered with beakers and flasks stood in the center of the room. On it a notebook lay open. I flipped through the pages. Might as well be hieroglyphics.

The footprints led to the wall at the far end of the basement. Between the blackboards was a pair of sliding silver doors that could lead to an elevator. Odd, no elevator on the first or second floors. Was my attacker hiding in a subbasement?

I raised the poker and pressed the single button. A chime rang. The doors slid open, but the elevator was empty. Inside was a control panel that could only be designed by a mad scientist. Buttons, dials, displays, readouts, more Greek letters. In all that mess I found a button marked with a down arrow and pressed it.

The lights dimmed and a high-pitched whine filled the air. The elevator rattled, moved sideways, and the bottom of my stomach dropped out. I fell to my knees, gasping for air. The lights returned. A bell rang and the doors opened. I fumbled for the poker, stood on wobbly legs, and stepped out. It looked like the room I had come from.

Same scribbling on the blackboards. Identical notebook on the worktable. It *was* the same room. What a crazy elevator.

Noise coming from above. I snuck up the steps and tiptoed down the hallway. Someone was on the second floor, opening and slamming doors and cabinets, making no effort to be quiet. I hid in a closet as he rumbled down the stairs. Waited for him to pass by, stepped out, and walloped him good with the poker.

He dropped like a tomato can when the fix is in. He wore a cheap gray suit like mine. Must share the same tailor. I rolled him over to get a look at his mug.

He was wearing mine!

* * * *

Not sure how long I stood over what appeared to be my unconscious body. I figured this must be a dream. Or was I on another bender?

I rifled through his—my?—pockets and found a wallet with a City of Philadelphia PI's license in my name and three crisp fifties. I compared one of my bills. The serial numbers matched. The wallet slipped from my shaking hands.

I couldn't catch my breath and slumped to the floor. Must have finally flipped my lid. The guys in the little white suits should be along any minute.

Didn't feel crazy or drunk. But what other explanation could there be? How could I be staring at another me, with the same ID and identical bills? Time Travel? H. G. Wells? That's comic book stuff.

I looked at my watch for a test. Mickey's big hand was on the two and his little hand on the four: 4:10. I checked the right wrist of the fellow on the floor, a lefty like me. Same Mickey Mouse watch: 3:40. Now to break the tie. In Hainsworth's study, I dialed the operator and asked for the time.

"Three forty-one p.m.," the female voice said.

I had traveled thirty minutes into the past.

* * * *

The question wasn't where the professor was, but when. Was he watching Napoleon march across Europe? Or did he travel to the year 2000 with its flying cars and moon colonies?

Me? I'd settle for a copy of tomorrow's *Racing Form*.

Finding the professor was the least of my worries. I couldn't stay here. Or rather, now. I wasn't around when the earlier me woke up. Based on the footprints, it looked like I'd returned to the basement.

Back in the elevator I re-examined the buttons and dials. Last time I pressed down and ended up thirty minutes in the past. Might as well try the opposite. Holding my breath, I pressed up. The doors slid shut and the process repeated: lights dimming, the whining noise, sideways motion, and my stomach doing the jitterbug.

The elevator opened. With the poker in hand I crept up the steps. My unconscious body was no longer on the hallway floor. I called for the time: 4:25, just like my watch read. Back where, or rather when, I belonged.

Car doors slammed outside. Through the window, I spied a man with a scar on his cheek approaching the front door. The wind caught his jacket, revealing a holstered pistol.

I scrambled through the house. At the back door lurked a guy so big, it was like someone stuffed a gorilla into a suit. Armed with only the poker, I couldn't take on both of them. This situation required finesse.

The front door creaked open. I rushed to the foyer and confronted the man. Doing my best impersonation of an upper-crust Main Liner, I asked, "Are you the gentleman from the caterers?"

Scarface gave me a puzzled look.

"Nicolosi Caterers? You need to start setting up now. My guests will be arriving shortly."

"I am not a caterer," he said in a German accent.

"Where are they?" My arms flailed like a windmill. "This is the social event of the season. If this party isn't perfect, I won't be able to show my face in polite society."

"Who are you?" he replied.

"Who am I? Who are you? You're not the caterer. Surely, you can't be part of the band?" I stepped past the confused German and opened the front door. A Plymouth De Luxe boxed me in. "You will have to move your car."

Powerful hands locked around my neck. The gorilla! As I scuffled with him, the sleeve of his jacket pulled back to reveal a stylized SS tattoo. He clamped down and twisted my head until I faced Scarface.

I dropped the accent. "Hey, pal. Leave now and no need to involve the cops." I struggled, but the gorilla's grip was tight as a boa constrictor. "You know you're trespassing."

Scarface grabbed my wallet from my jacket. "As are you, Herr Private Detective Sturgis. I presume you are searching for the professor."

"Professor?" I shrugged as best I could with my neck in a German vice. "What professor? I'm looking for a missing cat. A Siamese with one blue eye and one green. Very temperamental. Belongs to the wife of Commissioner Hurley. Do you know the commissioner? He's s—"

Pow! Scarface laid a right cross on my jaw.

You're going to pay for that, Fritz.

"You are searching for Herr Professor Hainsworth, yes?"

No way I can win this one. "You got me. I'm looking for the professor. But this place is a bust. No one's been here in forever. There's a month of dust on the floor, and the mailbox was full. Now, how about easing up a bit?"

Scarface nodded to the gorilla, who released his hold.

I straightened my tie and smoothed my jacket.

"What do you know of Herr Professor's work?"

"Nothing. The house is filled with textbooks, but I can't even understand the titles." Scarface smiled at this. "I didn't find anything he was working on. No notes or journals."

"And who is your client?"

"You're not going to like this." I frowned. "I can't tell you. It's a matter of professional ethics."

"Hans." Scarface nodded at the big guy.

Hans slugged me in the gut.

I gasped for air. "Said you wouldn't like it."

The big guy raised his fist again.

I held up my hand. "I've always been flexible in the ethics department. Under the circumstances"—I glared at Hans—"I can tell you that his daughter hired me."

Another punch from Hans dropped me to my knees.

"The professor doesn't have a daughter," Scarface said.

Doubled over, I said, "I was afraid of that."

"Hans."

The gorilla loomed over me.

"Wait, I'm telling the truth. She claimed she was Nancy Hainsworth, the professor's daughter. But it didn't add up. She said she was engaged, but no ring. I was suspicious from the start."

"Yet you took the case?"

I stood and shrugged. "She paid my fee. In cash."

"Describe this Nancy Hainsworth."

"Blue eyes. Blond hair so bright it'll make you squint. Great legs. A real dish."

"Accent?"

"That's funny. She didn't have one. Almost like she was trying to cover one up."

Hans and Scarface conferred back and forth in German. I caught the name Marta and the word *Russisch*.

Great, not only are these has-been Nazis looking to give Hitler a do-over at Stalingrad, there's Nancy or Marta or whoever working for the Commies. They'd love to turn back the clock and develop the Atomic Bomb first.

"Look," I said. "Considering the circumstances, I'm willing to take on new clients. I have a pretty good idea where the professor is."

"Where?" Scarface asked.

"Not so fast. I get fifty dollars a day, plus expenses."

Scarface pulled out a Luger and pointed it at me. "Tell me and I will let you live."

So much for my fee. "Pretty sure he's got an apartment in University City, near the campus. A place where he likes to meet the ladies."

"How do you know this?"

"I'm a private detective. It's what I do."

"Where is this apartment?"

"I don't have an exact address, but I know the city. You don't. You beat what I know out of me and go stumbling around looking for the professor, you'll never find him. But you'll attract a lot of unwanted attention."

"What do you propose?" he asked.

"We all go together. I deliver the professor, you release me."

Scarface and Hans stepped away to confer. From their tone they weren't likely to take my offer. Time for Plan B. Run outside to my car and drive off? Doubtful. Most likely end up with a bullet in the back.

I could try making a mad dash for the elevator. Go back in time before they show up and get the drop on them. The problem was the future Fourth Reich stood between me and the basement.

Scarface and Hans ended their conversation. "We don't trust you. Give us your best idea where the professor is, and we will search for him ourselves."

I didn't answer.

Scarface raised the Luger and aimed at my chest. "Tell me."

Plan C. "Okay. Real truth. Professor Hainsworth is here in the house."

"What? Where?"

"In the basement. Come on. I'll show you." I pushed past the pair, but Hans collared me.

"Not so fast," Scarface said. "I'll take a look. Hans, keep him here."

Hans grinned, while twisting my right arm almost out of its socket.

With gun in hand, Scarface descended the steps.

One-on-one now. Time to break loose and make for my car. I'd wait another twenty seconds until Scarface was exploring the basement, stomp on Hans's instep, twist out of his grasp, and head for the door. Okay, this was it. Now or ne—

"Hans!" Scarface shouted from the basement. "Come down here. Bring the detective."

Hans squeezed my neck and dragged me to the top of the stairs. "Go."

I shuffled down the steps, trying to come up with another stall. Maybe I could maneuver myself near the machine, jump in, and close the doors before they plugged me.

As I neared the bottom of the steps, I saw Scarface on the other side of the room with his hands up. A guy was holding a gun on him. A guy who looked just like me.

I squinted. It *was* me. But an older version. A future me.

"Shhh." He raised a finger to his lips.

I raced across the room and picked up Scarface's Luger from the floor.

I met Hans as he rumbled down the steps and marched him over to his pal.

"Is talking with you going to destroy the fabric of the universe?" I asked Future Guy.

"Relax," he said. "This has all happened before."

Scarface glanced from me to Future Guy and back. "It works! You've used it and it works. We are willing to pay. We have gold. We will make you very rich men. Just release us and give us the machine."

"No sale," Future Guy told Scarface. To me he said, "Tie their hands behind their backs while I cover you."

"You are making a big mistake," Scarface said.

"Gag him, too."

Once I had them bound and gagged, we led the Germans up the steps and out of the house. We loaded them into the Plymouth, and I tied their feet together.

"There's a service station down the road a couple of miles," Future Guy said. "We'll dump these clowns there and call the sheriff."

Future Guy drove the Plymouth, while I followed in my Ford. We pulled into the closed service station, parked around back, and both got out the cars. In the daylight I got a better look at him. His suit was expensive, custom-tailored, not off the rack. Lines in his face. A few gray hairs. The beginning of a paunch. He must be ten, fifteen years older.

"When did you come from?" I asked.

"That's not important right now. We need to get these Germans off the playing board."

I nodded. "Also Nancy or Marta or whoever is some sort of a Russian agent."

"Way ahead of you. Remember, I've been through this before. I tipped Lt. Callahan down at the Red Squad. He should have her on ice about now. Go ahead and drop a nickel on the Germans."

"Why me?"

"Cause that's what happened last time."

Couldn't argue with that. I found a pay phone around front and asked the operator to connect me to the Sheriff's Department.

"Deputy Fowler," a bored voice said.

"I've got two Nazi war criminals waiting to be picked up."

"Stop with the gags. This line is for official business."

"No joke. You'll probably get a bonus or a commendation for bringing them in."

"Okay, where're you at?"

"Ludman's Service Station. Corner of Old Kennett Pike and Brandywine Creek Road. Got them tied up around back in a green Plymouth."

"Yeah, I know the place. Your name?"

"Just a concerned citizen."

"Wait I nee—"

I hung up.

Back at the Plymouth, I gave the Nazis the good news. "Cops will be here to pick you up soon. I hope you've enjoyed your stay in our country. Don't come back." I loosened Scarface's gag. "There's one last thing I need to tell you."

He glared. "What is that?"

"This." I socked him in the jaw with a right cross.

* * * *

In the basement, I stared at the silver doors of the time machine. "Whatever happened to the professor?"

"You'll see." Future Guy shrugged. "Guess I should be getting back to my time."

"And when is that?"

"That's not really important."

I was getting pretty steamed that he wasn't giving me any straight answers. "Actually it is. Because at some point in the future, I have to come back and rescue myself. How will I know when?"

"Trust me, you will." He reached into his pocket and handed me an envelope.

"What this?" I slipped it open. Twenties and fifties.

"Youngstown Kid to win." He grinned. "I switched the bet. You're all settled up with Joey."

I counted the bills, over a thousand dollars. An idea crossed my mind. "This is a nice score. We could make some easy money playing the ponies, betting college football, maybe get sophisticated and try the stock market."

"But we won't."

"Why not?"

"Because I already lived it and I didn't do it, so I know you won't."

I fumed. I wasn't some puppet. My fate wasn't predestined. I made my own decisions.

"You're thinking you're not a puppet."

"Stop that."

Future Guy sighed. "Okay, you want a better reason. You don't want to attract any attention to the time machine. We've already got Nazis and Reds looking for this thing. Someone even worse could come along. Remember freezing our ass off in St. Vith? You want that to be all for nothing?"

He was right. I was being selfish. Needed to think about the big picture. "Yeah, damn Nazis and Reds."

"Damned Nazis anyway," a female voice said, her Russian accent no longer stilted. Standing on the steps, Nancy, amazing legs and all, held a gun on us.

I nodded. *"Miss Hainsworth."*

She clicked her heels in salute. "You may call me Major Varenakova, GRU. But you suspected that. How fortunate that American police officers are not so clever as American private detectives. And I offer my gratitude for flushing out and eliminating the German competition." She looked at us back and forth and squinted. "The professor did make a time machine and it works, yes?"

"I don't know what you're talking about," I said. "This is my brother, Mark."

"Spare me your protestations and hand over your guns. You first." She pointed her pistol at me.

As I reached in my jacket, Future Guy went for his gun. But the major was too quick, a regular Russian Annie Oakley. She fired twice before he could raise his weapon. He fell to the floor with a thud. Before I could retrieve the Luger, she had me covered again.

"Your gun, very slowly, unless you want to join your *brother*."

"No, I don't." One dirt nap was enough for the both of us. I pulled the gun out and dropped it on the floor.

She gathered up the weapons and slipped them in her purse. "Now, show me the machine."

I said nothing. My eyes fixed on Future Guy, Future Me, dead on the floor. His empty eyes staring back at me.

She cocked the gun. "You will tell me."

I swallowed hard and remained silent.

She aimed at my left knee. "I don't have to kill you all at once, Mr. Sturgis. A series of gunshots in strategically chosen body parts would prove to be quite the motivator."

I grimaced. "Fine. It's right here." I pointed to the silver doors between the blackboards.

"I searched this house a month ago and walked right past it." She laughed. "I only hired you because all my efforts to find the professor failed. And here it is." She shook her head. "How does it work?"

"Just like an elevator." I pressed the button. The doors slid open. "Come on in."

She followed and gaped at the control panel.

"I haven't figured out all the controls, but I can go forward and backward thirty minutes."

"Forward, please."

I pressed the up button a half-dozen times and braced myself against the wall.

The lights dimmed, the high-pitched whine filled the air, and the elevator slid sideways. The major's legs wobbled. As she doubled over, I leapt at her, knocking the gun from her hand.

I grabbed her head and banged it against the wall. She scratched at my face. I pinned her throat against the wall with my left forearm. She tried kneeing me in the groin but caught my thigh. I pressed harder, trying to choke her. She fumbled in her purse, clutching another gun. With my right hand I slammed her gun hand against the wall, but she held tight to the weapon. Tried to point it at me. I forced the barrel away.

A shot rang out.

The major made a gurgling noise and stopped struggling. I let up, and she slumped to the floor in a pool of her blood. I checked for a pulse. Nothing.

The doors opened. Future Guy was still dead on the basement floor. I'd seen plenty of death: wholesale in the Ardennes and retail on the streets of South Philly. But this was me lying there dead.

I didn't understand, couldn't understand. More than once, Future Guy said he lived through these events from my viewpoint. He must have known the major would dodge the police, show up here, and kill him. Why did he let that happen? Why wasn't he prepared? Was he resigned to his fate having already seen it before?

That wasn't going to happen to me. I'd be ready for the major when the time came for me to go back and relive this day. Even better, if there were no more time machine, I could never go back and get shot.

I took one of the guns and fired at the time machine's control panel till it was empty. The bullets embedded themselves in its hard plastic. The machine had to be dead, but I wasn't taking any chances. Using siphoned gas from the Buick in the garage, most of the professor's liquor cabinet, and any other flammables I could find, I doused the house. I stuffed my turpentine-soaked handkerchief halfway down the gas tank, struck a match, and ran.

Heavy clouds blocked the stars. No light except from the fire. I parked on the road and drank straight from the bottle of Mammoth Cave whiskey I'd liberated. I lit a cigarette, turned on the radio, and listened to the King of Swing perform magic with his clarinet. While the flames consumed the house, I wondered where in history the professor had deposited himself and if we'd ever actually cross paths in person.

When there was nothing left but ash and embers, I drove off, determined—but not fully convinced—that I'd never be back.

James Blakey writes short genre fiction and his works have appeared in *Mystery Weekly*, *Crimson Streets*, and *Over My Dead Body*. His story "The Bicycle Thief" won a 2019 Derringer Award. James lives in suburban Philadelphia, where he is a network engineer for a data consulting company. When not writing or working, he can be found on the hiking trail (he's climbed thirty-eight of the fifty US high points), or bike-camping his way up and down the East Coast. His website is www.jamesblakeywrites.com.

THE LAST PAGE

Barbara Monajem

There's a reckless streak in my family. Sometimes it leads to downright stupidity, which is how I ended up in so much trouble, and why I found myself in the haunted room of Warbury Castle, awaiting my fate.

I didn't expect to see the ghost. But maybe I should have. According to legend, a medieval knight found a small circlet of gold in a nearby field. Depending on which version you believed, it was either a giant's ring or a fairy's headdress. Either way, supposedly it brought luck to the knight's family—health, wealth, an earldom. All was well for hundreds of years, until 1801, when a cousin of the then Earl of Warbury committed suicide and the circlet disappeared. Now the ghostly knight haunted his own house, guarding this room—the last place the circlet was seen—and scaring people to death, making them vanish into thin air, and other weird things. There were plenty of stories, none of which made sense.

But while other people were frightened by this ghost from the past, my troubles were with a ghost from the present—my old boss, who was alive and well and after me—my fault for getting involved in organized crime.

Things had started out innocently enough. A year ago I got a job tending bar in a Montreal strip club. Dumb, you might say, but I was broke, behind on the rent, and the job paid okay. Not only that, René, my boss, advanced me money to pay my landlord. How was I to know I'd get dragged into something shadier? Besides, I needed the work. I had studied history in university, but jobs in my field are rare. I didn't get on with the few remaining members of my family, so help wasn't likely to come from them.

René, on the other hand, was happy to help, with the bartending gig and the advance—and by offering me a job stripping. "It pays better, Lise," he said, "better tips, too," but I wasn't that desperate. Apart from tending bar, René had me run errands, and after a while he made me collect from some of the nearby businesses. I didn't know it was protection money. It didn't dawn on me *what* I was mixed up with until he sent me to deliver drugs.

I drew the line at that. All right, maybe I should have drawn it way earlier. René gave me an ultimatum. "Like I said, Lise, you can strip instead." In other words, deliver drugs or strip…or else.

My natural recklessness, aka stupidity, kicked in. I sold the drugs elsewhere, kept the protection money, and flew to the UK, where I was born. I figured I could hide out among the sixty-five million Brits. The money I'd stolen was a lot to me, but peanuts to René. He would write it off and forget me.

Or so I told myself. Six months down the road, all seemed well. I had the job of my dreams, working at Warbury Castle, dressed in costumes of various periods, doing everything from dusting the exhibits to baking bread in a medieval kitchen. I even acquired a British accent for the sake of the tourists. The only drawback was minor. My boss, Sarah, was a super snob, and she would have been super annoyed if she realized I looked a lot like one of the long gone Warbury countesses, which I did when dressed in Regency-era garb. So I avoided that era. Easy enough.

Sarah was an archaeologist and historian, so obsessed with the castle and its history that she was writing a book about it. She was distantly related to the current earl and never let anyone forget how special she was. Fine, whatever, but I had a similar reason for choosing to work at Warbury Castle: I was descended from a cast-off scion of the Warbury family who'd emigrated to Canada more than two centuries ago with the missing circlet, or so said *my* family history. I didn't mention this to anyone because, coupled with my resemblance to a long-dead countess (who wasn't even related to said scion), people might have thought I was snobby like my boss. We're all related to someone of note, if you look back far enough, but so what?

I read all the primary sources I could find, hoping to learn more about my ancestor. I was tidying up the exhibits one afternoon when something struck me. Sarah was right there, and curiosity overcame my better judgment. I asked, "What's the primary source for the legend about the stolen circlet and the suicide?" One of the exhibits said that the cousin who killed himself stole the circlet, but that couldn't be true if my ancestor had taken it with him to Canada, as I'd been told as a child.

She glowered as if I were a peon. I'm half and half, French and English, and that got my back up—the French half anyway. I could just hear Grandpère's bitter growl about the accursed English. He was the best of my family. I'll always miss him.

"I read the diary of Christopher Bowering from 1801," I explained. He was the Earl of Warbury at the time. "He mentioned his cousin's gaming losses and feared he might steal something valuable, but said nothing about the circlet going missing or the cousin killing himself. The last page of the diary has been torn out. Is there another volume? I know there's a late Victorian anecdote, but that was written almost a hundred years later."

Sarah looked down her long English nose and said in her hoity-toity English accent, "Questioning the source material does not come within the purview of menials, Lise."

What? I wasn't questioning anything; I just wanted to read the original material because it seemed to conflict with my knowledge of our family history.

She gave the exhibits I'd been dusting an imperious glance, sniffed as if I were the lowliest, grubbiest drudge in the castle, and said, "You've done enough here. Get back to the scullery." I didn't mind leaving, because I like kitchen work, but what a bitch!

An hour later while kneading bread, I was thinking about what a horrible boss Sarah was, and I glimpsed a familiar face in the crowd, another bad boss. René. Damn. At the strip club, I had chatted about wanting to go to merry old England someday. Big mistake. I kept my head down as I shaped the dough, hoping he hadn't recognized me. No such luck. René lingered when the demonstration ended and growled in my ear, "I'll be back at closing time, and then together we'll get my money. Don't even *try* to get away, *petite*."

I was dead meat unless I paid him back, with interest and more. That was impossible, so it was him or me. I didn't want to kill him—I was horrified at the thought—but I wasn't ready to die. I considered calling the police, but cops don't have much sympathy for thieves. I didn't think they would take me seriously until they found me dead, and what good would René's arrest do me then?

So I had to find a way to protect myself. It's hard to get a gun in Britain, not that I had tried or could try given that I was at work. I didn't have my pocket knife because we can't bring weapons into the castle. They even make the female employees use those ugly see-through handbags, in case we try to steal the Sèvres snuffboxes or whatever.

Instead of going to the locker room to change into street clothes at closing time, I hid inside the huge copper cauldron behind the scullery. Once all was quiet, I slipped along to the gun room, where they do demonstrations, and found what I needed—a flintlock pistol along with the necessary black powder and lead shot.

I loaded the gun, but I was scared. I felt René's vengeful presence lurking in the castle, looking for me. Was I really going to shoot him? It would be self-defense, but the very idea gave me chills. That's why my next step was to hide in the haunted room. It's totally dark in there at night, and René believed in ghosts. I didn't, but oh, how I hoped I was wrong. I wished the ghost of the guy who committed suicide would help the knight scare René off for good—not only to save me from shooting him, but also because my curiosity was killing me, and I couldn't wait to get back to my research.

THE LAST PAGE, by Barbara Monajem | 133

Sure, tales passed down through families are often inaccurate, so maybe my ancestor was another family member or no relation at all to the man who supposedly stole the circlet, but I wanted to *know*. Hence my question about primary sources. Sarah's attitude made me want to dig deeper. Which I intended to do. If I were still alive after tonight. And not in prison.

Of course I'd brought this situation on myself, stealing René's drugs. I'd been both stupid and dishonest. I could put up with stupidity—it's in my genes, and I needed to work on it—but dishonesty had been going too far. I should have given René the protection money, left the drugs behind, and run—broke, yes, but I could have gone somewhere he wouldn't expect. Toronto, maybe. Or Nunavut. Would he have followed me there out of spite? I didn't think so.

I looked around, trying to distract myself from my nerves. In the daytime, the haunted room is used for demonstrations. There's a shelf with display items, a chair, and a deal table with the accoutrements for powdering hair and making wigs stay on. Sarah lectures here while we flunkeys take turns rubbing disgusting pomatum onto each other's hair, then dusting it with orris root or flour. We wear masks, but it's still totally gross. Since Sarah is a stickler for accuracy (that's why there had to be a primary source about the suicide), the pomatum is made of mutton suet and lard. It not only stinks, but it's slippery as all get out.

I lit a candle purloined from the kitchen. The more I thought about it, the more I knew I couldn't kill René. I guess the imminence of death got me thinking about my immortal soul. My reckless side kicked in with an idea. I cleared the table and tipped it over, so he would think I was hiding behind it. It was heavy and fell with a thud. I cursed—what if he'd heard? I wasn't ready yet!

The little pomatum pot was almost empty, so I took down the ceramic container that usually contains several weeks' supply of pomatum. Sarah replaces the pomatum herself, saying the container is too valuable for us to touch. Too bad. I swiped my hand through the muck and spread it on the floor in front of the door. René would charge into the room, slip, and fall. I would dash out of my dark corner, jump over the gooey area, and run for my life.

Praying as the seconds ticked past, promising to be a model citizen from now on, I spread more muck. I crept back for a third handful, but my hands were too slippery, and the container fell with a crash. It broke into pieces, scattering shards across the floor. The base of the pot landed at my feet. Cursing myself for making even more noise, I leaned down to pick up the base and noticed a little leather bag in the remnants of the pomatum. I extracted the bag from the muck, wiped my hands on my apron, and opened the drawstring. I tipped the contents into my hand. It was a metal circlet—larger than a ring but smaller than a bracelet. It gleamed gold in the flickering light of the candle. Strange characters were engraved along the inner side.

The lucky circlet? Could it be? It certainly fit the description in the legend: a giant's ring or a fairy's headdress. The characters might be some sort of magic spell.

What was the circlet doing in here? Sarah must have found it, but why had she hidden it? To steal it? No, that didn't make sense. She was a snob, not a criminal. On the other hand, the last page of the earl's diary was missing. Had she torn it out? If so, why?

This jumble of speculation ran through my head, but as I gazed at the beautiful circle of gold, a realization struck me. Here in my sticky hand lay my salvation. My way to repay René. I would toss it at him as I leapt out the door. "Paid in full," I would say, "with interest." Once he saw what he had, he would be in way too much of a hurry to sell it on the black market to worry about stupid little me.

No. The circlet belonged here, not in the secret vault of some filthy-rich collector.

Oh, what did I care? Nobody would know the difference except me. Sarah couldn't admit to having hidden it. They might catch René—tough luck for him.

No. The circlet belonged *here.* No way would I give it to him.

Come to think of it, the circlet would be worth quite a bit melted down. I could use the money to run somewhere else, far, far away. New Zealand. Mozambique. The moon. Well, maybe not that far, but I could get away with it. I knew I could.

No. I clutched the little circle of gold. "Please, please, *please*," I whispered, hoping some magical being was listening. "I can't help being a bit reckless, but I want to be an honest person, truly I do."

The only answer was a growl from outside the door. "Lise." René must have heard the ceramic container fall. He shook the door. I had latched it, but that wouldn't stop him for long. "Come on out, Lise. I won't hurt you. We just need to talk."

Like hell. I had to leave the circlet here. But where? The walls were plain plaster, the shelf too obvious. Maybe I should take it with me....

No. I didn't trust myself. What if I succumbed to temptation, once I was free of the castle and René?

The answer came in a flash of light. No, not celestial light—just ordinary light from below. A trapdoor? I'd never seen it before. Had it been hidden under the deal table? I shoved the circlet into my dcolletage and scrambled behind the table, the gun in one hand while I felt frantically for a way to open the trapdoor with the other.

"Time's up!" *Thud. Crash!* René was breaking down the door. My hand went to the circlet again. *Please help me do the right thing. I just want to start over.*

The trapdoor swung open beneath me, and I fell.

Boom!

I opened my eyes. I had landed somewhere soft and bright—a bed, with sunshine pouring through the windows. Beside me lay the gun. Above me, a familiar hole in the plaster, made by a lead ball long ago, marred the exquisite painted ceiling. But there was no trapdoor. Odd.

"Damnation," a male voice hollered. I turned my head, still blinking at the light. Not far from the bed, a man scrambled down a tall ladder, brandishing a paintbrush, scowling dreadfully. "You've ruined my beautiful ceiling."

"I didn't," I said, sitting up. "That hole has been there forever." The result of some fool playing with a gun during a drunken revel, according to the guidebook.

And yet the smell of gunpowder told me my pistol had just been fired. I must have squeezed the flintlock's trigger as I fell. I picked the gun up as the guy stormed toward me. I didn't recognize him. He was dressed in period costume, first decade of the nineteenth century by my estimation. Knee-breeches, riding boots, and a good quality linen shirt. A rumpled cravat, stained with paint, hung loose around his neck.

Some people look great in period costume; others don't. This guy was tall, dark, and handsome, like the cover model for a historical romance, except that his clothes were accurate. He was clean-shaven, unlike the current fashion for stubble. He had to be one of the restoration people working on the ceiling of this room—a bedroom back in the day—but why had I never met him before?

He appropriated the pistol. "I don't hold with women handling guns." His frown deepened. "Particularly not *my* guns. Who the deuce are you?"

"This is *your* gun?"

"It's my Lamotte. Got it on my grand tour before France fell to pieces." I must have looked dubious, for he pointed to an inscription on the hilt: CB 1787.

I rolled my eyes. "I suppose that makes you Christopher 'Kit' Bowering. Thirteenth Earl of Warbury."

"The same." He gave a curt nod. "Again, who are you? Why are you in my bedchamber?"

Clearly a lunatic, but he didn't seem dangerous. Then it hit me: thirty seconds ago, it had been nighttime. Now it was broad daylight. What was going on?

"Occasionally, I invite a woman to grace my bed," he continued, "but not if she's a thief."

"I'm not a thief." But I was a bit perplexed because I hadn't the slightest notion what to say about the gracing-the-bed bit. He was a gorgeous specimen, but I didn't do casual sex. "I borrowed it to protect myself."

He narrowed his eyes. "From whom?" He tapped the gun back and forth as if he pondered using it on me. Fortunately, it was no longer loaded.

"Uh, from René, my, uh, former employer." Why was I suddenly tongue-tied? I was definitely confused, and that comment about gracing his bed hadn't helped.

"My good woman," he said, all stiff and stern. "If you have displeased your protector, it's no concern of mine. It certainly won't make me likely to take you to my bed instead."

"I don't want to be in your bed." I slid off it to prove my point. "Protector?" I grimaced. "That's such an archaic concept, and René wasn't my anything."

The lunatic flapped a hand. "You're a pretty little thing, but I'm not in the mood for a mistress. I have enough problems with my cousin...." He shook his head, as if ridding himself of an unpleasant thought, and wrinkled his nose. "Darling, you'd better bathe if you want to attract a man. You smell like a sheep."

"It's the pomatum to hold the orris root." My hands were still sticky. I wiped them on my apron.

He burst out laughing. "You powder your hair? That's frightfully out of fashion, love, as is your clothing. The waistline is too low, for one thing, and—"

"It's for demonstration purposes only." I was 1780s that day.

He raised a languid brow. "And what, precisely, do you demonstrate?" His voice brimmed over with innuendo. "Your decolletage is too high as well. Show your wares, darling. A fellow wants to know what he's buying."

"You are the rudest man I've ever met! I'm not selling anything."

He smirked. "Then why, oh why, were you in my bed?"

"Because I fell onto it," I said. "From up there."

He followed my gaze to the ceiling. "From up there."

His mocking tone was the last straw. "There's a trapdoor. I was trying to get away from René, it opened up, and I fell through. I don't care if you don't believe me because it's *true*."

His whole voice and manner changed. "You're from Up There." Definitely with capital letters. He scowled at the ceiling.

I looked up again, then scanned the whole ceiling. Huh. Most of the familiar painting was there, but not in the area where he'd been working. Behind me, a crowd of cavorting fairies was missing, too, but not as if they'd been painted over. As if they hadn't been painted there *yet*.

"Show me," he said. "Where is the trapdoor?"

"Must be right up there." I pointed. "I fell straight down onto the bed."

He moved the ladder closer and climbed it, but there was no sign of an opening in the ceiling, not even a faux window or anything rectangular that could have been painted to cover it up.

"I didn't see it when I was painting." He glared. "And I don't see it now."

"I didn't see it from the haunted room either," I said. "It must have been hidden under the deal table."

"Haunted room? Deal table? Are you mad, woman? The room above this is the steward's office." He came slowly down the ladder. "And there's no trapdoor where you're pointing. If there is one at all, it's several feet that way. A woman opened it the other day by lifting it, not by dropping it open. It was too small to fall through." He approached, anger and threat in his stance. "But after she shut it, I couldn't find it. Or her. Or my circlet." He glared at me, his eyes steely and his jaw tight. "I want the truth from you, and I want it now."

My heartbeat ramped up. Out of one frying pan and into another. I backed toward the door. "I did tell you the truth. One minute I was wishing as hard as I could to escape from René and start over, and the next I was here." I made it to the door. If I could just lift the latch and run...

"You were wishing when a trapdoor let you fall through," he said, suddenly pensive. "And I was wishing when another trapdoor—a smaller one—was lifted."

"Wishing for what?" I fiddled with the latch behind my back.

"An honest woman," he said bitterly. "And what I got was a female thief with a long nose." He huffed at me. "Where do you think you're going? I have only to shout, and my servants will prevent you from leaving the castle."

Servants? Grand tour? Day, not night—and through the window across the room from me, where there should have been a parking lot, was an alley of oaks bordered by swaths of lawn. And he was dressed a decade or two later than me.... "What year is this?"

"What?" He moved me away from the door—gently though, I had to give him credit for that.

"Please tell me what year it is." I put my hands to my temples, trying to think. If he was indeed the thirteenth earl, whose diary I had read, and not some nutjob...

"Eighteen hundred and one," he said. "Now answer me: Who was the long-nosed woman Up There who took my circlet of gold?"

Wow. It *was* 1801, as I'd suspected. He truly *was* the earl. I had somehow fallen not just through a trapdoor, but through *time*.

I pulled myself together, sort of. "Uh...that must have been Sarah. I work for her."

Kit narrowed his eyes. "I see. And what are *you* here to steal?" He loomed over me. His eyes widened. I blushed and tried to cover my cleavage—men are so obnoxious—but he batted my hands away, dipped into my décolletage, and plucked the circlet out. "Aha! How did *you* get it? Did you steal it from her?"

I quivered with indignation, a bit of shock, and more than a smidgen of excitement. What can I say; it was 1801, and my breasts reacted happily to the touch of his hand. "I didn't steal it. I found it by accident, and now, in case you haven't noticed, I brought it back."

"So you did," Kit said gruffly. "Thank you. You have no idea what this means to me."

"Yes, I do. It's a valuable circlet that has been in your family for centuries." Maybe it granted wishes, for it had saved me from René by sending me here. To eighteen-oh-frigging-one! Now what was I going to do?

Well, I had promised to be a good person from now on. I should run with that.

"Where did you find it?" he asked, and then, like an afterthought, "And when?"

"Um…maybe ten minutes ago, hidden in a pot of pomatum." It was the truth, just not all of it. But he'd have thought I was insane if I'd said ten minutes and two centuries ago.

"Why did you ask me what year it is?" He narrowed his eyes at me.

Oh boy. An honest person tells the truth, even if it sounds crazy or like a lie. Here goes. "Up There, it's the year two thousand nineteen." I closed my eyes, waiting for the blow—whether physical, for people were brutal back then, thinking nothing of boxing people's ears or beating them with switches—or merely sound and fury.

"Magic," he cried. "I thought it must be, when I couldn't find the trapdoor the thief peeked through. Seemingly, the circlet's magic opens trapdoors when and where it chooses—up, down, smaller, larger, past, present, and future…. How superb!"

I opened my eyes. He was grinning, and wow, was he gorgeous when he smiled. Not only that, he believed in magic.

"The circlet really does grant wishes." He looked up at the ceiling again, and the smile disappeared. "Or perhaps it simply used your wish to return here where it belongs. It certainly didn't grant *my* wish." He cocked his head at me. "How will you return where *you* belong?"

I hadn't had much time to mull this over, but… "I suppose I could wish on it again." Even as I spoke, he was shaking his head. No way would he let me hold it again, and rightly so. Not that I would steal it on purpose, but how could he know that? "Of course, it might not grant my wish. Anyway, if I go back, René will kill me."

"Tsk," he said, still contemplating me, which was unnerving but not entirely unpleasant. "Then you'd better stay here."

This was unexpected, and I had to think it through. What would I *do* in 1801? "Could I work for you? I can cook and clean, and I'm good at keeping accounts." I could do math without a calculator. I even knew how to add up pounds, shillings, and pence. "I can copy correspondence, although not in good copperplate, but with practice I would improve." I paused. "Do you have children? I could be a governess. I have plenty of general knowledge, and I speak fluent French."

"I have a couple of bastards, but no legitimate children yet. No wife, you see. That's the honest woman I was wishing for." He sighed. "All women want me for is my title."

"And your looks," I blurted. If I'd turned pink before, now I was crimson.

He grimaced. "That, too. I'm just an ordinary man, when it comes down to it." He picked up a leather-bound book. "Make the bed, will you...what's your name?"

"Lise," I said.

"Very well, Lise. Tidy the room, too, while I record this occurrence."

I began to obey—I was now a servant—but then I recognized the book. "It's your diary!"

He raised a haughty brow.

"I read it up till sometime in...1801." At his appalled expression, I added, "It's in the castle library in 2019. I work—worked there, so I had access."

"To my *private thoughts*?"

"You were dead then," I retorted.

"I'm not dead *now*." He flushed beneath his tan.

"It was all good, nothing embarrassing," I said. "About how much you loved your mother and miss your father, how you dealt with various tenant disputes, how boring you found the vicar's sermons, how you enjoyed helping with the harvest." I skipped the rants about the women who pursued him. "How worried you are about your cousin..."

"Yes?" He looked down his nose, daring me to stick mine into his business.

I had no choice, for this was my chance to find out the truth about my ancestor. "You wrote that your cousin Alfred ran up a huge gaming debt. You couldn't decide what to do—for if you paid the debt, he would only gamble more. But the last page of the volume was torn out, so I wondered what happened next."

The earl scowled. "Aye, he's penitent now, but once his debt is paid, he'll be unable to resist the dice and cards again. I refused to pay it for him.

He threatened to take the circlet and sell it, so I kept it close by. I took my eye off it for a second to remonstrate with him, and that woman stole it. Then I lashed out at him, which made it worse. He started talking about suicide, and I found him searching in here for my gun."

"What happened next? In the last page of the diary?"

"I haven't written it yet." He glanced about. "Where's the gun? I laid it down a few moments ago." He scowled accusingly at me.

I shook my head, showing my empty hands. I looked around—and realized that the door was ajar. Someone had opened it while we were talking. Had Alfred sneaked in and taken the gun?

My heart began to thud, for I now knew exactly where we were in 1801. "This is really, really important because your cousin Alfred is my ancestor." We had to hurry. "We have to go find him. We have to make sure he doesn't kill himself."

His brows drew together. "Or you'll suddenly cease to exist?"

"This isn't about *me*," I said. Another surprisingly unselfish thought. "I don't think the universe is that fragile." But that was beside the point, too. "I just know that's not what's supposed to happen."

"We're agreed on that." He took me by the hand—a large, warm, imperative sort of hand. We dashed along the corridor, down the grand staircase, and across the great hall to the library.

A roar of rage greeted us. A sandy-haired man lifted a lyre-backed chair over his head and brought it down hard on a writing table, smashing a pounce box and sending a bottle of ink flying. I dove and caught the bottle just in time to save the carpet. I was totally thinking like a servant—or maybe I just had to make sure the carpet remained as pristine as it would be in 2019.

"Well done, Lise," the earl muttered. "Don't be an idiot, Alfie." He lunged for the pistol, which lay on the table, but his cousin got to it first.

"I read what you wrote in your diary—that I'm worthless. Very well, I'll relieve you of the burden of my idiotic existence." He waved the gun around. Was it loaded again? I didn't see any powder and shot, but he could have gotten them elsewhere.

"Alfie, please don't," Kit said. "I was angry. I didn't mean it."

Alfred pointed the gun at his temple. And then his mouth.

"Please don't do that," I said, my voice trembling. "I have a better idea."

He lowered the gun and turned to Kit. "Who the devil is this?"

Kit studied me as if he wasn't quite sure, so I stood forward. "I am Lise from Canada, bringing you a plan for your life."

Alfie looked to his cousin again. "I repeat, who is she?"

"She is a lady who knows the secrets of my heart," Kit said, a hint of a smile at the corners of his mouth. "She knows how much I love you. How much I want you to live and have a good life."

Somehow, I had graduated from servant to lady.

"She is honest and will speak the truth," Kit said. "Listen to her."

I was honest? Hopefully he wouldn't change his mind about that, after what I was about to say. "Kit is willing to pay your passage to Montreal, where you will take a new name and start a new life." That's exactly what he had done according to the stories in my family—disappeared from existence in England and reemerged in Canada. Those stories were the only proof we had of our relationship with the Earl of Warbury.

Kit smiled and nodded his assent, while Alfie stared. "Montreal? Why?"

"It's a wonderful city, young and vibrant and full of opportunity." I knew a fair amount about my ancestor's life. "Once you're settled and know your way around, you'll buy a piece of land and grow apples."

"Apples?"

"Montreal has the perfect climate to grow the crispest, tastiest apples ever. Not only that, you'll purchase a forest and produce maple syrup." The more I spoke, the more my enthusiasm grew. "Your *cabane à sucre* will become renowned for the excellence of its cuisine." I paused. "You do speak French, right?"

He nodded.

"You won't treat the French like serfs?"

He looked perplexed, but said, "Of course not." He laid down the gun.

"Then you will love Montreal." Tears came to my eyes. "The food is marvelous. *Tourtière* is amazing, and our *soupe aux pois* is famous around the world. As for the leaves in autumn…" Homesickness overwhelmed me.

"You already miss your home," Kit said.

I nodded, swallowing my tears. Gravely, he passed me a handkerchief. I dabbed at my eyes.

He took the gold circlet from his pocket, turning it over and over in his hand. "Maybe if I give it to you, it will grant your wish to return."

Humbled by his kindness, his sudden trust in me… I shook my head. Risk his circlet again? No way.

"You can come visit me," Alfie said suddenly. He had picked up a globe and was twirling it to find his future home. "Once I've become established and have a proper house in which to receive you." He smiled, and I burst into tears.

"What?" Kit pulled me into his arms. "What is it, darling Lise?"

"When he smiled…" I sniffled. "He looked just like my *grandpère*. Younger, of course, but so much alike." I pulled myself together and half-heartedly tried to withdraw from his embrace—because this time when he called me *darling,* he sounded as if he meant it.

He didn't let go. "Will your grandfather miss you?"

"No, he's dead. No one will miss me. I don't have any close family."

"It's settled then," Kit said. "In due time we'll travel to Canada to visit Alfie. You'll have to marry me, though. Otherwise it wouldn't be proper to travel together."

From courtesan to servant to lady to wife? This was happening way too fast.

"You will marry me, won't you?" His smile was rueful now…and a little anxious.

I didn't know what to say. Marriage in the nineteenth century was nothing like the twenty-first. My husband would pretty much own me. I would be obliged to have children, perhaps many of them. Too many, but in an age of high child mortality, that made sense. Death in childbirth was common, surgery was barbaric, and there weren't any antibiotics or immunizations, and—

He took my hands and brought them to his lips. It couldn't get more romantic than that. "You wished to escape, and I wished for an honest woman," he said. "You're beautiful and educated and intelligent—just what I need. It seems meant to be, don't you think?"

It did, when he put it that way. I couldn't return to the future. I liked him more with every passing minute, and besides that, life as a countess was as close as I would get to a twenty-first century standard of living.

But in the interest of honesty… What if my marrying him would skew history another way? Before I had a chance to pursue this train of thought, he scooped me up and kissed me.

My reckless streak totally went for that. It was a great kiss, and everyone knows that back then a kiss led straight to marriage.

"No more diary for me," Kit said. "I suppose I mustn't destroy this one, but henceforth, I'll keep my secret thoughts to myself." He released me, tore out the last page—the empty one—and tossed it into the fire.

And everything fell into place.

Sarah hadn't torn the last page out. She wouldn't have dared, because others had read the diary before her. She just used the missing page to her advantage. She must have been in the haunted room when light suddenly shone from the floor, and she'd lifted a trapdoor…to find Kit painting the ceiling whilst berating Alfie (and wishing for an honest woman). The circlet glowed next to his palette, and Sarah couldn't resist. She grabbed it, slammed the door shut, and proceeded to rearrange history. The cousin had disappeared from all records except hearsay from a hundred years later, so why not?

She would "find" the circlet…in the moat, or the dungeon, or inside a wall, thus substantiating the hearsay. She was an archaeologist and could probably fake it convincingly. She would gain renown for her incredible find. Her book would be a bestseller. She might even end up on TV.

But the circlet couldn't leave it like that—because now that it was lost, Alfie really was likely to kill himself. It roped me in to make sure history stayed precisely as it was supposed to be—and, incidentally, to fulfill two heartfelt wishes and make an honest woman of me.

Which Kit soon did. No wonder I resembled the Regency-era countess. I *was* her. I still am.

And what about the circlet, you ask. At the dock, just before the sailors rowed the excited but anxious Alfie out to the ship, Kit put the circlet in his cousin's hand. "It will grant your dearest wish," he said. Our farewells were tearful but full of hope. Kit and I watched, hands clasped, as the ship moved slowly out of sight.

Where is the circlet in the twenty-first century? Nobody knew when I was there, and I have no way of finding out, seeing as I'm back in 1801. Go have a look for it, if you're concerned—but I'm not. The golden circlet is magic. It can take care of itself.

Winner of the Holt Medallion, Maggie, and Daphne du Maurier awards, **Barbara Monajem** wrote her first story at eight years old about apple-tree gnomes. After publishing a middle-grade fantasy, she settled on paranormal and historical mysteries and romances with intrepid heroines and long-suffering heroes (or vice versa). Barbara used to have two items on her bucket list: to make asparagus pudding and to succeed at knitting socks. She managed the first (don't ask) but doubts she'll ever accomplish the second. This is not a bid for immortality but merely the dismal truth. She lives near Atlanta with an ever-shifting population of relatives, friends, and feline strays. Learn more at www.BarbaraMonajem.com.

REYNA

David Dean

Reyna lay between the sheets of her small bed, the house around her quiet in the coolness of the dawn, her brothers and mother sleeping, her father not yet returned from his night shift at the gas station. Around her the room took form and color with the coming of the unseen sun, its distant radiance tinting the walls a rose-petal pink.

Glancing to her left the eleven-year-old saw her wheelchair awaiting her as it did every day. Beyond it stood a small table on which her parents had placed statues of Our Lady of Guadeloupe and Saint Padre Pio. A spray of flowers formed a backdrop to the little shrine. Reyna's mother often brought home flowers to place in a vase next to the Blessed Virgin, flowers that she had rescued from the homes of the wealthy people she cleaned for each day.

On the wall opposite, the faces of young pop stars alternately beamed or pouted down at her, faces that filled her heart with secret yearnings.

With a sigh, Reyna closed her eyes to them, took a deep breath, and focused her thoughts, tunneling deep within herself for that hidden resource, that spark that glowed there always, if not always brightly. It took all Renya's concentration to find and grasp it, to gently coax it into an incandescence that would fill her inert body. After a few moments, she was looking down on herself. It always began this way.

Knowing that she didn't have much time, she paused only long enough for a glance, a reassurance that her body would be there to come back to. Once Mama woke Mateo and Gabriel, Reyna feared someone coming into the room and discovering the empty husk of her crippled body and mistaking it for coma…or worse yet…death. They had suffered so much already because of her accident.

Her first out-of-body experience had been a fumbling, and somewhat terrifying, tour of her small room. On her second attempt she had fared better, exiting her room and drifting through her family's tiny bungalow like her own ghost, eventually discovering Mateo's collection of dirty magazines.

Reyna had been shocked, though not surprised, as Mateo, being the eldest, was always precocious and full of mischief. Naturally, she revealed her findings to Mama later that morning—little Gabriel had to be protected from such influences, as he was the youngest and idolized his older brother.

It was only after her mother asked how she knew of the hidden magazines that it occurred to Reyna what she had done. She had the choice of telling the truth or lying. She lied, telling Mama that she had overheard Mateo discussing the nudies on the phone with a friend. She couldn't think how to explain the truth.

Later that morning she heard Papa confronting Mateo over the magazines. He was restricted to the house for seven days, except for scheduled school activities—he was on the football team at St. Charles Borromeo and had to make practices.

Not knowing how his parents had discovered his secret stash, he accused Gabriel and made him miserable the whole week Mateo was grounded. Reyna swore not to snoop after that.

She had been unable to resist, however, when her mother's wedding band went missing.

The simple gold ring never left her finger till she pinched her hand shifting furniture one day while working. Arriving home later that evening with a swelling hand, Renya's mom complained that the ring was hurting her and used some liquid soap to get it off before the inflammation grew worse. Exhausted, and in some pain, she went to bed early. When she awoke in the morning, the swelling had subsided somewhat, and she thought of the ring. It could not be found.

Though Reyna's mom and her crew worked long hours cleaning and neatening other people's homes, her own was less tidy, and showed the results of two active boys and parents who worked long hours. Unable to recall exactly where she had taken the ring off, she spent a fruitless hour searching for it before having to leave for work again. Reyna's father did likewise, having come home to the crisis and been enlisted. After lifting and sifting through furniture, cushions, and strewn clothing, he, too, gave up, seeing Mateo and Gabriel off to school, then going to bed to catch a few hours' sleep. Reyna had heard everything through the open door of her tiny room.

With the house now silent, and her tutor not due for an hour, she closed her eyes, stilled her breathing, and tunneled inward searching for the ember. Finding it more easily each time, she seized it, blew it into life, and rose from her inert body like an exhalation. Moments later she drifted through the house, an invisible cobweb floating along the ceiling, her view of the cluttered floor below that of a hawk circling a lonely, distant field. Studying the mix of surfaces that presented themselves in search of a glint, a glimmer, of the lost gold ring, she discovered nothing. Willing herself to descend, she repeated the process, skimming along the carpeted and hardwood landscape of her home. When even the stained tiles, tub, and toilet of the bathroom revealed no evidence, she hurried to her parents' bedroom and slid beneath the door.

Ignoring her father's gentle snoring, she slipped beneath the bed and scrutinized the lightly furred surface of the hardwood floor. Within the dusty cumulus a golden arch shone in the dim light, and she glided over to it—her mother's wedding band lay trapped in a crevice between the wall and the floorboards' edge. Were she not above it she would never have seen it.

That afternoon, after both her physical therapist and her tutor left for the day and her papa came in to visit, she told him where to find the ring. There was nothing else she could do, as she lacked the power to move any object.

Upon hearing this, her father tilted his head to one side and asked, "How could you know that, Reyna?"

She shrugged in answer and he left the room. A few moments later he returned with the ring, the expression on his stubbled face a mix of joy, disbelief, and perhaps, Reyna thought, a touch of fear. "How?" he repeated. "Did one of the boys hide it as a joke and tell you?"

"No, Papa," she answered. "I just knew." Again, she couldn't think how to describe her newfound ability.

"Just like St. Anthony—the finder of lost things," he murmured, supplying his own answer. "God gives what's needed."

"Yes, Papa," she replied, smiling. "He does."

After that Reyna noticed that everyone treated her differently than before, even the boys, with a deference that she'd only seen when older relatives, or their priest, came to dinner. She wasn't sure she liked it.

It had been the story of Padre Pio that had begun it all. Shortly after the inexplicable accident that made her such a burden, Reyna's mother placed the little statue of the saint in her room. "He was a worker of many miracles, especially healings," Mama explained, setting the portly and bearded ceramic figure next to the one of the Blessed Virgin. "He was so holy," she continued, "that he had the stigmata at times—the wounds of the cross— just like Jesus! Can you imagine?"

Reyna found that she didn't want to; the thought of bleeding wounds both frightened and sickened her. Since the car had run her down, she had become very squeamish about such things. Seeing this on her face, her mama added, "Did you know that he could also be in two places at once?"

"I wish I could be," Reyna responded without hesitation. "If I could, then I would leave myself behind and go outside...go wherever I wanted to."

"Well, I don't know about that, but I do know that we can pray for his intercession and healing...and that is what we'll do."

"Yes, Mama," Reyna answered, and she did, but it was the thought, the idea, of bi-location that fascinated her.

It was during one of those prayerful meditations that she found she had been granted the same ability as the miraculous monk—she left her body and was free.

And today she was determined to venture outside the house.

Feeling much as she imagined a balloon might, Reyna bobbed along the ceiling, struggling to master her ethereal self and control her movements. Taking a last look at the pale girl with her long dark braids and thickly lashed eyes closed in apparent slumber, she crossed the room to the window, paused for courage, then passed through it and into the wakening world.

Preening himself on a glistening holly tree, a cardinal caught her attention, and she entered his tiny, fragile body as quickly as a thought, something she had not intended to do, nor even knew she could accomplish.

As if startled, or struck by a stone, he threw wide his brilliant wings, and before Reyna knew what was happening, took flight, and she with him.

Darting from tree to shrub, shrub to bush they dashed along, Reyna as startled as he now, even as she was exhilarated by the bird's speed and aerial dexterity. Feeling breathless, though she knew it was only a feeling, she focused herself and found her proud host calming, as well. Lighting on a branch, his head turned this way and that, as if searching for Reyna, his tiny heart beating hard. Reyna soothed him with thoughts like soft strokes, her will subsuming his instincts, and soon he began to sing—he was hers.

But what to do? Reyna feared just going along for a ride, uncertain where they might end up. She wasn't sure she could find her way back.

Then it occurred to her—her school. She had not been back since the accident on her way home. She missed her teachers and friends, missed playing with others.

She knew how to get *there* and back. She was sure of it.

The bright-red bird launched itself, abandoning its usual pattern of short, cautious flights and winging straight and level across the shingled roofs of Reyna's neighborhood, following the streets that she knew well from having walked to school and back so often with her brothers.

It had been that one rare day she walked home alone that everything had come unraveled. Mateo stayed on at school for football, or maybe it was soccer, Gabriel at home with a bad cold. That was the day she could neither remember with clarity, nor explain—why *had* she turned back after safely crossing the street and run into the path of an oncoming car? The driver couldn't avoid her, according to his testimony. The only witness, a large, long-haired man in coveralls whom the driver had caught a glimpse of, was never located. Her life, and those of her family members, was forever changed in that moment.

To care for Reyna, her father had to work night shifts while her mother worked days. In this manner one was always available (even if sleeping). Reyna's sense of guilt for these hardships was profound.

Passing over the very spot where her family's troubles had begun, she looked down on the suburban intersection, which appeared no different from so many others—two-lane blacktop framed by cracked sidewalks and shaded by trees whose leaves were tinged with the yellow and russet of coming autumn.

She and her cardinal alighted on one of these. Reyna saw no evidence of what had happened to her at this very spot almost a year ago—no scattered books, no blood—all trace of the accident gone. *Why did I turn back?* she asked herself for the thousandth time.

With that thought, she felt herself leaving her little host and saw him flit quickly away through the canopy of branches. This time, however, she felt herself not rising, but sinking, dropping through wavering layers of shadow and light, like a diver descending to the bottom of the sea.

Before she had a chance to become frightened, she stopped and found herself exactly where she had been before the sensation overcame her—looking down on the fateful intersection.

Fewer cars were parked along the streets now, and the sun was much higher in the sky than it had been moments ago. A group of children were crossing the street, the boys laughing and shoving one another, the girls ignoring them, speaking with their heads close together. All of them wore backpacks or carried books and wore the uniforms of St. Charles Borromeo. Reyna could see from the direction that they walked that school had just let out. But how could that be? It wasn't time yet.

As the children reached the other side of the street a battered white panel van pulled up to the curb nearby, its engine coughing into silence. A large, heavy man sat behind the wheel, his big arm resting on the open windowsill, a cigarette clasped between his thick fingers. Beneath a great tangle of shoulder-length bushy hair he peered across the street and down the sidewalk.

Reyna looked in the same direction as the man…and saw with a start her own self approaching…alone. It was *the* day…the moment drawing near.

The man flicked the cigarette away and opened the driver's door, stepping out. She could see now that he wore coveralls stained with dark splotches, like a car mechanic. Taking a few ponderous steps, he arrived at the van's side door and slid it open. Leaning in, he appeared to busy himself with something inside. A faint mewling came from a cardboard box he was reaching into.

Reyna looked back to her former self in her school uniform of plaid skirt, white blouse, and knee socks, scanning for traffic before crossing the shadowed street. Satisfied, she stepped out. The big man turned, smiling, his grizzled jowls quivering.

"Hey there! Wanna see some newborn puppies?" he called to her from the opposite curb.

Reyna saw herself hesitate in the street, still several yards from the van and its open door. As if on cue, the pups began to sing and whine.

"Take a look," he offered. "You can have one, if you like."

She saw herself smile just a little as he held up one of the squirming, fluffy creatures for her inspection, its eyes barely open, its belly soft and pink.

Don't, she ordered her former self, beginning, at last, to remember. *Keep going.... Run home!*

But it was no good. These things had already happened; Reyna of the year before would make the same choice as before—the puppies were adorable, irresistible.

Her smile wide now, her former self hurried toward them, closing the distance.

The big man's arm shot out like a piston, seizing her in a terrible grip, and hauling her toward the waiting van.

With a small cry of terror, Reyna watched as she tried to pull in the opposite direction but was dragged forward. She saw now the interior of the van and a second larger wooden box behind the cardboard one containing the puppies. It had a lid like a coffin and an open padlock dangling from a clasp mounted on its side. She understood in that frantic glance that she mustn't allow herself to be placed in that box; that if that happened she would never see Mama and Papa or her brothers again.

In desperation she bit the man's grubby hand, her small, sharp teeth sinking deeply into the thick flesh. His blood tasted of salt and iron.

With a high-pitched squeal he snatched his hand away, releasing her. Reyna turned and ran as hard as she could in the opposite direction, aware only of an impending roar and a rushing shadow before everything went black and red.

Responding to a call that his wife had gone into labor, the driver was hurrying to the hospital a half mile away. Reyna knew that her former self would not recall any of this.

Unable to watch the bloody carnage done to her by the vehicle, she hastened to reverse the process that had brought her back to this day, ascending like a scream through the filmy elements of time and catching up to the present.

Moments later, she opened her eyes in her small sad bed, her wheelchair standing guard nearby.

Beyond her door she heard Mama in the kitchen and smelled the aroma of the dark, thick coffee she and Papa liked. Across the hall she heard Mateo and Gabriel arguing. Soon, Papa would come home, tired and bleary-eyed from his night shift. He and Mama would kiss as they always did, and she would hurry off to work herself. Reyna would lie in her bed and wait for her tutor, wait for her physical therapist, wait for her visiting nurse, wait for her life to someday resume....

"No!" Reyna cried to the pop singers on her wall, the statuary on her table. "Saint Padre Pio, I don't want to wait any longer! What can I do?"

As if in answer, there was a pecking at the window. Looking over she saw the cardinal peering in at her.

An idea began to form in her mind.

If having inhabited this beautiful tiny creature had created a bond between them, then how much more of a connection might be formed with her earlier self? If she could not will the earlier Reyna to avoid the trap laid for her, could she not reunite her present and former selves to do so? Armed with foreknowledge of their fate, Reyna could simply take another route home, avoiding the terrible intersection and its rapacious troll altogether.

But having conceived the possibility, Reyna understood that it wasn't enough to avoid her fate at the hands of the monster. There must be justice, as well—for her year of pain and suffering, for the hardships imposed on her parents, for the innocent driver, and perhaps for the other little girls who would not, or did not, escape. There must be a reckoning, and it must be now...and she thought she knew a way.

Heedless of her family finding her vacant body, Reyna once more closed her eyes and sought out the transforming energy within her broken frame. Within moments, it seemed, she was hurtling back to the moment, the place.

She met herself traipsing down the buckled sidewalk and entered her younger self. The merging of her past and present selves only resulted in a tremor within her brain, a small pebble disturbing a placid pond.

How wonderful to feel her legs once more, to be walking beneath the autumn elms, smelling the aroma of burning leaves, catching glimpses of a faint blue sky between the branches overhead. It was exhilarating to be whole and free once more...and she intended to stay that way.

Nearing the intersection, she saw the big man sitting in his rusty van, smoking. He was looking in her direction. She could not yet make out his expression. She freed one arm from her knapsack and let the bag dangle from the opposite shoulder. Without breaking stride, she unzipped it.

Looking back up, she saw that the ogre had tossed his cigarette onto the street and was exiting the cab of his vehicle. He turned away from her to slide open the van's side door, leaning in to stir the pups. A faint whimpering and yipping reached her ears, and terror pierced her like a sickness.

Forcing herself forward, Reyna entered the intersection and walked toward the other side.

Turning around, the monster held a squirming puppy in one giant hand, the hand she had bitten, and this reminded her that she had tasted his blood—he was human. Her resolve swelled once more.

With a hitch of her narrow shoulder she allowed her school books to fall out onto the street from the open bag.

Squatting to gather them up, Reyna called out to him, her teeth near chattering, "Hey mister, would you help me?" Somehow, she smiled.

He looked confused at this unexpected development. She had not even allowed him to make his pitch about the dogs. Reyna noted him taking a quick look around before answering, "Sure...I'll help you. Then you can come look at my puppies. You'll love them."

She kept smiling at him across the twenty feet that separated them. "Okay!" she answered.

He turned to place the puppy back with his siblings. Reyna teased some papers out from between the pages of a book while he was distracted.

Smiling also, the big man lumbered toward her, his bloody eyes gleaming and eager. Reyna allowed the breeze to send the papers fluttering along the asphalt. As he knelt, she sprang up to chase them.

Thwarted, he called after her, "I'll pick these up and you—"

But he never got to finish. With a roar of acceleration, the car raced into the intersection just as Reyna knew it would, the young father-to-be distracted with his cell phone and on the way to the hospital. The man in the coveralls was kneeling, turning just in time to see the grill of the car before it smashed into him, sending him and Reyna's books flying. She screamed and turned away. A pedestrian coming upon the scene pulled out his cell phone, shouting to the stunned motorist, "I'll call nine one one!"

When all was silent once more, she turned back. Scrambling from his vehicle, the driver rushed toward the coverall man, who lay on his back. Splashed with crimson, his large frame appeared crushed and deflated, his eyes wide as if studying the scudding white clouds above.

"Oh my God!" the young man cried. "I've killed him!"

In the distance a siren began to scream.

Only just beginning to understand the magnitude of what she'd done, Reyna went to him and placed a hand on his shoulder as he knelt over the big man. Startled, he looked up into her face, tears streaming down his own.

"He was trying to get me into his van," she told him in a clear, steady voice, and pointed at the waiting, open door of the battered vehicle.

"What?" he asked, unable to focus on her words.

The siren drew closer.

"He wanted to put me in a box," she explained.

The young man turned now and looked to where she was pointing.

"A box?" he repeated, still not understanding.

A police car pulled up to the scene, its siren fading as the officer exited and hurried toward them.

"You'll see," she promised. "It wasn't your fault."

And with those words, Reyna focused herself on the task of returning, separating her selves once again so that she could go back. She had to go back and see.

When her eyes opened again in the early-morning gray of her room, the aroma of the coffee was still fresh, her brothers' argument ongoing. It was when she heard her papa laughing at something her mother said that she dared to hope.

Turning her head a little to the left, she looked for her sentinel through slatted eyes—the wheelchair was no longer standing guard; her little statue of Saint Padre Pio was missing, as well.

"Reyna!" her mama called down the hallway. "We're waiting breakfast for you! Wake up, you sleepyhead!"

Throwing back her covers, Reyna leapt to her feet, and with a cry of joy rushed to join her family.

David Dean's short stories have appeared regularly in *Ellery Queen's Mystery Magazine*, as well as a number of anthologies, since 1990. His stories have been nominated for the Shamus, Barry, and Derringer awards, and "Ibrahim's Eyes" won the EQMM Readers Award for 2007. His story "Tomorrow's Dead" was a finalist for the Edgar Award for best short story of 2011. He is a retired chief of police in New Jersey and once served as a paratrooper with the Eighty-Second Airborne Division. His novels *The Thirteenth Child*, *Starvation Cay*, and *The Purple Robe* are all available through Amazon.

AND THEN THERE WERE PARADOXES

Cathy Wiley

"I hope this is an easy one." Detective Chief Inspector Trevor Ashcroft of the Thames Valley Police paused to study the outside of the building, as he always did before entering a crime scene. It had suited him for the last forty years, and he had no plans to change his pattern.

Sergeant Geoffrey Howlett stopped as well, used to this habit of his superior. "I agree. You deserve an easy last week before retirement."

"I do. Although if I had wanted easy, I shouldn't have joined the police." Ashcroft studied the building before him, ignoring the various TVP officers guarding the front door. The morning sun shone on the mid-terrace brick cottage, probably from the Victorian era—Winterbrook was full of eighteenth- and nineteenth-century homes. There was moss growing on the roof and ivy creeping halfway up the building. His wife, who loved watching those property-buying television programs, would probably call it charming, and admire the period details. He sighed to himself. Once he was retired, Shirley was probably going to make him watch hours of those programs. "What do you see?"

Howlett examined the scene; then, following a habit of his own, took out a smart phone and snapped a picture. "Well, depending on whether or not the victim owns the place or is just letting it, we may have a well-to-do individual." He tapped on the mobile phone. "The report lists that the victim was a Dr. Simon Bamford, so I'm leaning toward owning the home and being well-off. But it looks like the doctor isn't as concerned about appearances, based on the unkempt garden. So Dr. Bamford is probably too busy to mind the garden and either can't afford a gardener, or, as I mentioned, he doesn't care. The bright blue door—you'll notice the adjoining neighbors all have red doors—shows that he doesn't mind being unusual."

Ashcroft nodded in approval. "Or, if he was letting the place, he doesn't have the option to make changes. But don't forget to look up. There are a number of wires and antennas on the chimneys, so I think we are dealing with a high-tech individual." He walked to the door, acknowledged the officers' greetings, and stepped inside.

Once inside, Ashcroft again took a moment to study his surroundings. The front room had a small sitting area and an ornate cast-iron fireplace. He could see into the dining room and kitchen, where an officer was trying to calm down a distraught older woman. While he waited for the constable to finish with the woman, Ashcroft continued his perusal of the house. Again, the owner didn't seem to care about appearances. It's not that the place was dirty. In fact, Ashcroft could smell the lemon odor of furniture polish. But there wasn't much surface to polish, as almost every horizontal surface was covered in papers and books. Now here was a way to find out something about a person—check out what they read.

Ashcroft saw novels by H. G. Wells, Madeleine L'Engle, Michael Crichton, Stephen King, Douglas Adams, and Isaac Asimov. It was odd, Ashcroft noted, not to see anything by Agatha Christie, considering they were in Winterbrook, the small hamlet where Dame Christie had lived and died.

But the victim wasn't just a connoisseur of fiction. Ashcroft spotted books and articles by Stephen Hawking, Albert Einstein, and a number of people he didn't know, but who had lots of titles and letters before and after their names.

Howlett leaned over to him. "Have you noticed over half of these books have the word 'time' in their title?"

He had. "Somehow, I don't think this is going to be an easy case."

The officer from the kitchen came over.

"Hello, Constable Norcott," Ashcroft said, recognizing the woman from other cases. "Can you give me a description?"

"This is going to be an interesting one, Inspector," she said. Her cockney accent was evident, even though Ashcroft knew she struggled to divest herself of it. "We have what is essentially a locked-room mystery. Our witness, one Clara Coleman-Hines," she inclined her head toward the agitated woman now seated at the dining room table, "is the housekeeper for Dr. Simon Bamford. It took her a while to get over her nervousness of speaking to the police, but when she did, she gave us an orderly, chronological report."

"You two must have gotten along then," Ashcroft said. "I can always count on you for precise reports."

A slight blush crept up Norcott's face, but she looked down at her notes and continued. "Mrs. Hines came in today, her usual cleaning day, at seven o'clock and started her tasks as normal. However, when it was time to clean his office, she was stymied. She has a key to the house, but evidently Bamford kept his office—his laboratory as he called it—locked up tight. He would allow her in there for fifteen minutes each week for a quick clean. But this time, he didn't answer her knocks on the office door, so she looked in the small window in the door and saw the doctor, spread-eagled on the floor, his head covered in blood, and a pistol at his side. She called nine nine nine at eight twenty-two. Officers arrived at eight forty-three and were unable to enter the office. A battering ram was deployed at nine fifteen."

"A battering ram?" Ashcroft said, raising an eyebrow.

"The door is made out of thick metal and has an electronic locking system."

Howlett nudged him with an elbow. "Good call on the high-tech, Inspector."

"It's quite high-tech," Norcott continued. "It's helpful in some ways. When the cyber division finally arrived, they were able to interrogate the lock—electronically interrogate it, that is—and we found out that the doctor went inside at eleven thirty last night and the door hadn't been opened again until we broke in at nine fifteen. And trust me, the battering ram was needed. Not only did he have the lock, he also had two chains and three deadbolts. All five of which were in place before we knocked down the door. The housekeeper says Dr. Bamford was highly paranoid."

"No other way in?" The sergeant asked as he peeked around her down the hall, where the door—completely off its hinges— rested against a wall. "Was it suicide?"

Norcott looked down at her notes. "There are no windows in the back room. It was originally a large larder. There's a closet inside the room, but it doesn't lead anywhere. No trapdoors, no secret rooms, no nothing. As for suicide? Doubtful. While the angle of the wound could have been suicide, there are signs that he struggled with another individual. A bullet is embedded in the wall next to the closet. Papers are scattered all over the place. Bamford has a gunshot wound under his chin, which looks like it was done in close quarters and looks to my eye like it was instantly fatal. But there are no fingerprints on the gun. Not even the doctor's and he's bare-handed." She paused. "Like I said, a locked-room mystery. Dame Christie herself would have been proud to write this." She nodded in a northerly direction, where Ashcroft knew sat Winterbook House, Dame Christie's home, which had probably served as the model for the fictional home of Miss Marple.

He again exchanged glances with Howlett, then headed to the back room. Howlett could question the housekeeper.

Ashcroft put on latex gloves before entering the room, although he didn't plan on touching anything. He tried never to handle anything at a crime scene, and once he walked in and saw all the electronic equipment around, he definitely avoided it. He and technology didn't get along.

As to the locked-room aspect of this case, Ashcroft knew there had to be an explanation—though one wasn't apparent. He saw no means of exit or entry into the room other than the door. Some type of tussle had obviously taken place between the victim and someone else. Papers were scattered on the floor, a rolling chair had been shoved away from a stainless steel desk and now lay on its side, and some type of electronic device was on the floor in front of the body. The doctor still had one hand on the device. Perhaps he had been holding it when he had fallen forward.

Taking out a pocket torch, Ashcroft entered the closet and conducted a search of his own. He trusted his people but wanted to confirm for himself that there was no other access to the outside.

"Why are you knocking on the walls?" Howlett said from the door. "Looking for secret passages?"

"Looking for something." He walked back into the main room. "But this does seem to be a crime scene worthy of Dame Christie. I'm, well, baffled."

"Too bad we can't ask Hercule Poirot or Miss Marple to solve this murder." Howlett crouched next to the body. "Very odd."

"Well, they're fictional, so that would be difficult. Did you find out anything more from the housekeeper?"

"Not really. She said she last spoke to him last night at around ten o'clock. That's the last that anyone heard from him, according to Constable Norcott." Howlett crept closer to the palm-sized round device. It had a slick, reflective surface, like a mobile phone, but there didn't appear to be anything written on the surface. "What is this? I've never seen anything like this."

"There's some type of technology that you don't have?" Ashcroft teased. "How did you let that happen? I thought you bought everything as soon as it came on the market." He bent over and studied some of the papers on the floor, then leaned back on his heels. Yes, definitely an interesting last case. "Well, here's the problem. I don't believe time machines are being sold at Hughes," he said, naming a local electronics store.

"Time machines." Howlett laughed. "What have you been drinking, Inspector? That's all a load of rubbish."

"Perhaps. I'm sure you think I'm bonkers. But it certainly does appear to be what the good doctor was working on." He pointed at the papers. "I'm no scientist, so while I might not understand the schematics for a machine and definitely won't understand the physics behind it, my reading ability is fairly decent. And I can read 'Diagram of Time Machine prototype 35.6' fairly clearly."

Howlett came over and considered the papers. "Blimey." He stood up straight, then took a few steps toward the device in front of the victim.

"Getting your hands on this would be one hell of a motive," Ashcroft said. Unlike Howlett, he decided to back *away* from the device.

"It would. It would also be amazing as an investigative tool. Or you could use it to go back in time and prevent the murder."

The inspector considered that. In his career, there were many, many deaths he wished he could have prevented. "That is quite tempting. But I think we're not supposed to alter the past. Aren't there supposed to be all sorts of bad ramifications from that?"

"Paradoxes, you mean?" Howlett asked. Both men studied the device—the potential time machine—on the floor. "You're probably right. Still, I'm gobsmacked. You could use it for anything—we could even use it to talk to Miss Marple."

"I told you, she's fictional." Ashcroft tried not to roll his eyes at the younger man.

"We could ask Dame Christie then," Howlett said. "She wrote amazing locked-room mysteries. She can solve this one for us."

"What, we'd just go back in time and ask her?" Ashcroft said with a snort.

"Sure!" The sergeant took out his phone again, tapped a few times. "She lived here from 1934 until she died in 1978. So we could pick some random time, like 1943 or something."

Ashcroft shook his head. "I'd prefer not to be here during the Second World War, thank you kindly."

"Okay, so let's say something like 1938, eighty years ago, before the war. That would be fine, right?"

"As long as we're dreaming, why not just go back to last night so we can see what happens?" Ashcroft said. "Or yesterday evening so we can hide in the office before Bamford arrives?"

Shrugging, Howlett said, "We could, but that's not as much fun."

Ashcroft smiled. "And of course there's another problem." He paused for effect. "Assuming it works, we don't know how to use the time machine, do we?" Thinking of the time, he checked his old-fashioned pocket watch, a gift from his wife: 10:43.

Howlett pursed his lips as he picked up the device with gloved hands. "Good point. Too bad it doesn't respond to voice command. For example, we could say 'Okay, Time Machine, take us to the fifth of November, 1938.'"

* * * *

Ashcroft felt terrible. He was sick to his stomach. He hadn't felt this badly since his stag party thirty-two years ago. And what was wrong with his vision? Everything was dark.

"Sergeant Howlett?" the inspector asked, flailing his hands in front of him. He immediately hit a body, a live one.

"Ow." Howlett said. "What happened? Why did the lights go out? Here, let me grab my mobile."

The inspector heard fumbling, then a bright light flared out. He sucked in his breath. The beam shone on the floor, spotlighting the time-travel device. But there was no longer a body beside it, nor any papers. The floor, which had been a white vinyl, was now aged wooden planks. He took out his torch from his pocket and shone it around. His beam showed a string coming from the ceiling, so he pulled it. An incandescent light bulb turned on, illuminating the area. They were in what appeared to be a large larder, surrounded by tin cans, wine bottles, and other supplies. There were no signs of the laboratory.

"Have we gone barmy, or did the time machine actually work?" Howlett asked.

"I think both, actually," The inspector said, turning. The door was re-attached to the frame, and it no longer had a small window, or chains or an electronic lock. "Yes, I believe both." He jumped back when the door opened.

The woman on the threshold, wearing a black maid's uniform, appeared even more surprised than he was. She screamed loud enough that he figured they heard it back in his timeline as well.

"It's all right, madam. It's all right. We're the police. We apologize for disturbing you. Excuse us." He nudged her to the side and stepped out. "Howlett, follow me. And for God's sake, bring the device."

The maid followed them. "'Scuse me, sir, how did you get in there? There's no other entry into the larder."

They walked quickly through the house, stumbling a bit since it wasn't quite the same configuration as the house in their timeline, and stepped out-side—into a whole different world. *It really was 1938.* Ashcroft gawked at the antique cars on the street, then worried how conspicuous he must look. Glancing down at his clothing, he silently thanked his wife for sticking to the classics. He didn't appear too different from the people on the street. Peeling off his latex gloves, he glanced back at Howlett. His clothing, too, wasn't way out of fashion, even if the younger man tended to wear all black. Ashcroft sighed in relief, then did a double take. "Howlett, put that thing away!"

"I can't get a signal. Not even one bar."

Ashcroft reached back and impatiently tapped the phone in the ser-geant's hands. "Of course not. Mobile phone towers didn't exist in 1938. Put it away!"

The sergeant gaped at him. "You really think we're in…" He turned, slowly taking in the scene around him. "Brilliant."

Ashcroft shook his head. "Follow me." He quickly strode down the street. Luckily, the neighborhood hadn't changed much. He took a left at the next road.

"Where are we going?" Howlett asked as he struggled to keep up.

"To see Agatha Christie. That was your idea, wasn't it?" Since they were in 1938—as hard as it was to believe—they might as well take advantage of it. Besides, he'd love to meet her.

"Right. Right." Howlett yanked on his jacket. "Inspector, we could make such good changes. This is before the war, right? We could stop it. We could prevent it."

"We're not altering the timeline, remember?"

"But I lost a great-uncle in the war. My grandmother never got over losing her favorite brother. Couldn't we—"

"Things happen as they do for a reason. If we change one thing, perhaps what replaces it is worse."

They didn't say anything else until they were in front of the large Queen Anne house. It looked odd without the blue plaque declaring that it was Agatha Christie's home. They opened the short iron gate and strode up the path. Howlett stepped forward, took a deep breath, and knocked.

A fiftyish woman with gray hair and a gray uniform answered the door. "Yes, gentlemen. How may I assist you?"

Howlett cleared his throat. "May we speak to Dame Christie, please?"

Ashcroft knocked him with an elbow. She wasn't a dame yet, and while she still wrote under Agatha Christie, she would probably be known for her current marriage to Max Mallowan. "That is, we would like to talk to Mrs. Mallowan." He pulled out his warrant card and prayed that they hadn't changed too much over the years. "The police would like to consult with her."

The maid gestured them inside, then walked into a back room. "Let me check with the missus. You are in luck. She just returned from a trip this morning."

When they were alone in the hall, Ashcroft shook his head. "She wasn't promoted to the Order of the British Empire until the 1970s. Don't give her ideas."

The maid came back and ushered them into the sitting room. Ashcroft blinked a few times. It suddenly hit him that he was meeting *the* Agatha Christie, the author of some of his and Shirley's favorite novels. His wife would be so envious.

"Good afternoon, ma'am." He bowed. "Detective Chief Inspector Ashcroft and Sergeant Howlett at your service."

"Please, call me Agatha. It makes it easier than worrying about which last name to use."

"Yes, ma'am. Um, Agatha." Now that he was here, what was he supposed to do? Tell her that he was from the future?

"Something is very unusual about you two," Agatha said, looking at them with shrewd, intelligent eyes.

"Yes, ma'am." Ashcroft struggled to figure out how to phrase this.

"We're from the future," Howlett blurted out. "Don't glare at me, Inspector. We don't have much time."

"We have nothing *but* time," Ashcroft said.

Agatha Christie laughed. "Oh, this is intriguing. From the future, you say? And do you have proof of this?"

Howlett took out his phone. "Here is proof. Look at this device. It's a handheld telephone."

Agatha gingerly took it from his hands, inspected it, and returned it. "It is a very interesting trick of lights and wires. Please demonstrate it and ring my phone." She recited her number, but Howlett was already frowning.

"It doesn't actually work right now," Howlett said, his shoulders sagging.

"So like I said, an interesting trick."

Ashcroft closed his eyes, thought about his book collection at home. He loved Agatha's works, and unlike Howlett, he didn't need a Wikipedia article to recall details about her. "Let's see, it is 1938, right?"

She nodded, clearly amused.

"So you've already published some of the Hercule Poirot books. *Appointment With Death*."

"Yes," she agreed. "That came out this May."

"And soon, I believe, will come *Hercule Poirot's Christmas Book*." He read that one each Christmas. He quickly summarized the plot.

She nodded slowly. "Very impressive, Inspector Ashcroft. However, those in the publishing companies have already read it. Perhaps you know someone who works for them."

What was next? Oh, right. "Now you are probably working on a novel set on an island, right?"

The amusement left her eyes, and she was clearly shocked. "I haven't shown that to anyone yet."

"There are ten characters. They die one by one."

Agatha ran her hands over her hair, smoothing down the curls. "Well, Inspector. I do believe it's possible that you might be telling the truth. And I'm quite fascinated now that my maid mentioned you originally asked for *Dame* Agatha Christie."

Ashcroft glared at his sergeant. "Never you mind that. We do not want to do anything that might alter the future that we live in, so please don't ask us for details. I will say, however, that you will be very famous, very beloved by readers worldwide." He was rewarded with a wide smile from his favorite author.

"However, ma'am, we are actually here to ask you a question," Howlett said quietly, then turned toward his superior and waited.

Ashcroft nodded his approval.

"We have found ourselves with a murder case worthy of your novels.

You see, we have found…"

Ashcroft listened to Howlett's recitation of the facts of the case. He watched Agatha, saw her brow furrow as the crime was detailed.

"And you found the time machine." She shook her head. "You should visit H. G. Wells. He's not too far from here. He'd be delighted to find out his writings aren't completely fictional."

"Unfortunately, ma'am, we would like to get back to our timeline," Ashcroft said.

"Well, then," Agatha smiled craftily. "I'd suggest doing what I've had my characters do before. Hide and watch."

Ashcroft tried not to smile. He'd hoped Agatha would come up with another solution, a better one, perhaps. But he was also delighted that he'd had the same idea as she did. Maybe he should try his hand at writing after he retired.

"You said there was a closet in the room, correct?" she continued. "Sneak into there, use your time machine to send yourself back to before the death, and watch."

"Then we can prevent the murder!" Howlett said. "It doesn't have to—"

"It is very brave and fine of you to want to prevent a death," Agatha interrupted. "But there are people who may, in fact, deserve to die. When the victim is also the villain."

Ashcroft checked his mental timeline before speaking. "Like your victim in *Orient Express*?"

"Exactly so." Agatha nodded. "Hopefully your Dr. Bamford is not that evil. But there are many whose deaths we don't regret. What do you know of him?"

"We know that he built a working time machine. So he's brilliant, at the least," Ashcroft said. "But we know nothing about him otherwise."

"So you will return to your timeline before the murder and carefully watch. Then you will know what course of action to take." Agatha stood up, shook both of their hands. "And I will resist the urge to write science fiction and continue my writing. Dame Agatha, you say."

"Dame Agatha." Ashcroft repeated. "You do need to have some patience though." He started to walk out of the door, then turned around. "Excuse me, Eventual Dame Agatha. That book you are writing now, the one that takes place on the island?"

"Yes?" she asked.

"Don't use the title you're currently contemplating. You don't want to use the title of the nursery rhyme."

She raised an eyebrow at him.

"Trust me, that name won't go over well with the Americans. Why don't you just use the last line of the rhyme instead?" After saying his piece, he turned around and walked outside.

"I thought we weren't supposed to alter the past," Howlett complained. "Why did you just do so?"

Ashcroft rolled his eyes. "Trust me, this change is a good thing." He headed back to the cottage. "How are we supposed to get back into that larder?"

Howlett shrugged. "We use our warrant cards."

It worked. Housekeepers in both time periods were afraid of the police, so the maid whom they had frightened a half hour before let them back into the house and back into the larder. They let themselves into the closet, which in 1938 held a great deal of wine.

"Can't we just take a bottle with us?" Howlett asked.

Ashcroft shook his head, even though he had considered it as well. "Theft, Howlett? Really."

"Think how good a 1938 vintage would taste in eighty years." Howlett furrowed his brow. "Or would it not taste aged at all, since it just traveled through time?"

"Let's not worry about it. Time travel hurts my head. So, how do we go back to a certain time with the device? I suppose we should be in there before half eleven, when the doctor went inside the room."

Howlett took out the device, stared at it. "Okay, Time Machine, take us to the fourth of November, 2018, at ten thirty at night."

* * * *

It was just as bad going forward. Ashcroft felt like he had drunk ten of those bottles of wine from the larder closet. Blinking, he saw the closet no longer had wine, just random papers. He looked over at Howlett.

"My God, man. You're already using your mobile?"

Howlett looked up guiltily from the phone. "I wanted to make certain I had a signal again. And that it worked." He showed the display, showing that it was the fourth of November, 2018, at ten thirty.

Ashcroft cautiously nudged open the door. The laboratory was dark, other than some light coming through the small windowpane in the door. Through it, he could see the time machine on the laboratory counter, near some paperwork. He glanced back, saw that Howlett also was holding their copy of the time machine. He shook his head. "Yep, time travel makes my head hurt, literally and figuratively. Now, let's wait." He glanced back. Next to the original time machine device lay a pistol, the murder weapon, he realized.

They waited. As eleven thirty approached, Ashcroft held his breath. And heard the snick of the electronic lock opening. He listened in through the partially opened closet, heard Bamford lock all the deadbolts—one, two, three—and engage both of the chain locks. But he didn't hear anyone else come in the room with the doctor. He risked a glance.

Bamford, now alive, was standing at his counter, one hand caressing the time machine, the other holding a smart phone.

When Howlett nudged him softly, Ashcroft switched places with him, so Howlett could see and listen better.

Still no one came into the room. Bamford, however, began to speak. "Miri, record my voice for posterity. Today, on the fourth of November, 2018, I, Dr. Simon Aloysius Bamford, have completed my life's work. I have in my hands a fully functional, fully accurate time machine. I have tested it already and briefly visited the year 1940. This scientist was careful not to make any changes, not to alter the future. Then."

Ashcroft shuddered at the menace contained in that last word.

"Now, I will use it and alter history. I will go back in time, to May of 1940."

To assassinate Hitler, Ashcroft thought. Of course. Everyone always wanted to assassinate Hitler if they could.

"I will go back," the doctor continued, "and I will assassinate Winston Churchill. Without Churchill, the English won't be strong enough to resist the Germans."

Churchill! Ashcroft sucked in a breath. Realizing Banford's evil intent, he decided that Agatha was quite right indeed that some deaths shouldn't be prevented. He felt Howlett vibrating next to him.

"When is the killer going to come and stop him?" Howlett hissed.

Ashcroft wondered the same.

"Okay, Time Machine," Bamford began. "Take me back to—"

Howlett burst into the room. "No!" he cried as he raced toward the doctor.

Bamford swiveled around, shock on his face. He grabbed the pistol and fired wildly at Howlett. Ashcroft ran out as well, wincing as the bullet flew by him. He saw Howlett and Bamford grappling, the pistol aimed toward the ceiling, wedged between their chests. Howlett was getting the advantage as he managed to push the pistol toward Bamford.

The gun went off again.

His sergeant stared down as Bamford fell on the floor, his face unrecognizable from the wound. "I couldn't. I couldn't let him do that. My great-uncle died in that war. He sacrificed himself, believed in the cause."

Ashcroft stood and stared a long time. Then he reached into his pocket and took out his latex gloves. He slid them on, gently took the gun from Howlett, took out a handkerchief, and wiped down the gun, removing all fingerprints. He placed the gun on the floor, near the body.

Then he reconsidered. Picking up the gun, he placed it in the doctor's hand, wrapped Bamford's fingers around the trigger, and fired at the original time travel device. The device shattered into a thousand pieces. He considered doing the same to Bamford's mobile phone with the recording, then just pocketed it.

Finally, he picked up the papers from the floor, put them in a neat pile, slid the chair back into place, and closed the closet door.

"So it will look like a suicide?" Howlett said.

"So it will look like a suicide," Ashcroft said. "The doctor was devastated that his life's work didn't actually work, shot the machine, then shot himself."

"But...but I killed him. I killed a man."

Ashcroft stopped straightening up the room and walked over to his subordinate. He placed a hand on his shoulder. "You tried to stop someone with an evil intent, and a weapon went off. Did you pull the trigger?"

Howlett shook his head vehemently. "No. The gun just went off. Still there will need to be an inquest."

"And who would believe us? Believe that we went back in time?"

"We have the time machine." Howlett looked down at the remaining device, but Ashcroft noticed he didn't make any move toward it.

Ashcroft took out his handkerchief again, indicated that Howlett should wipe off the blood that had spattered across his face, then blot the drops on his clothing. "I'm glad you wear all black. The drops won't be noticeable except under a black light, so I think we should be fine. Besides, most of the blood went up on the ceiling."

He shook his head as he looked back down at the time machine. It looked sleek and simple, but the existence of such a thing was anything but simple. Such a remarkable invention created by such an evil man.

"I think it would be best that no one knows about this device," Ashcroft said. "In the wrong hands, even if those hands are those of our own government, it could cause havoc. Even in the right hands, we don't know what would happen. No. It is better if we make this look like a suicide, that we erase any evidence that even hints the machine ever worked."

"But this morning, when we saw the scene it looked like—"

"This morning hasn't happened yet. Now, when Constable Norcott arrives, it will look like this, with no signs of struggle. Luckily, the angle of the wound already looks like a suicide."

"This seems so unlike you," Howlett protested. "So unlike your usual rule of doing everything by the book."

But Ashcroft was thinking of other books, ones in which justice was still paramount, even if not exactly in keeping with the law. "As Agatha said, there are times when the victim is a villain."

Howlett looked around the room. "So we've altered the timeline?"

"Looks that way," Ashcroft said.

"But then, who killed Bamford in the first place? I wasn't there the first time he died, so I couldn't have killed him then since I wasn't there—here—until now. So I don't understand—"

"Stop." Ashcroft carefully glanced around, confirming that the scene appeared correct. Gingerly, he picked up the second time machine from the floor, where Howlett had dropped it when he ran out of the closet. "Like I said, Sergeant, time travel makes my head hurt. Let's just forget about it, okay? Especially since the murder hasn't happened yet—and now it won't, as far as anyone else will know, because we've turned it into a suicide. Nice and clean." He paused, then said, "Okay, Time Machine, take us back to the fifth of November, 2018, at ten forty-three a.m."

* * * *

Ashcroft was never going to get used to this. But as his vision cleared, he saw the shocked faces of Howlett and of himself as they blipped away to the past. He took a moment to compose himself before he opened the door and called out to Constable Norcott.

"So, Inspector. Do you agree it looks like suicide?" she asked.

"Agreed. I believe the medical examiner will confirm." He nodded encouragingly at Howlett, who still looked pale.

Norcott looked down at the scene on the floor. "Can you believe he thought he could make a time machine? At least it made your last case slightly interesting."

"More than slightly," Ashcroft said with a smile, slipping the device into his pocket.

Cathy Wiley is a member of Sisters in Crime and Mystery Writers of America. She's written two mystery novels set in Baltimore, Maryland, and has had several short stories included in anthologies organized by the Chesapeake Chapter of Sisters in Crime and published by Wildside Press, one of which was nominated for a Derringer Award for best short story. She lives outside of Baltimore, Maryland, with one spoiled cat and an equally spoiled husband. For more information, visit www.cathywiley.com.

ALEX'S CHOICE

Barb Goffman

If you had asked me a year ago for my favorite month, I would have said June. No hesitation. June meant summertime. No more school. I could spend my days hanging out with friends, playing with my yellow lab, Maxwell, and surfing the web.

If you had asked a month ago as June loomed, I would have said this summer was going to be incredible because Uncle Preston, my guardian, was finally going to let me explore the city beyond the few blocks of our neighborhood. I was twelve years old and responsible, he admitted. I had earned a little freedom. Besides, I had Maxwell to protect me.

But now June had come, and everything had changed. My life had cracked into a gazillion pieces, all because of a stupid speeding car.

When that car zoomed around a corner twenty-six days ago and hit Uncle Preston, he died on impact. I barely had time to process what had happened—how the man who had raised me since my parents died a decade ago was now gone, too. Grandfather arrived from Maine and whisked me and Maxwell off to his seaside home. His mansion. Where it was safe, he said. Where it was quiet.

And boy was he right about that last part.

There was no Internet connection at Grandfather's house—my house now. No TVs or iPads or computers even. No technology. Just old-fashioned phones that connected to the wall. It was like living in a time warp. These things hadn't bothered me on previous visits because Uncle Preston, Grandfather, and I had always kept busy. But now, with Grandfather working all day, Maxwell and I were on our own. Well, we had Cook, but she just made our meals.

Grandfather said he wasn't worried about me. Between books and my imagination, he was sure I'd be able to fill my days and get used to my new home. To my new life.

As if I could ever forget the old one.

I knew Grandfather was trying to help me adjust the best he could. He was mourning, too, after all. And I was trying to settle in. Really. But I could only read so much, and it had been raining almost incessantly since we arrived. So instead of playing on the vast lawn, Maxwell and I had been spending our days looking at old photos. Instead of exploring the village and cliffside, we'd been staring out the windows, down the hill at the churning ocean, as the wind whistled and the sand blew and I wished that my life was different. That I wasn't so alone.

Which is why I was excited to see this morning that the ocean winds had finally blown the clouds away. The sun rose strong and bright, raising flowers from their beds and my spirits along with them. This was how June was supposed to be. Now I could go outside. Now I could be distracted.

With the salty breeze beckoning me, I threw on clothes, and Maxwell and I hurried outside, straight to the large garden shed. Cook would be vexed that I'd skipped breakfast—she always talked like that—but I'd spotted a rainbow-colored kite in the shed a few days ago and had been itching to fly it.

I let the cord out a little as I stepped onto the spongy lawn, and then I began to run, Maxwell at my side. I ran fast, then faster, releasing bits of the cord as I went, the kite soaring so high I could have sworn it melted into the sun. I ran so far that Grandfather's house seemed to shrink. No longer an imposing mansion, it looked like a postage stamp as I approached the cliffs that marked the edge of Grandfather's land. The roaring surf below enticed me.

I'd never been this close to a beach before. Until now, I'd only visited Grandfather each year on Christmas, and Uncle Preston had made sure I never went near the water on those trips. You can't trust the ocean, he'd always said. It entices you with its splendor, but danger lurks within. As Maxwell and I stared down at the rocky shore now, the beach grass rustling, the waves tumbling in and out, all I could see was the peace Grandfather had promised—and I heard a girl laughing in the breeze.

I twisted around but saw no one. I inched to the cliff's edge and peered down. The beach—even the part directly below the cliff—was empty. I *had* heard laughter. No way I'd imagined it. But from whom?

The kite tugged my arm. The wind had picked up, and with no answer to my mystery in sight, I shrugged my questions off and let the kite lead me and Maxwell away from the cliff. Off I ran again, watching the kite rise and fall like the tides, and dreaming of it pulling me up, up, up into the clouds, where everything was all right in my life again.

But like all dreams, this one had to end. As we approached the house, the breeze suddenly faded, and the kite fell like a stone, crashing into an ancient boxwood hedge, its string tangled up in the branches. Maxwell trotted inside, and I tried to unravel the cord. As I was struggling, something caught my eye. A bicycle. It was leaning against the garden shed, so unusual looking that I couldn't tear my eyes away. Someone had painted every inch of it a glossy white. The frame. Seat. Basket. Bell. Even the tires. I ran to it.

"Where'd you come from?" I asked aloud. "You weren't here before."

It might sound nuts that I was talking to a bicycle, but I was glad to have someone—or something—to speak to besides Maxwell. Of course, it didn't answer.

I pulled the bicycle to me. Its chain squeaked as I moved it, like the creaks and cracks Grandfather made with each step. Yet it had no rust anywhere. No dirt sullied its brilliance. It was as if it had sprung from the air, waiting for me after years in careful storage.

I rubbed its smooth frame, cool and almost silky, like the fur behind Maxwell's ears. Then I threw my leg over it and perched on its seat. Had it been molded for me? My feet connected perfectly with the pedals. My fingers rested naturally on the handlebars.

As I pushed down with my right leg, the tires started whirling. And we were off, my new friend and I, gliding over the grass. We rode out to the cliffs, then backtracked out to the far edge of the property where several old family dogs had been buried. It was past lunchtime when we returned to the house. Cook would be cross that I'd stayed out so long, but the farther and faster I'd pedaled, the more my sadness had faded. The bicycle and I were one, calm and assured. Happy and free.

I didn't ever want to let that feeling go.

* * * *

That night at dinner, Grandfather and I sat as always at the long dining room table. He at the head, me to his right. The room was silent, except for the clicking of our silverware against the china plates, Maxwell's panting beneath the table, and Grandfather's soft cough as he cleared his throat, preparing to tell me about his day.

Grandfather once told me that long ago, when Uncle Preston was a boy, this house had always been filled with noise and people. Friends came and went. No invitations necessary. By day, people laughed and ate and told stories. In the evenings, music and dancing spilled out onto the lawn. Even Uncle Preston, who I could only remember being as stiff as the starched shirts he'd always worn, apparently used to joke and play games under the moonlight with my mother. They were, Grandfather said, boisterous ones.

But then one day, when they'd grown and I was two, everything changed. My parents, Uncle Preston, Maxwell, and I had all come to visit. Some sort of accident happened—no one would ever discuss it—and my parents died. I couldn't even remember them. I only had pictures to remind me. Uncle Preston had packed up my things and moved Maxwell and me to his brownstone in the city, where I would be safe, he said. My grandparents stopped hosting parties. Stopped accepting visitors. Then my grandmother died too—from heartbreak, Uncle Preston had said. And Grandfather's life was left in pieces.

But he persevered, as he expected me to do now. Grandfather stayed on in the manor house with his cook and his maid and his driver. Every day he went into town, where he ran the bank. Every night he came back and ate at this table. He used to eat alone with his newspaper. But since Maxwell and I had come to live with him, he left the paper for later.

The first half of the meal always consisted of him telling me about his day. Grandfather believed it important for children to learn about the world, the obstacles people face, and how they overcome them. The second half of the meal was reserved for me to report my doings. Grandfather would look at me closely when I spoke, paying attention to my every word. He found delight in the same things I did. When God created the world, Grandfather said last week, he created summertime so children would have the chance to imagine and grow. I think he missed being a child himself so he placed particular importance on how I spent my days. I was beyond eager when my chance to speak finally came tonight.

"So, Alex," Grandfather said, "I hope you went outside today, now that the weather has finally turned."

I nodded repeatedly, a bobblehead doll come to life. I told him of flying the kite until the wind abruptly died and the kite dropped to the earth. I told him about the cord getting caught in the hedge and that I had to detangle it. And I told him how, as I worked, I spotted a bicycle.

"It was leaning against the shed," I said. "But it hadn't been there before. It just appeared. Like magic."

Grandfather set down his glass of wine, his hand shaking a bit, and leaned forward. A smile crept across his whiskery face.

"Did you ride it?"

"Oh, yeah. It fit me perfectly. When I was on it, I felt…light, somehow, as if I were the kite and could fly. Where did the bicycle come from, Grandfather?"

He took a long drink as he stared at me. It felt like he was taking my measure, and I somehow knew something important was about to happen.

"That bicycle has been a part of this family for many generations," Grandfather finally said, leaning back in his chair. "It appears when it's needed. When it can do some good."

"I don't understand."

He chuckled. "Quite appropriate. Magic isn't meant to be understood."

Magic? My eyes popped to my brow. I didn't believe in magic, but Grandfather wasn't one to make up stories.

"Did anything else unusual happen today?" he asked.

Besides finding a supposedly magical bicycle? I almost said no, but then I remembered. "I heard laughter in the breeze. A girl laughing. But when I looked around, no one was there."

He closed his eyes for a long moment. When he opened them, they were bright and watery. "Where were you when you heard it?"

"By the cliffs. Over the beach."

Grandfather smiled tightly, his lips glued together. Was he going to cry? Instead he pushed away from the table and waved me toward him.

"Come," he said. "Let's take a walk."

* * * *

Nearly twenty minutes later, Grandfather, Maxwell, and I approached the cliffs. Grandfather was puffing by then, and he settled on a stone bench overlooking the beach below to catch his breath. He'd been quiet on the way over. Something was bothering him, I could tell. So I'd walked silently beside him, watching the sky turn pink as the sunlight faded amidst the roar of high tide. When we finally reached the bench, I found a stick on the ground and threw it. Maxwell ran joyfully across the grass to retrieve it.

Grandfather watched him, nodding. "Appropriate Max should be here. How old is he now?"

"Almost eleven."

"So he was barely a year old then," Grandfather said. "Just a puppy the day of the accident. The day your parents died."

Uncertain I heard correctly, I sat next to Grandfather. My surprise must have shown on my face, because he said, "Yes, Alex. It's time you learned what happened."

Maxwell returned. Grandfather tugged the stick from his mouth and tossed it across the lawn. Maxwell set off again.

"It was ten years ago tomorrow," he said. "A lovely day. Sunny. Breezy. Nearly eighty degrees, but cooler right down by the water, of course. In fact, the temperature dropped quite a bit in the late afternoon. Your parents bundled you up in a sweatshirt and took you on a dinner picnic down there on the beach. Maxwell too." He sighed. "Elizabeth always loved that beach."

"Where was Uncle Preston?"

"Back at the house. He'd twisted his ankle badly that morning and was resting on the deck with a book and binoculars. Watching the birds...and you. He always had a soft spot for you."

I swallowed hard. I felt the same way about him.

"That's how I know what happened," Grandfather said. "Because your uncle saw it, even though he couldn't do anything to stop it."

Grandfather stared at the horizon for at least a minute. He was seeing something far away—in time, I suspected, not in distance. Meanwhile Maxwell returned, panting. He dropped the stick and sat by our knees. Grandfather left his daydream and patted Maxwell's side.

"You and your mother were sitting on a blanket, watching your father play with Maxwell," he said, resuming the story. "Max was a real bundle of energy back then. He could chase birds or play fetch for hours without growing tired. He'd just returned a stick for the twentieth time or so, and your father threw it again. I'm not sure if your father misjudged his throw or if the wind shifted, but the stick landed in the water as the waves were flowing in. Max raced after it."

The hair on my arms rose. I stared at Maxwell. He was here and clearly fine, but something in Grandfather's tone made me scared for him.

"The waves rushed out once more, taking Maxwell with them. He disappeared under the water. Your father raced after him, straight into the surf." Grandfather paused, staring now at the ground. "Your mother jumped up, pacing, staring out at the sea. When neither of them surfaced, she ran into the ocean too."

Tears began sliding down his face. I reached out and grabbed Grandfather's ropey hand. He looked at Maxwell. "They loved you, boy."

Maxwell peered up from his spot on the grass, and his mouth fell open into a smile.

"By this point, your uncle had been screaming for help, but no one could make it down to the beach in time. Somehow, a few minutes later, your father managed to clamber out of the frigid water, cradling Maxwell. He dropped the dog on the sand, and they both lay there for a few moments, exhausted, I suspect. Until your father realized that you were alone. He must have figured out your mother had gone into the ocean. He dove back in to save her."

He exhaled the deepest breath I'd ever heard. "He'd been wearing blue jeans and a heavy sweatshirt. The soaked clothes must have weighed fifty pounds.... They never surfaced, not him or your mother. Not until they washed up about a hundred yards down the shore an hour later." His voice had grown so soft, I leaned closer to hear him. "First your mother." He was crying full out now. "Then your father."

After a few moments, Grandfather pressed his handkerchief to his face, composing himself. "I wouldn't have told you all this. Your uncle and I agreed to never tell you the details. But apparently," he began smiling, "fate has other ideas."

"Fate?"

"The bicycle. It takes people to the past so mistakes can be corrected."

I gaped at him. That had to be a joke. But Grandfather appeared quite sincere.

"I know how it sounds, Alex. A time-traveling bicycle. I thought the stories incredible when I first heard them many years ago. Your mother never believed them. But I've seen its power with my own eyes. If you believe"—he clutched my hand—"and if you've directly witnessed something the bicycle thinks was a mistake, it will take you back to that time so you can fix the past."

"And you think it wants me to...save my parents?"

"The bicycle seems to like significant dates. The accident was ten years ago tomorrow. Plus you heard laughter in the breeze as you looked at the beach. Elizabeth used to play down there all the time as a child, always smiling, always laughing."

Was that the answer to my mystery? Had I really heard my mother laughing? Was she somehow calling to me from the past, wanting me to save her, to piece together the shards of our family? I blinked at Grandfather, hopeful but uncertain.

"The date and your mother's laughter, those are the signs. Reminders of people wrongly gone from this world." He grasped my shoulders. "What you need to fix."

"But how?"

"All you have to do is keep Maxwell out of the water."

My brain swam. "Grandfather, I was two years old when this occurred. How could I do that?"

"When you go back in time, there'll be two versions of you. The original you, two years old, sitting on the blanket. And there'll be the Alex I'm speaking with right now. Twelve years old. Your parents won't know you at this age. They'll think you're a stranger. All you'll have to do is stop your father from throwing that stick into the water. And everything will right itself."

His eyes glistened with hope. "Please, Alex. Please do this for our family."

Nodding, I stared down at the beach and gulped. He made it sound so easy.

* * * *

On the walk back to the house, Grandfather explained what I had to do—get on the bicycle, concentrate on where and when I wanted to go, and start pedaling. The bicycle would take care of the rest. Late the next afternoon would be the right time, Grandfather said, mirroring the time of the accident.

I wasn't sure I believed all of this, or any of it, but the bicycle *had* appeared from nowhere, and I *had* heard that laughter, and Grandfather had never lied to me before. So I decided to trust him.

By the time we reached the house, Grandfather was winded again and shuffling his feet. He went off to sleep early, while I sat on the sofa in the library, flipping through photo albums from when I was a baby. I swept my fingers across the clear page covers, trying to feel what I saw. My mother's long blond hair, parted in the middle. The freckles sprinkled across her cheeks and nose. She beamed in every picture.

My father was in far fewer photos. He'd probably taken most of them. His dark hair was wavy, often falling across his forehead. When it was brushed back, his black eyebrows stood out. And there were a ton of pictures of Maxwell and me, always together. Me hugging him around his neck. Him crawling on my chest with impossibly small paws. I knew I couldn't really remember those days, but as I nestled on the sofa, with Maxwell sleeping by my feet, it felt as if I could.

I hoped Grandfather was right, and I could change the past. Because as much as I loved Uncle Preston, the thought of growing up with my own parents filled an emptiness in my heart that—I realized now—had been there long before Uncle Preston died.

The chiming of the mantel clock reminded me the hour was growing late.

"C'mon, boy," I said, patting Maxwell's side. "Let's go to bed."

He opened his eyes and yawned, probably thinking that *he'd* already been asleep. But slowly he rose, stretching his back legs. Maxwell had slept on my bed every night for as long as I could remember. He usually settled down by my feet, but at some point during the night, he'd end up snoring beside me, stretching over most of the bed, his paws pressing into me.

After we got in bed, I tried to sleep but couldn't drift off. So I sat up, opened my eyes, and began talking to Maxwell. I told him about the plan for the next day. How I prayed it would work. I reminded him to stay out of the ocean, even though this version of Maxwell had already done those things ten years ago.

A clock down the hall chimed, then it began to gong. Once. Twice. After the twelfth clang, a bright light shone in the window. I slipped out of bed, pulled back the curtain, and rubbed my eyes to be certain I wasn't seeing things. The bicycle was standing beneath my window. Glowing. Its wheels spinning. Its bell began ringing.

This was real. It was time.

I threw on clothes and dashed down the hallway to Grandfather's room. "Wake up." I shook his arm.

He rolled over quickly, his eyes wide in alarm. "What's wrong?"

"It's time, Grandfather. The bicycle has told me. It's time."

He flung off his covers, grabbed his robe and slippers, and he, Maxwell, and I hurried downstairs. Grandfather flipped on the outside lights, then we stepped onto the lawn. The bicycle rolled to us as if it had an invisible rider.

"I thought late afternoon would be the right time," Grandfather said. "The same time as the accident. But I guess the bicycle has other ideas."

I could hear it humming. "I think it's too excited to wait."

The bicycle stopped in front of us. My stomach fluttered as I straddled it.

"All you have to do is ride toward the cliffs," Grandfather said. "Remember to focus on that day and keep pedaling. You ready?"

I took a deep breath. "Yes, I'm ready." I hoped.

"You can do it. I know you can." Grandfather winked at me, the way he sometimes did for encouragement. He seemed desperate and eager all at once. "Be brave."

"I will." I pushed off and started pedaling. Maxwell ran by my side, but I kept concentrating on the beach, on what happened that day, and soon I couldn't hear Maxwell anymore. Just the wind in my ears as the bicycle's front tire leaned upward, and then we were flying. Up and up. The stars grew larger and brighter, and a peaceful feeling overcame me. I kept pedaling because Grandfather had said I should, but somehow I knew the bicycle was in charge now, and my legwork was no longer necessary. I looked down. Grandfather seemed as small as the teddy bears I used to play with. He waved at me. I couldn't make out his facial features anymore, but I was certain he was smiling.

The roar of the ocean called my attention back to my task. I concentrated on the day my parents had died, and the bicycle tilted back toward the earth. We flew into a mist that kept growing thicker, until I couldn't see anything. Gritty sea spray stung my cheeks, and in the distance I heard Maxwell barking—his happy bark, growing louder and louder. The smell of seaweed tickled my nose as the fog lifted. And suddenly it was daytime, and the shore was a few feet below me. The bicycle skidded onto the beach. I yanked my legs off the pedals, dragging my feet through the warm, rocky sand. Then I spotted myself farther down the shore, a toddler standing on a blanket with my parents.

It had worked!

I jumped off the bicycle, wheeled it behind a dune where it would be safe, and strode toward my family. *My family!* My mother was blowing soap bubbles in the wind, and the smaller me was giggling and jumping, trying to catch them. I stopped short, my feet sinking into the sand. That toddler was me. I knew it, yet I could hardly believe it.

Bark. Bark. Bark.

My gaze shifted to the dog speeding to me. Maxwell. He was so skinny. And I'd forgotten how rich and golden his muzzle used to be. He reached me and jumped up on my legs, panting, happy. He stared into my eyes. I think he knew me.

"Hey, boy," I said, easing him off. I leaned down to pet him. Maxwell rolled over onto his back, and I rubbed his tummy while his tail flapped against the sand.

"You must be a real dog lover," a deep voice said as a shadow fell over us.

I looked up, and my heart beat wildly. It was my father. He had the same nose as me. Our hair was the exact same shade of brown. I hadn't been able to tell that from the pictures.

"Hi," I said, scrambling for something more to say.

"Maxwell doesn't often take to new people," my father said. "You must be special."

I gulped, patted Maxwell's tummy twice, then stood. "Well, I have a dog just like him. But older."

Maxwell noticed the stick in my father's hand and nudged his knee, doing the throw-it dance I knew all too well. My father threw the stick toward the blanket where my mother and Little Me now sat, and for a second I smiled as Maxwell raced after it. Then a feeling of panic overcame me. *Oh, no. I'm supposed to prevent this.*

"Be careful," I called, running after him.

Maxwell ignored me, jumped in the air, and caught the stick. Wow. I hadn't seen that move in years. He raced back to me, his fur rippling in the wind, as my father jogged up.

"Don't worry about Maxwell," he said. "He always comes back." My father pitched the stick again. It flew behind a dune, Maxwell on its trail.

"Who's this?" my mother asked.

I stood just a few feet from her now. The wind had pushed her hair around, leaving it wild and messy, but she still was beautiful. All children probably thought that about their mothers, but in this case, it really was true—even more than I'd expected. Her eyes had a twinkle that her photos hadn't captured.

"Maxwell has a new friend," my father said, turning to me. "I'm Tom." He tapped his chest. "This is my wife, Elizabeth. And that's Alex." He pointed at Little Me.

I couldn't get over the fact that I was staring at my two-year-old self. My face was pudgy, my cheeks pink.

"Hi." I glanced at each of them. "Nice to meet you. My name's Alex, too."

"Small world," my father said.

He had no idea.

"You look familiar, Alex," my mother said. "What are your parents' names? I probably know them."

I hesitated. I didn't want to lie to her, but these were unusual circumstances. "I'm sure you don't know them. We're just visiting." Best to change the subject. "That's a great dog you've got."

I nodded at Maxwell, who was trotting back, the stick in his mouth again. While my parents turned to admire him, I quickly glanced around. How was I going to keep Maxwell from going into the ocean? There was nothing to tie him to. And nothing to tie him with. No leash or anything like it. Why hadn't I brought a leash?

I devised another lie. "He seems to be limping a little. Maybe he needs to go home."

Please take him home.

"A limp?" my father asked. "I don't see a limp. Do you, Elizabeth?"

"No," my mother said.

"Are you sure?" I asked. "That back left leg looks off."

Maxwell trotted up and began his throw-it dance again, no limp in sight. *Thanks a lot, boy.* My father rubbed Maxwell's neck.

"He seems fine to me." My father threw the stick again.

My stomach clenched as I watched the stick land near the water. Maxwell chased it and scooped it up. A bunch of seagulls squawked overhead, and Little Me started following them, nearly colliding with Maxwell, who had begun jumping up at them too. He always adored chasing birds.

Smiling, my mother ran after Little Me, while my father laughed.

"Hey, Max," he said. "You're never going to catch those gulls. C'mon." My father gave Maxwell the *come* hand signal.

Maxwell, always well-trained, grabbed his stick and dashed over to my father. They began playing tug-of-war. Finally Maxwell dropped the stick, and my father threw it yet again. This time the stick flew even closer to the surf. My father chuckled once more as Maxwell raced after it.

The tide was rising, and the crashing waves were higher than they'd been just minutes before, stopping a few yards from the blanket. When Maxwell returned, his legs were wet. A few more throws like that, and Maxwell would be sucked into the ocean—the very thing I'd come back to prevent.

"Could I throw the stick?" I asked.

"Sure." My father handed it to me.

I lobbed the stick toward the base of the cliffs, but the wind carried it to the surf. Maxwell pounced on it and bounded back to my father, his paws leaving wet marks in the sand. My father hurled the stick once more. And it flew right back to the water. As Maxwell grabbed it, my stomach clenched. Would this be when he'd get pulled in? But Maxwell returned to us.

"Could I try again?" I asked.

Again my father handed me the stick. Again I flung it at the cliffs. Again the wind carried it to the surf, luring Maxwell into the waves. The wind was working against us.

I walked toward the water. From this angle, I could see the bicycle waiting for me. *Help*, I pleaded. But the bicycle didn't hum or move or do anything. I got the message. It had taken me here, but I had to finish this on my own.

When I turned back, my father had thrown the stick again, and Maxwell jumped into the ocean just as a large wave crashed onto the sand. The wave retreated, and Maxwell tried to shake dry, his jaws clamped around his prize. Then he trotted to us, water dripping from his fur. It wouldn't be long now.

"Tom," my mother called. "I need help changing Alex's diaper. This wind is making things much more difficult than usual."

"On my way," he said.

He walked to the blanket, and Maxwell came to me, dropped the stick, and begged me to throw it. I swallowed hard, fighting off tears as I watched the waves crashing in. I knew that no matter what I did, the stick would land in the water. Maxwell was destined to get sucked in. I couldn't stop it. All I could do was prevent my parents from going in after him.

Should I tell them who I was? Why I was there? I remembered Grandfather's words. My mother hadn't believed in the bicycle and its powers. Even if I showed the bicycle to her, she'd think I was lying. Playing a cruel prank. No, the truth wouldn't work.

I could snap the stick into pieces so Maxwell couldn't chase it. But there were several more to choose from on the beach. And my father surely wouldn't be able to deny Maxwell the joy of chasing a stick when he did his throw-it dance. I never could.

I stared at my parents' backs as they changed Little Me's diaper. The only way to save them, I realized, was to sacrifice Maxwell. Maxwell, who slept with me every night and made me laugh every day. Who comforted me when Uncle Preston died. Who had been my best friend all these years. I took a raspy breath and rubbed the side of his head.

"I love you, boy."

Then I hurled the stick as hard and as far as I could into the ocean. Maxwell dashed after it, into the surf, under the waves. And he was gone.

I stood there a few moments, checking to see if he'd surface. But the waves rushed in and out again, and Maxwell didn't reappear. Choking back tears, I stumbled down the beach. I didn't want my parents to see me cry. And I couldn't let them realize Maxwell had been carried out to sea, or else they would try to save him and the whole disaster would begin again. I hid behind a large dune, fell to the sand, and let the tears that had been building spill down my face.

Oh, Maxwell. I'm sorry, boy. I'm so sorry.

I'd killed my own dog.

I sobbed for a couple of minutes, the ocean roaring in my ears. I never wanted to hear its sickening sound again. Finally I wiped my eyes and lumbered back to my parents. They had moved the blanket a few yards closer to the cliffs, farther from the water, and were sitting, playing with Little Me.

"There you are," my father said. "Where's Maxwell?"

"He went racing after some gulls," I said, pointing down the beach. My voice cracked while I spoke, but I doubt they noticed it over the thunderous waves beating against the shore.

"That silly dog," my mother said. "He certainly has a prey drive when it comes to birds."

My father stared down the beach. "I don't even see him. He must really be running hard." He turned to me and wrinkled his brow. "Hey, you look upset, Alex. Don't worry. Maxwell always comes back."

I nodded, wishing it would be true this time.

The sand beneath me began vibrating, and a bell chimed. The bicycle was calling. Time to go. I'd done what I'd come for—and sacrificed my best friend in the process.

Tears pricked my eyes again. "Well, I better go home," I said. "It was nice meeting you."

"You too," my mother said.

She and my father waved goodbye as I trudged to the bicycle. I wasn't so eager to see it now. If it weren't for this stupid bicycle, Maxwell would be alive.

I think the bicycle felt sorry for me because when I sat on it and pushed off, away from my parents, the pedaling came easily, even though it should have been difficult on the sand. A few seconds later, I rode into a heavy fog that came from nowhere. And once again the bicycle glided into the air, and we were flying high into the sky. Into the future.

* * * *

The smell of cinnamon pulled me from my dreams, and I opened my eyes. It was morning, and I was back in my bed in Grandfather's house. I didn't remember getting there. But I did remember everything that happened down on the beach. Did it not work? Why was I back here? Where was Maxwell?

I dressed quickly, rushed downstairs, and hurried into the kitchen.

"There you are," my mother said.

She was standing at the stove, making my favorite cinnamon pancakes. Her face had more freckles and lines than I'd noticed on the beach. Her hair was shorter, and she was older. But most importantly, she was alive.

"We were beginning to think you'd miss breakfast," my father said.

He was carrying a plate of bacon to the kitchen table. He'd gained some weight in the past decade. But his smile was the same. I couldn't help but smile back.

Someone sighed loudly behind me. "I was hoping you'd miss breakfast for once so I could eat your food."

My breath caught. Uncle Preston? I wheeled around. "Is it really you?"

He tilted his head. "Who else would it be?" Then Uncle Preston laughed. *He never laughed.* "I promised I'd help you fly that kite today, didn't I? Do I ever go back on my word?"

I hugged him. "No, Uncle Preston. You don't."

"Alex, are you okay?" he asked.

I pulled back. "Yeah. I am. I really am."

"Well, good," my mother said. "Because breakfast is served."

We all sat at the kitchen table. I couldn't recall anyone ever eating here. Things clearly were different now. I was just swallowing my first bite, staring at the three of them so intently they must have wondered if something really was wrong, when I heard shuffling. My grandmother entered the room, just as chipper as she'd seemed in so many old photos. And then Grandfather walked in, too. He appeared the same, except his eyes were brighter. I suspected mine were as well. All our lives were whole now. Well, almost. Except for Maxwell.

I'd done what I'd had to. Saved my parents. Restored my family. It's what my soul had longed for. What Grandfather had begged me for. But would I have gone back in time if I'd known in advance the price I'd have to pay? I wasn't sure. Maxwell had been my family, too, just the same as my parents. The same as Grandfather. More so, in some ways. The fact that he was a dog made no difference to me, and as happy as I was that my parents were now alive, I was heartbroken that I'd sacrificed Maxwell in the process.

How could I ever forgive myself?

"Good morning, sleepyhead," my grandmother said as she sat at the table.

"Did you sleep well, Alex?" Grandfather asked as he took the last remaining chair. "Any interesting dreams?"

I looked straight at him. "As a matter of fact, I dreamed about an all-white bicycle."

Uncle Preston started laughing while my mother swatted Grandfather's arm.

"Have you been filling Alex's head with silly stories about that woo-woo bicycle?" She smirked as she glanced my way. "I'm sorry, honey, but there's no such thing as a time-traveling bicycle. Your grandfather simply has a good imagination."

My heart lifted at the idea. If that were true, it would mean my parents never died. I hadn't killed Maxwell. Had it all been a dream? I studied Grandfather, certain he would give me a sign, but his face indicated nothing.

If it was a dream, I'd remember the last ten years with my parents. I'd remember...and suddenly I did. All the birthdays. Family dinners. Celebrations. Memory after memory flooded my mind, which meant...the bicycle. How I saved my parents. None of it was real. The laughter in the wind—I must have imagined that too.

"Better eat up, Alex, if we're going to make haste with that kite," Uncle Preston said.

I nodded and swirled my pancakes in the syrup on my plate, basking in my memories, until a clicking sound interrupted me. Nails against the floor. A lump grew in my throat as I dropped my fork. Maxwell? He walked into the kitchen as if nothing bad had ever happened.

I leaped from my chair. Hugging him, we sank to the floor, my face wet from his slurps and my tears.

"Alex, what's going on?" my father asked. "You're acting like you haven't seen Max in years."

How could I explain? Of course Maxwell was alive. Still, I was overwhelmed to see him.

"I had a bad dream last night," I finally said. "Maxwell always makes me feel better."

Maxwell licked my nose, then rolled onto his back for a tummy rub. I obliged.

It definitely was a dream. They're all here. My parents never died. I never lived with Uncle Preston in the city. He never stepped in front of that car. Grandmother never died of heartbreak. And Maxwell never drowned. It was just a dream. It—

My gaze settled on Maxwell's rear left leg. It had a big furless patch, and a jagged line ran up the middle.

"What happened to Maxwell?" I asked.

"What do you mean?" my mother said.

I pointed at his leg.

"That old scar?" she asked.

I nodded. Maxwell never had a scar.

"Alex, are you sure you're okay?" my father asked. "Maxwell has had that scar since he was a puppy. You know that. He'd been chasing birds down the beach, and somehow he ended up in the ocean. We didn't even realize it until he crawled out from the surf, frozen and exhausted. His back left leg was all scraped up."

My heart thumped loudly in my chest. "He escaped from the water."

"Yes. He did." My father came over to us and joined me in rubbing Maxwell's tummy. "You always come back, don't you, boy?"

Maxwell's tongue lolled from his mouth as he panted and thumped his tail against the floor, steadily, happily. He was the glue that held this family together. I hugged him again, and he licked my face.

So it all *had* happened. The deaths. The time travel. Maxwell being pulled out to sea. But he was here now. Happy and alive.

I'd gone back and saved my family. And Maxwell had come back, saving himself—and me in the process. If Maxwell could forgive me for throwing that stick into the ocean, maybe, just maybe, I could forgive myself, too.

I stared at Grandfather. "It wasn't a dream, was it?"

Grandfather simply smiled at me. And once again, he winked.

Barb Goffman has been delighted to coordinate and edit this anthology. She's won the Agatha, Macavity, and Silver Falchion awards for her short stories, and she's been a finalist for national crime-writing awards twenty-seven times, including a dozen Agatha Award nominations (a category record), six Macavity nominations, five Anthony nominations, and three nominations for the Derringer Award. Her work has appeared in *Ellery Queen's Mystery Magazine*, *Alfred Hitchcock's Mystery Magazine*, and *Black Cat Mystery Magazine*, among others. Her book, *Don't Get Mad, Get Even*, won the Silver Falchion for the best short-story collection of 2013. Barb runs a freelance editing service, focusing on crime fiction. She lives with her dog Jingle in Virginia, and she hopes to one day go back in time to spend one more day with her beloved dog Scout, who partly inspired this story. Learn more at www.barbgoffman.com.

Made in the USA
Lexington, KY
21 December 2019

58904362R00112